C000016452

The Deadly Promise

GILOU BAREAU

Folrose

THE DEADLY PROMISE

CONTENTS

MORE PRAISE FOR THE DEADLY PROMISE

PREFACE

PROLOGUE

PART ONE

1   8

2   18

3   31

4   36

5   46

6   50

7   52

8   62

9   66

10   72

11   79

PART TWO

12   82

13   85

14   89

15   92

16   95

17   97

18   102

20   107

19 108

21 112

22 115

23 120

24 129

25 135

26 139

27 144

28 153

29 156

30 158

31 161

32 165

33   167

34   170

35   172

36   174

37   176

38   181

PART THREE

39   186

40   191

41   197

42   202

43   206

44   209

45   213

46   215

47   219

48   222

49   224

PART FOUR

50   232

51   243

52   247

53   255

54   258

55   262

56   272

PART FIVE

57   278

58   287

Epilogue   291

Glossary   293

MORE PRAISE FOR THE DEADLY PROMISE

'This thriller is a great read. It is shaped around differences in Jewish views of Israel and on this is informative and readable. The suggestion that such differences lead to violent attacks is way over the top, but with this reservation I strongly recommend the book.'

Clare Short, former British Secretary of State for International Development.

'Gilou Bareau's family drama provides an exceptional eye for detail into the drug and music culture of the time, 2014. His well-written thriller draws us deeper in and gradually reveals important insights into Israeli/Palestinian politics. More specifically, Gilou raises important questions of Jewish identity. Food, culture, ethnicity and religious belief each contribute to differing degrees. However, no element is exposed as more toxic, and therefore more vital to understand, than the violent racism of Israeli Zionism. Engaging and insightful, *The Deadly Promise* is a must read if you like political thrillers with a touch of family drama, and even if you don't. Thoroughly enjoyable.'

David Cannon, Chair of the Jewish Network for Palestine (personal capacity).

For Palestine

"Perhaps, when this accursed Russian war in Ukraine is over, the world will acknowledge there is no difference between one occupation and another, and will dare to draw the necessary conclusions."

Gideon Levy, *Haaretz* columnist

PREFACE

Israel, made in the name of Jews, shames me. I am not alone. There are many thousands of Jews around the world who feel the same. We are a significant minority. We're Jews who support Palestine, and this novel is my way of showing why.

My aim, from the beginning, was to script a narrative that would have wide appeal. If you don't know much about Israel and Palestine, you'll still be able to enjoy *The Deadly Promise.* It is, first and foremost, a thriller.

As Clare's endorsement highlights, my novel is shaped around differences in Jewish views of Israel. Other themes run through the narrative. What it means to be Jewish, which sounds straightforward but isn't. The relationship between European Jews (Ashkenazi) and Oriental Jews (Sephardi) is also not straightforward; they clash culturally and politically. Also under the spotlight are the traditions of orthodox Judaism, and Zionism, the belief in a Jewish state, which cuts through everything. At the back of the book there's a Glossary, which I hope is useful.

I am incredibly grateful to Clare Short, David Cannon and Ilan Pappe for taking the time to read *The Deadly Promise* and supporting it on its journey to publication.

The Deadly Promise has been written under the pseudonym Gilou Bareau.

#Jews4Palestine

PROLOGUE

Albany Street Police Station, Regent's Park, London.

2nd May 2014, 2am

Zach winced at the CCTV image, a shot of his brother running for his life. Abe's terrified face left the screen and a new picture appeared of a hooded white man with the build of a heavyweight boxer. He was chasing Abe, just seconds behind. Zach knew what happened next. He'd read the accounts on social media, seen the photographs. Now Zach couldn't get the pictures out of his head. Abe, hit by a car. Sailing through the air. Landing headfirst. Lying dead, blood seeping out of cracks in his skull. The distraught driver, inconsolable. The hooded man running away.

Beside Zach, Hepzibah let out a low agonised howl and dug her nails into his hand. He put up no resistance. His body temperature was fluctuating wildly. A moment ago he'd been boiling, now he was freezing, drenched in cold sweat. He couldn't think. He'd absorbed the information: Abe was dead. But he couldn't process it. He forced a question out.

'Why?'

Detective Inspector Murrell looked unsure. 'Why what?'

'Why run into the road?'

'Probably he thought the lights were on red. They *were* on the other side, but not on his. That's what confused him, we think. He was running down Eversholt Street in a panic. When he reached Euston Road, he saw cars on the other side stopped at the lights. He ran across. But they were on red to let traffic turn right into Upper Woburn Place. Eastbound was still flowing. I can see it happening.'

PART ONE

The First Step

1

A steady stream of Sephardi mourners wound its way through the grounds of the synagogue towards the funeral chapel. Their path through the trees was covered in a carpet of pink cherry blossom, which was kicked up in a swirl as they tramped through. The men led. They wore sombre clothing, wide-rimmed black hats and freshly polished shoes that caught the late afternoon sun. The women walked silently behind, their heads covered with a black *tichel*. Walking with them, the hushed children were their parents in miniature. Boys in oversized dark suits, girls in black headscarves and starched skirts that reached their ankles.

Hanging back in the car park, Zach watched them file in with an unpleasant taste in his mouth. These people – the Lombrosos, the Cardozos, the Pintos, the Obedis, all of them – they loathed Abe and everything he stood for. Why were they there? Tradition. In the community, a funeral was not to be missed. Certainly not the funeral of a son of Dov Peretz.

Fuck tradition. It has no place at Abe's funeral.

But there it was, dominating the stage.

Zach pulled out his tobacco, yet again delaying the moment he would join these hypocrites who had come to mourn his brother's death with a snigger behind their sorrow. Zach's hands shook as he rolled a cigarette, still more so when he held the lighter. He'd been in shock since he received the call from Hepzibah not long after one that morning.

'Abe's dead,' she'd said.

Zach's legs gave way. Who'd look after him now? Abe had always been there for him, whatever Zach had done. He put Zach up, fed him, gave him wine to drink – though he did always frisk Zach before letting him leave, checking for stolen items and nicked cash. Their lives could not have been more different. Abe: the successful academic, professor of mediaeval history. Zach, who had lost everything. His job, his home, his daughter. And now he'd lost Abe.

Overnight, Zach had become the solitary family atheist. Zach was now alone in the battle against religious conservatism. A hard task. Sephardis tended to integrate less than the Ashkenazi, in south Manchester as well as the more renowned north. And his family were as traditional as they come.

Once, Zach tried to explain. It was a paradox. He'd turned his back on Judaism, but he hadn't become any less Jewish. He'd lost none of the culture, the history. Being Jewish was an identity. Before anything else, he was a Jew, and if it wasn't the first thing he told people, it was the second. But his family wouldn't hear it. All they could see was that he wasn't preserving the faith.

Zach knelt in front of a wing mirror in the synagogue car park. From what he could see through his thick black curls, he looked like shit. He had sunken bloodshot eyes and pupils that looked on the edge of exploding.

People were going to stare.

Fuck 'em. Zach was what he was, and today he didn't care who knew. He drew on the end of his fag in short drags and threw it away. Then he fished out a black tie. He was as ready as he was ever going to be.

At the chapel doors he took a *kippah* from a basket and placed it on his head. That couldn't be avoided, but he ignored the ceremonial kissing of the tiny *Torah* embedded in the doorframe. Abe would have smiled at that.

It took Zach a moment to adjust to the candlelit chapel. His father was a few feet away. Dressed in a prayer shawl, Dov Peretz sat beside a simple pine coffin, rocking back and forth, reciting psalms in a low melodic voice shot with sadness. He was performing *Shemira*, guarding Abe's body until burial, and wouldn't acknowledge anyone, not even with a glance.

The small chapel was packed with South Manchester Sephardis. They stood solemnly, communicating with no one. Their long shadows swayed like reeds across the stone floor as their weight shifted from one foot to the other. Only Dov's low rumbling voice could be heard, along with sniffles and quiet sobs. When Zach blew his nose, the mourners stared at him in disapproval. More so when he inspected the tissue. It was dotted with red specks of mucus.

Zach met their censure with a shrug. They didn't belong at his brother's funeral, whereas Abe's friends and colleagues were conspicuous by their absence. Once the rabbi had persuaded the police to release the body, Dov made it clear they would not be welcome. Hepzibah was also barred on the basis that she was now Abe's ex, although technically they were still married.

Zach scanned the chapel for his brother and sister. He spotted Ester, sobbing noiselessly, head bowed. She held a tissue to her mouth to stifle her weeping. Nissim, by her side, called Zach over with a lift of his eyes and a jerk of the head.

Instead, breaking with tradition, Zach approached his brother's coffin. Dov didn't cease chanting, nor did he look up. No one shouted or ran over, but he could hear disapproving murmurs and feel eyes like daggers in his back.

Abe's coffin was draped in a *Mogen Dovid*. Inside, he would be dressed in a kippah and a prayer shawl, religious paraphernalia he rejected as a young teenager. The shawl would be cut, signalling his death. Rituals. Zach wanted to see his brother, to free him. What would happen if Zach pulled the drape off and opened the casket? Would God appear and strike him down with a bolt of lightning from an outstretched fingertip?

Zach felt a hand on his shoulder and turned to see Nissim. His tears quickly dried. Their relationship was distant. They embraced stiffly and Nissim led him away through the crowd of mourners.

His brother was fifty-two, twenty-one years his senior, and his sister Ester was fifty. Both were old enough to be his parents. They were from a different generation, the 1970s: the era of punk rock and the Anti-Nazi League. But those times passed them by like a ship in the night as they embraced the religious, insular life Dov charted out for them. Nissim worked in the family business, while Ester's fate lay in the home.

In contrast, Abe began to rebel not long after his Bar Mitzvah. Zach remembered one day in particular. Abe was fifteen. He stood in the middle of the living room and insisted, *in English*, on attending a non-religious school in preparation for life at university, where he would study anything but a business-related subject. To top it all, he announced he was socialising with goyim. Zach could still recall the stunned expression on his father's face. Dov turned puce. He lapsed into Arabic. He swore, he cursed, but Abe stood his ground. Six-year-old Zach watched in awe as Abe faced up to both his father and his mother, then left to meet his new friends. The moment the front door shut, Dov and Malka began arguing. In Arabic, always Arabic. They blamed each other, only Dov's voice was louder, his language more colourful. When they were finished, they lectured Zach together, in both Arabic and English, on tradition and respect for your parents.

Abe had integrity in spades, and a strength of character Zach admired, even if he found it unfathomable. Abe would stand up to any-one, but when it turned nasty he never fought back, on principle. He stood up when others wouldn't and always got knocked down. Zach, on the other hand, had a habit of fighting back (on principle), and when violence was unavoidable, he made ssure he landed the first punch.

Nissim, the older brother Zach barely knew, brought him face to face with Ester. Beneath her weighty orthodox garb she had a figure most women would envy. Despite concealing her body in heavy clothing, hiding her hair, and occasionally wearing a wig, Ester was captivating. Tall, slim, dark-skinned. Her only unconventional feature was a prom-inent bridge on her nose, a family trait. In a different life, she could have mixed with Hollywood stars and had any man she wanted.

Ester stopped weeping and collected herself enough to register dis-approval. It was the first time she'd seen her younger brother since a family argument a year earlier. As always, her censure was brief, but the point had to be made. He'd been very naughty, and she'd been very cross. After a moment, Ester cocked her head to one side and opened her arms. She smiled in the way people do when they share a loss: a sad sorrowful smile. They hugged.

Zach cried in Ester's arms, not for the first time. Wrapped up like a baby, he was reminded of his childhood. She'd been his refuge then.

A deeply resonant voice rang out, singing words from the Torah. Dov ceased his lament and the rabbi entered, chanting. The congregation gathered round and Zach caught sight of his father leaning on a stick. He looked a broken man. He was more than grief-stricken; he was destroyed. His eyes, lined with black rims, were empty of life. He was burying his child. A son he had loved despite their disagreements.

Chanting the eulogy of sorrow, the rabbi approached Dov and tore his jacket above the heart. He performed the same rite with the other males in the family: Nissim, three of his children, and Zach – but on the opposite side of the jacket. It was done two-handed, with force. The blessings complete, pallbearers – members of the community Zach dimly recognised – lifted the coffin with due reverence and stepped out into the bright sunshine.

Nissim and Dov led the mourners behind the coffin, followed by Ester and Zach. The pallbearers took one step at a time, slow enough for Dov to need only his stick. He looked smaller than when Zach last saw him, a shell of the tall upright man he used to be.

The pallbearers stopped, and Zach hoped his father would turn to him. He didn't. Six more times they paused on the way to the gravesite. Not once did Dov look round. Zach thought of reaching out but stayed his hand, sensing his father was deliberately ignoring him. Yet he remained positive. Surely today they would embrace and cry together. Zach wiped his runny nose and blew. More tiny red specks of mucus.

'You don't look well.' Ester's tone was flat, but her eyes betrayed her concern. They roamed his face looking for answers. 'If you carry on like this, you're going to kill yourself.'

He knew she was right, but that didn't stop him fingering the wrap in his back pocket. Zach was addicted to cocaine. He didn't use needles, he didn't smoke crack, he didn't sniff glue, and he didn't abuse alcohol (much), but he would still end up dead. It would just take a little longer.

The procession stopped at his mother's grave. Zach gripped the wrap and didn't let go. The anticipation was sweet. But today it was mixed with a sadness heavy with anger. His fanatical father had hijacked the funeral and now Abe was to be buried next to his mother. What a bitter irony, and not one Abe would find amusing. Close only in birth and death.

As the rabbi chanted a eulogy to the dead, the mourners crowded round and watched the coffin being lowered into the ground. The pall-bearers stepped back, allowing Dov and Nissim to shovel earth into the grave. Zach followed Ester. Her words hissed inside his head.

You're going to kill yourself.

He knew she was right, but he still salivated at the thought of a line.

The grave filled, final prayers were recited. It was time for the family to leave for home where they would sit *shiva* for seven days. The mourners formed themselves into two rows and offered the traditional words of consolation as the family passed through. People Zach didn't know told him how sorry they were in Hebrew, a language he didn't speak. If he thought they cared, he might have been touched. But it was all appearances.

Tradition.

Zach caught up with his father at the outdoor taps. As yet, they hadn't exchanged so much as a glance. Up close Zach could see Dov no longer fitted his black suit. It hung like a sack over his frail eighty-three-year-old body. There was a rasp in his breathing, loud enough to be heard above the sound of running water. His chronic bronchitis saw to that.

Nissim finished at the taps and suggested with a look that Zach join in the ritual washing.

The water was cold. How could his father stand it for so long?

'Hi Dad,' Zach said, more in hope than expectation.

Dov didn't reply or look up. His eyes were fixed on his wrinkled bony hands. He was turning them round and round under the water. They must have been freezing. Zach had pulled his out and was now looking for something with drying properties. In the end he resorted to sandwiching his wet hands between his arms and the sides of his chest.

'Dad,' Zach tried again, but he was beginning to suspect his father couldn't bring himself to look at him, never mind embrace him. He was a drug addict, a thief, a no-good bum. Dov had told him often enough.

Zach turned the tap off. Only then did he realise Dov was crying. He put an arm around his father but was pushed away, roughly, and abused in Arabic.

'*Cusumac,*' Dov hissed, impugning the integrity of Zach's mother, his dead wife. He turned to Nissim, his eldest, and said, '*Yalla.*'

Nissim took his arm but did not lead him away. 'Perhaps, given the circumstances, it is time for us all to be a family again.' Nissim's reasonable tone belied his nervousness, an anxiety they all felt challenging the patriarch. 'Maybe Zach could come to the house.'

Dov exploded. Swearing loudly in Arabic, he pushed Nissim away, but quickly lost his balance and would have fallen had Zach not caught hold of him. Dov made sure their eyes did not meet, and he said nothing. Instead, once he had composed himself, he shoved Zach away with both hands, and said in Arabic:

'Get me my stick, Nissim. I'll make my own way home.'

'There's no need,' his eldest said with a sigh.

Zach watched them shuffle slowly towards the cemetery gates. His father's anger hadn't lessened in twelve months. Indeed, it had strengthened. Zach wanted to shout, 'Come back Dad, please!' but instead tears rolled down his cheeks.

Ester handed him a tissue with no real sympathy. 'You're not surprised, surely? Not after what you did when Malka, *your mother*, lay there dying.'

Zach had done what he had to. He didn't expect them to understand. But forgive? Yes. Nissim and Ester managed it. Was he surprised Dov hadn't? Yes, because when it came to his father, Zach always lived in hope.

Ester pushed up her bundle of hair, a habit of hers. 'You're ruining your life, Zach. You've lost your job, your daughter ...'

'I haven't lost Rachel,' he snapped. Only he could say that.

'So when was the last time you saw her?'

Zach kicked through the blossom, sending hundreds of tiny pink petals into the air. 'Over three weeks ago.' One day shy of a month, in truth.

'You haven't seen her in more than three weeks? Zach, she's three years old. You should be there for her all the time.'

'Do you think I don't want to be?' Zach kicked through the blossom again, this time with more anger. 'Things are difficult between me and Beth.'

'Of course they are. You're a drug addict.'

Her voice was cold and flat. There was a trace of love, but he had to listen hard to hear it. Deep down, Zach knew he had to kick his habit, yet he still found her tone impossible to bear.

'It's either drugs or your daughter. It's as simple as that, Zach.'

He didn't answer. Instead, he fingered the wrap in his back pocket.

'I'm happy to help you go to a private clinic. So is Nissim.'

'Thanks,' he said, smiling weakly.

'You'll at least go and see the doctor?'

'Sure, soon as I get home.' Zach shifted about uneasily, not realising he had hit a nerve.

Ester's fuse had been lit. '*Home*? You call that place *home*? You live above a *Laundromat.*' It was a dry cleaner's, but he didn't correct her, partly because the flat was no longer his, but mostly because he couldn't be bothered. Ester flapped at her bundle of hair. 'Ring me when you've seen the doctor.'

'Sure.'

She leant forward and kissed him goodbye on the cheek.

He returned her kiss and said, 'I haven't got any money to get back.' This was true. 'I spent all I had on the train fare to get here.' This was a lie.

Hepzibah paid. She also gave him Abe's black suit, which he wore to his brother's own funeral. And now it was torn.

Ester pulled at the cotton ruff around her neck, a sign she was stressed. 'I can't keep giving you money, Zach. You're thirty-one years old. You should be able to get back from your brother's funeral under your own steam.' She raised a finger, Ester's way of telling Zach she was being serious. Nevertheless, it wasn't long before she opened her purse. 'This is the last time,' she said.

Zach nodded, having heard it all before, many times. Ester brought out fifty quid, all she had. 'That should be enough, I hope.'

'Only just. I've got extra tube and bus fares.' Zach pocketed the money and smiled in gratitude.

Ester looked at him suspiciously. 'I'm not financing a visit to one of your druggie friends, am I?'

'I'm going to see Heps.'

Ester fiddled with her headscarf. Her bundle of hair bobbed up and down. 'Yes, well, it's good you're going.'

'Yeah, seeing as she was banned from the funeral.'

'What are you saying, Zach?' Ester looked at him in amazement. 'We couldn't have *those* people here, not today. Surely *you* understand that.'

'Look Es, you know my views, but no I don't understand. Abe was one of *those* people.'

'I don't need reminding, thank you.'

'And he wasn't a good person?' Zach could feel tears welling up, but he fought them back.

'Of course Abe was a good person. I loved him dearly, as you know, but that's not the point.'

'Oh? So what is the point?' He didn't wait for an answer. 'Bye Es.'

'Ring me? Tomorrow?'

'Sure,' he said, and headed back to the synagogue.

'Where are you going?'

Zach didn't answer. He was soon fingering that wrap again, Ester's warning pushed away. In some sick way having a gram of cocaine on his person helped enormously. Alone in a toilet cubicle, he prepared a big fat line. Now he could forget about his father, his mother, and even Ester, and push all his hurt, all his anger, confusion, and guilt to the back of his mind. In a moment Zach would feel on top of the world.

2

Midnight was approaching and Zach was on the upper deck of the 253, heading for Hepzibah's. A couple of drunks eyed him aggressively across the aisle. One of them said something; Zach had no idea what. He was on planet zog, where he felt like shit. He'd come right down, too far, and his body temperature was going crazy. Right now, he was red hot. Soon he'd be ice cold.

Peering through the window, he saw they were in Stamford Hill. Not long to go. He clenched his fists and willed the bus on.

More looks.

He ignored them and stared out into the night. The Prince of Wales on Lea Bridge Road was lit up, despite the late hour. Abe's flat wasn't far away, yet his brother had never set foot in the place. It was more a venue for a desperate, last-roll-of-the-dice Zach. The drinking hole wasn't dangerous, but the dealers were dodgy and the joint was frequently raided by the police.

The bus left the pub lights behind and drove through Millfields Park, the recreation ground on one side, the cricket pitch on the other. They were crossing into Lower Clapton. Almost there. Until then, Zach was trapped on the top deck with the usual late-night commuters. At the back of the bus, a group of alcohol-fuelled Arsenal supporters sang 'Ooh to Be a Gooner,' and swayed as they held imaginary scarves above their heads. In between verses, they belittled Spurs, their North London rivals, in less than decorative terms. Occupying the front two rows on both sides of the aisle, half a dozen giggly girls exchanged banter with a bunch of brash teenage boys sitting behind them. Then there was Zach, and the two drunks mouthing hostilities at him whenever he glanced over.

At last, he pressed the buzzer for Hackney Baths. Ignoring the glares and drunken provocations, he climbed down the stairs and stepped out into the cool spring night.

Zach's feet had barely hit the ground before the bus was gone. He couldn't linger, not at this time of night. The stretch of road linking Upper and Lower Clapton was called Murder Mile for a reason. The tag had almost been shaken off, but then there was another fatal shooting, a case of mistaken identity in a turf war.

Zach scoured the terrain. The raucous gang of white youths gathered outside the fast-food outlet up ahead were best avoided. He crossed over early and stepped past a homeless guy in the doorway of the chemist. There was always one. Tonight's was almost a kid. There but for the grace of his family went Zach. He left the main road, passed a great Greek deli, and turned a bend. Here, the street became residential. He broke into a steady trot, ready to sprint if he had to. Twice now he'd been mugged on that quiet stretch late at night.

Three hundred yards on, Hepzibah's two-storey terraced house stared back at him through its original sash windows. A nearby lamppost threw light onto the large, red-leafed acer planted in front of the bay window. Abe had been the gardener of the house. Zach could remember the day, ten years ago, when his brother planted out the small front garden – much to the approval of the elderly couple opposite. Zach walked to the doorway, which was adorned with a budding passionflower, and rang the bell.

An outside lamp flicked on and Hepzibah appeared, a shawl wrapped tight around her shoulders. Zach had always fancied her, from the moment she burst into his eighteen-year-old life as Abe's new twenty-seven-year-old girlfriend. Growing up she'd trained in ballet and had developed the body of an acrobat, strong and supple. Her figure hadn't changed over the years. The only suggestion Hepzibah might be forty and not twenty-five was the greying of her black hair at the temples.

Tonight, her hair was pulled back in a bun, a look Zach liked. It showed off her high cheekbones.

Under the light, Hepzibah looked as tired and drawn as she had twenty-four hours earlier. Her eyes, still vacant and dark-ringed, had a glassy sheen to them. She swayed on the spot, and Zach smelt alcohol on her breath.

'Hey Heps,' he said, opening his arms.

Zach towered over Hepzibah, as had Abe. He frequently found himself hugging her head. Tonight, the hug he gave her was brief, not long enough to be comforting. He hopped from one foot to the other, expecting to be let in. His gaze darted this way and that. Zach was desperate for a line – he hadn't dared have one in the train toilets. All the lids to the seats were missing. Once bitten, twice shy: never again would he place an open wrap on the toilet cistern of a moving train. Or an unopened one, for that matter.

Zach didn't read the look in Hepzibah's eye quickly enough. Before he had time to move, she lunged at him, raining down blows on his chest.

'Why couldn't it have been you, you fucking junkie? Look at you. All you can think about is your next fix.'

She was hitting him less hard now. With each thump her head dropped until her face was buried in his chest. He held her, feeling her body jerk with every sob. Hepzibah looked up at him, her face wet with tears.

'I'm sorry, I didn't mean what I said. You know that, don't you?'

"Course,' he replied.

Gently, she ran her fingers along Abe's black jacket until she reached the tattered breast pocket. 'You've torn it,' she said softly.

'The rabbi did that.'

'You got into a fight with him?'

'It's a ritual. All the male members of the family have their jackets ripped.'

'I'm glad I wasn't invited to their horrid funeral.'

'You'd have hated it.'

'Still, it was mean of them to bar me. But I guess they blame me for "turning" him all those years ago.'

Zach nodded. But his body said, 'enough of that, let's get in'.

She pulled her shawl around her once more. 'You better come in. You need that fix.'

'It's not a fix, Heps, it's a hit.'

She gave him a fake smile and added some fake pathos for good measure. 'Well, at least I know for the next time.'

Once he was past the coir mat by the front door, Zach's shoes tapped a simple rhythm on the sanded floorboards. He followed Hepzibah into the kitchen for some water, not realising she had guests. Half a dozen people were sitting around a large table, picking at olives and dipping pitta bread into *labneh*, a soft cheese made from strained yoghurt. Zach's gaze wandered to the sofa by the bi-folding doors, Abe's favourite space in the house. He'd sit there for hours, looking out at the garden, his focus often on the nearby birdfeeder poking through a large pittosporum.

Zach went over to the kitchen sink and turned on the cold water. Rather than search for a glass, he drank straight from the tap, and when he'd finished he wiped his mouth with his sleeve. Hepzibah's guests stared in disapproval, except for a young Middle Eastern woman who came to meet him. She wore jeans and a T-shirt. A black and white *keffiyeh* hung round her shoulders.

'I am so sorry,' she said. 'You are Abe's brother, I can see. He was a wonderful man.'

'Wonderful' struck Zach as odd. He put it down to English not being her first language.

'Yes, he was,' Zach replied, his tone neutral. The woman's body language suggested she wanted to embrace him, but when he gave her no encouragement, she put out a hand instead. It felt small and limp.

'My name is Fawz,' she said.

All Zach could think about was getting a line up his nostrils. His eyes couldn't settle on her, and he couldn't make conversation. She looked at him strangely, probably because his pupils were jittering about like pinballs on speed.

'Fawz,' she repeated. 'Abe told you about me, yes? I live with … in his flat.' She fought back tears. 'I will miss him terribly. I know you will too. You were very close.' Her voice trailed off when she realised she was having a one-way conversation.

Zach turned on his heels. Seconds later the toilet lid was down and so was he, on his knees snorting a line of cocaine with the gusto of a pig at a trough filled with cooked broccoli. Whoosh, up his nose it went, straight to the top of his head. Energy surged through his veins. Paranoia was banished. Confidence, mountains of it, flooded in. Now, post-hit, he felt as though every crack, every fissure in his body had been repaired. He smiled at himself in the mirror, pleased with what he saw. Tall, dark, and sort of handsome, with a prominent nose, thick lips and wild hair. Zach looked great. He felt great. Now he could do anything.

His black funeral shoes hit the sanded floorboards, announcing his imminent return. A hush fell over the kitchen as he walked in. Soon, the silence felt awkward. After his visit to the bathroom, Zach found this amusing rather than threatening, and let the others worry about it. He recognised them all except a tall blond man in his mid-twenties. This guy *was* handsome, with strong features that suggested northern European heritage. Pinned to the lapel of his jacket was a green 'Free Palestine Now' badge.

The table was littered with dozens of used glasses, paper plates and empty wine bottles. There was a little food left – a few slices of fried aubergine, some dolmades, a potato salad, bread, and an array of cheeses. Behind him, not a word was being spoken, and Zach imagined they were all staring at him, not that he cared. Okay, he wasn't displaying the best social skills, but they were an unfriendly bunch.

Zach wasn't hungry, nevertheless, he picked at a bowl of green olives and ate what was left of the aubergine with a squeeze of lemon. After a brief examination of the wine still on offer, he chose a red that sounded to his taste and poured himself a glass. He sampled it, approved, drank some more, then turned to find everyone looking at him. But Zach only had eyes for the blond.

'So, who are you?' The question cut through the air with the sound of a chainsaw meeting metal, shattering the silence.

The blond bombshell leant over the table and gave Zach his hand to shake. "My name's Seth. I met Abe through Jews Against the Occupation.'

Zach hadn't liked the guy before; now he liked him even less. He was a traitor. To make matters worse, he was an Ashkenazi, a *European* Jew. What about equal rights for Sephardis? The Europeans gave Arab Jews like Zach's father a name in the nascent Israel. *Mizrahi.* It meant eastern, denoting an outsider. Not from here (Europe, even though they were in the Middle East), but from *there.* Now Zach couldn't take his eyes off the 'Free Palestine Now' badge attached to Seth's very privileged European lapel.

He took Seth's hand with no enthusiasm. Seth was anti-Israel. And then there was the badge. Normally, when he was at Hepzibah's, he said nothing. But these were not normal circumstances.

'We're not at a rally, Seth. Take the badge off.'

Blondie was no taller than Zach, but he had a build that suggested he worked out every day, morning and afternoon, with just a short lunch break in between.

'The Zionist brother,' he drawled, 'I've heard a lot about you.'

Of course Zach was a Zionist. How could any Jew not believe in Israel? It was a Jewish state, there so Jews could be safe. Yes, he was critical of Israel's euro-centricity, but like the majority of Sephardis he'd paradoxically out-Zionisted the Europeans. Most pro-Palestinian Jews were European liberals like Hepzibah and Seth. Abe was the exception.

Jewish critics of Israel were infuriating people, not just traitors to the cause. With them it wasn't possible to lob in the usual firecrackers. Like the word *Zionist* being a racist euphemism for Jew. It worked a treat with gentile critics of Israel. Shut them up straightaway.

'My brother was buried today,' Zach reminded Seth. 'That's why you're here. It's a bit weird to come wearing a badge.'

Seth smiled, which pissed Zach off. His composure suggested he wasn't intimidated. If anything he was amused, which pissed Zach off even more. Seth pushed his chest out and said, 'Abe would have wanted me to wear this badge.'

A couple at the table agreed. 'Yes, he would,' they said. Others nodded in agreement.

'Let it go, Zach,' Hepzibah said.

She hadn't added, 'Or leave', but he knew it hung there, a silent clause, and he couldn't afford to. Finally, he rolled the cigarette he'd been waiting for, closed the door behind him and lit up. Once he got the fag burning evenly, he took a long drag. Zach found it intensely satisfying to take the smoke down deep and exhale ever so slowly, particularly after a line. He had always enjoyed smoking, but once he met Charlie the pleasure was heightened. Tobacco and cocaine went together like apple pie and cream. Ester's words rung doubly true, he knew, but he didn't care. He was high and he felt great, despite having had to climb down to Seth.

On his return, Zach made himself at home with that nice red, a blend of Shiraz and Durif from down under, and joined Hepzibah, Seth and Fawz at the kitchen table. Abe's work colleagues had gone. Seth raised a glass to Abe's commitment to 'the cause', prompting tears from Fawz. He touched her knee supportively as she said, 'Abe was staying with Hepzibah. I went to bed knowing nothing.'

Seth put a comforting arm around her and said softly, 'Maybe it was better that way.'

'How come Abe was staying here, Heps?' Zach asked. Abe hadn't stayed since he left, over two years ago.

Her words came out slurred. 'He was coming over with a recording of the meeting he'd just spoken at. We were going to use some of the material in the book we were writing.' She downed what was left in her glass, filled it up and planted the bottle gracelessly back on the table.

Abe used to hate the way she did that. 'You know,' she said, 'I'm sure the guy who chased Abe was at the meeting.'

Hepzibah hadn't answered Zach's question, but he let it go. What did it matter now? And there was something else on his mind.

'What was Abe doing speaking at a meeting? That wasn't his thing. It's more yours.'

'I suggested he try it. You know how strongly he felt about the lives of Palestinians in Gaza, and with an invasion imminent he said yes. I would have gone with him, only I had a deadline to meet. Maybe things would have been different if I had.'

Zach said nothing. He could see Hepzibah was on the verge of tears.

Gallantly, she fought them back and added, 'Anyway, maybe somebody saw something.' She turned to Seth. 'Are you sure you didn't see anything? Athletic guy, bigger than you, with a …'

The Ashkenazi was there. Zach spoke over Hepzibah to Seth. 'You were with Abe?'

'No, we'd already left.'

'Left what?'

'The pub, we had a drink after the meeting.'

'Why didn't Abe leave with you?'

Now it was Fawz's turn to lend support. She leant in close to Seth and put a hand on his knee. Their shoulders touched and they shared a look.

'He hadn't finished his drink,' Seth replied.

'How long does it take to finish a drink?'

'The others had left. I'd finished my drink, and Abe was about to ring Hepzibah. I had my bike with me and wasn't walking, so it didn't seem to matter.'

Zach glared at Blondie. 'It didn't seem to matter? You leave the pub and five minutes later Abe is dead.'

'I didn't mean it like that.'

'How did you mean it?'

Hepzibah downed what was left in her glass and put it down with a thud.

'Zach. Stop it. We need to focus. Who was the guy chasing Abe? If he was at the meeting, what does that mean?'

'Maybe it's got nothing to do with the meeting,' Seth suggested. 'You guys knew Abe better than me. Did he have any enemies?'

Fawz couldn't think of anybody, and neither could Hepzibah. Zach looked at his sister-in-law in disbelief. 'You can't think of anyone? What about Juris *fucking* Neilands?'

'Who is this?' asked Fawz.

'He's a PhD student. Abe was his external examiner. He failed him, and then the harassment started.'

Hepzibah put her glass down, carefully this time. It was full.

'He didn't harass Abe because Abe failed him,' she explained. 'They fell out because Abe told him he didn't support Israel. Neilands is a Christian Zionist.'

Now Fawz remembered. 'Yes, Abe did talk about him.'

Zach thought the concept ridiculous. 'What the fuck is a *Christian* Zionist?'

'*Jesuszach*,' Hepzibah said, rolling the two words into one. 'Exactly what it says on the tin. Christian and Zionist. They believe the bible prophesied "the return of Jews to the holy land", and that the creation of Israel is in god's covenant with Abraham.'

'He's still an anti-Semite.'

'In the land of the blind, the one-eyed man is king.'

'He's Latvian, isn't he?' Zach said, exaggerating what was for him a statement of the obvious. Why else would there be no Jews left in Latvia?

'Whatever, Zach.' Hepzibah rolled her eyes. 'But he's not the guy we saw on the CCTV last night, is he?'

'No,' Zach conceded.

Hepzibah continued. 'My money says the guy who chased Abe was at the meeting. He follows Abe to the pub and waits for him to leave. But why, that's the question.'

~~~

It was after two in the morning. Hepzibah was asleep in the rocking chair, snoring lightly. Seth and Fawz were sitting on the sofa together, talking energetically about some campaign or other. Zach stared into the embers of the fire and wondered whether it was time to wind up for the night with some of Hepzibah's brandy.

Fuck it, let's have another line.

He threw some kindling on the fire and it soon got going. Then he added a log. A spark shot out. It flew over three rows of sanded floorboards and the hearth, landing on the edge of a rug from somewhere exotic. Zach scooped it up before it had a chance to blacken the muted reds and oranges. He threw it back on the fire and left for the kitchen.

The tip of his tongue tingled as he prepared a small line on a worktop. He rolled a fiver into a narrow tube and snorted the powder up his nostril. Bang! *Off* again. Through the roof. He caught his reflection in the blackness of the window. Looking good. He did a twirl. Looking *good*.

A mac was draped over the banister. Zach slipped his hand into the inside pocket and pulled out a wallet. It belonged to the blond. *Sweet.* Inside was a debit card, a gym membership card, three different loyalty cards, and seventy quid. He took thirty. Searching the mac further, he found a brand spanking new iPhone. Zach had hit the jackpot.

The phone was already switched off. If he could've, he would have left there and then. But he couldn't; he had nowhere to go. He pulled on the borrowed, torn black jacket and went to the bi-folding doors at the end of the kitchen. They were locked. He opened the front. It was raining. *Damnit.* Now he couldn't leave the phone outside, which had been his plan. He kept it in his pocket. Risky, but for the moment he had no choice. He lit up in the porch and put the front door on the latch.

Half-way through his fag he heard a shout.

'Zach!'

Hepzibah had woken up and was on the warpath. The door had blown open. He was smoking. Bad news, because Hepzibah hated tobacco. He threw his fag away and closed the door. She was storming down the hall haphazardly, banging into the radiator on one side and the staircase on the other.

She waved a hand in front of her nose and kept her distance. 'You stink,' she said. 'I'm *already* pissed off with you. Now you're smoking in the house.'

'In the porch,' Zach pointed out.

'Why don't you go down to the shed and smoke?'

'The shed? It's pouring. Anyway, the doors are locked.'

'The keys are there.' She pointed to a bowl near the kettle. 'And there's an umbrella in the corner, by the front door.'

Even drunk Hepzibah had a reply, *if* she was talking, because frequently she wouldn't, for hours, sometimes days. She did yoga, she meditated, but she wasn't chilled. *Stuff* bothered her.

Zach raised his hands in surrender. 'Sorry, Heps.' She grunted and he directed the conversation away from smoke. 'The blond bombshell, I don't trust him.'

'*Who?*'

He nodded in the direction of the living room. 'The pretty boy.'

Seth came out, as if on cue, and lifted his mac off the banister. He grabbed his umbrella, turned to Zach and put on a smile. 'Nice to meet you,' he said.

'Likewise,' Zach replied, making no attempt at sincerity. He had Seth's phone and money in his pocket. Concealing a smile, he turned and went to the kitchen. There, he helped himself to bread, cheese, and more wine.

When Hepzibah returned, she was quiet. Zach let her be and washed-up stuff he knew she wouldn't put in the dishwasher: the delicate glassware, the bone china, and Hepzibah's Henckels knives, a gift from Zach in his more affluent days.

He dried his hands and looked over at Hepzibah. She was sitting at the table, her back to him, crying. His instinct was to comfort her, but he held back.

'Sorry if I was a bit sharp earlier,' he finally offered, though he wasn't quite sure why.

'God, you can be dense. I don't care about your stupid comments. I just can't believe I'm never going to see him again. I loved Abe more than anyone I've ever known. You were his brother, it's different. I was his wife, his companion for life. We would have got back together. I know we would.'

Zach stopped listening. In Hepzibah's world things were always about her as well as worse for her. In this world, she and Abe would have got back together. In fairness, she'd been given false hope. It was a mistake for Abe to seek her help. Zach told him so. Apparently Fawz did as well. But Abe worked with Hepzibah on the book for two months and now he was dead, her reality – that they would have rekindled their romance – was becoming unshakeable.

'I'm going to bed,' she said. 'Put the cushions on the floor, you'll be more comfortable. There's bedding on the sofa.'

'Why can't I sleep upstairs?'

'Fawz is in the spare room.'

'How come? Abe's flat's not far. A taxi wouldn't have been expensive.'

'What's the problem, Zach? That she's sleeping in the spare room or that she's Palestinian?'

'Both, probably.'

'You can make a joke out of anything, can't you? But behind all your liberal posturing you're as bigoted as the rest of your mad family. She'll be here when you wake in the morning. Can you get your head round that?'

'What sort of a question is that? I think I'll manage.'

'It'll be a first for you.'

'Oh, I'm sorry I haven't woken up with an Arab in the house before. That must make me anti-Arab.'

'Well, you're not exactly pro-Arab, are you?'

'Should I be?'

'Yes, when it comes to their struggle with Israel.'

Zach had heard it all before. 'Night, Heps. See you both in the morning.' He put his earphones in, switched on his iPod and scrolled down to the bottom of his playlist till he reached the Moby album with a number for a name. Perfect. Big enough beat to move him, sufficiently downtempo to calm him.

While he rocked to the music and drank Hepzibah's brandy, which inexplicably she didn't like, Zach emptied the contents of his holdall onto the sofa. Jeans, linen jacket and trousers, T-shirts, shirts, shorts, underwear, a pair of Wayfarers, a small tin bearing a cannabis leaf, a wash bag, and a framed photograph of Rachel. This was all he had to his name, bar winter clothing stored at Beth's, and his beloved iPod,. Oh yes, and an ancient android pay as you go phone.

Zach unzipped the pockets, turned the bag upside down and shook it over the coffee table. Some crumbs and a penny dropped out along with a ball of hash, large enough for two decent joints. Most stoners smoked weed, which Zach was partial to, but he preferred resin because you could inhale deeply without coughing your guts up.

He stuck three cigarette papers together and sprinkled some tobacco in. Then he tore the ball of resin in two and popped half in the tin, from which he took a long sewing needle, blackened at the tip. With this he skewered the other half and held it above a lighter till it smoked. He waited a second for it to cool before crumbling the burnt hash into the tobacco.

The track ended and the pace slipped down a gear as electronic music met gospel, a marriage made in heaven. He stuck a roach into one end of the joint and twirled the other round and round like a firecracker, ready to light. Before sparking up, he examined the contents of the wrap in his back pocket. After a day's use, that gram didn't look so healthy. What was left wouldn't last him much more than a day. The iPhone came just in time.

He sent a text from his trusty burner.

'Hi Jake, got any gear?'

3

Zach had another bad night wrestling with unsettling images of Abe. Eventually, he fell asleep. His first thought when he woke, Abe was dead. His second, did he have any missed calls or texts. He glanced at his phone. There was no green light flashing in the top right-hand corner. Nothing from Jake. He checked the time. 8.15. Still early, so no need to panic. He lay back down on the three cushions that posed as his bed and closed his eyes, fancying another half-hour's sleep. First, he saw Abe as he knew him, happy, smiling, but in seconds all he could see was Abe slumped down dead, blood seeping out of cracks in his skull. Zach opened his eyes and kept them open.

The smell of fresh coffee escaped from the kitchen into the hall and reached the living room. Zach pulled on his jeans and opened the door.

'Morning,' he said.

Hepzibah and Fawz were sitting at the kitchen table. Fawz, who'd been talking, stopped and looked over. She talked with her hands. Her manners were expressive. Hepzibah, by contrast, bottled things up before exploding. She was bottling something up now, whilst she glared at him. He ignored her, headed for the cafetiere by the kettle and poured himself a coffee. As he was opening the fridge for milk Fawz said,

'There is a bowl of green olives, next to the hard cheese. Can you bring both to me?'

The request shook Zach. That was his go-to breakfast, with toast. When he was growing up there were always two jars of marinated olives in the fridge, one green, one black, and bags of cheeses. Some people have marmalade in the morning. Zach had savoury stuff. *So did Fawz.* This should not have surprised him. After fleeing persecution in Spain, Zach's family lived peacefully with Arabs in Damascus for five hundred years. But the fight over Palestine in the 1930s and '40s fuelled Arab anger toward Jews and Zach's family fled again. He reminded himself that Fawz was, now, the enemy.

He sat down beside her at the table, but not close, and shared cheese and olives, dispensing with toast for the moment. The mood was not chilled. Instinctively, he knew this was not the moment to be popping bread into the toaster. Zach looked outside, avoiding Hepzibah's stare. The early morning sun bathed the back of the garden.

'Seth rang earlier,' Hepzibah said, her voice cold as steel. 'He can't find his phone. You haven't seen it, have you?'

Zach played it cool. He shook his head and sipped at his coffee. He looked innocent enough, and maybe convinced Fawz, but Hepzibah wasn't buying it.

'Really?' She raised an eyebrow.

'Really,' he replied, hoping that would be the end of the matter.

It wasn't.

'He said he had it here last night.'

'So? Maybe he lost it on the way home. Maybe it's behind the sofa. I don't know.' What was Hepzibah going to do? Say she didn't believe him?

'I don't believe you. You took it, didn't you?'

'No,' he said. What was she going to do? Search his stuff?

'Prove it. Turn out your pockets.' She knew Zach. He needed to be frisked before being allowed to leave.

Fawz looked on wide-eyed as Hepzibah patted Zach down like a pro. One leg at a time, up to the groin, round the bum. She'd watched Abe do it many times and taken over on several occasions. But all Hepzibah found was Zach's own phone and some loose change. She asked him to raise his arms for an upper body search. Zach was only wearing a T-shirt and it was apparent at a glance he didn't have another phone up his sleeve, because he didn't have a sleeve to hide it under.

Hepzibah stayed focused, much as Abe would have done. 'Where's your bag?' she demanded.

'In the living room.'

Fawz followed, not quite believing what she was seeing. She watched open-mouthed as Hepzibah emptied Zach's holdall, turning it upside down and shaking it. Nothing. This fazed Hepzibah, but she didn't let the setback deter her. She lifted the sofa cushions, checked the book-shelves, and searched the entire room. She widened her search to the hall and porch, taking her time. She even looked in the cupboard under the stairs. Still nothing. She combed the kitchen and investigated up-stairs. Fawz and Zach followed. Hepzibah was behaving as if she were on the set of a Poirot film, with her as Inspector. She looked under beds and mattresses, inside the chest of drawers in the spare room, and the wardrobe as well. She even looked behind the toilet. Nothing.

'OK?' Zach asked.

'No, it's not OK,' she replied, and made her way down the stairs. Zach and Fawz trailed behind her. Hepzibah opened the front door. Outside, she checked the porch and looked underneath a large terra-cotta pot filled with trailing geraniums. She scanned the small front garden. She inspected the beds, but could find nothing. Hepzibah put her hands on her hips and sighed.

'OK now?' Zach asked once more.

Hepzibah shrugged. 'I guess.'

Zach changed the subject entirely. 'So, how long have you known the blond bombshell?'

'What is this, the blond bombshell?'

'He's being rude. He's referring to Seth,' Hepzibah explained. She conferred with Fawz. 'A couple of months. We see him at meetings and stuff.'

'A couple of months. You hardly know him, yet he stayed till three in the morning.'

Hepzibah looked over to Fawz, who blushed.

'You like him,' Zach suggested.

'He seems like a nice guy.'

'Handsome, isn't he?'

'Yes,' she agreed.

'Well, I don't trust him.' Zach's suspicions were aroused when he nicked Seth's phone. It was switched off. Seth took his phone out, but switched it off whilst he was at Hepzibah's. Did he have something to hide?

'There's something about blondie that's not right. He likes to fight, I can tell. That's unusual for a leftie. There's more to the pretty boy than meets the eye.'

Zach made fresh coffee and hunted for bread to make toast, without bothering to ask Hepzibah. After that morning's inquisition, she said nothing and left to sit under the rose arch. It was in the middle of the back garden and still in the shade, but she didn't seem to mind. Fawz helped herself to coffee and sat with Zach at the patio table, where they ate Manchego and olives with toast. When he was finished, Zach rolled a fag and checked his phone again, hoping he'd missed a call or a text. He hadn't. It was 9.30. Jake had young kids. Surely he was up. Zach resisted the temptation to text him again. He grabbed his linen jacket and checked he had all he needed. Phone (his), money (other people's), lighter, skins, baccy, wrap. Ready.

'See you later,' he shouted from the kitchen. 'I'll cook tonight.'

Fawz called goodbye from the patio table, whilst Hepzibah came into the house and caught up with Zach at the front door. Gone was the scowl. 'Will you? That's nice. I've always liked your cooking.'

'It's not as good as yours.'

She didn't disagree. 'I'm glad you didn't steal Seth's phone. But I had to search you. I hope you understand. Abe would have done the same thing.'

'He would,' Zach agreed.

Hepzibah got up onto the tip of her toes to kiss Zach, but couldn't reach. He leant forward. She pulled him down and gave him a real smacker on the cheek.

'See you later. Hope it goes well today.'

'Thanks, Heps. Bye.'

Zach closed the gate behind him and lingered for a moment, checking whether Hepzibah was at the window. She wasn't. It was safe to retrieve his ill-gotten gains. He reached over the low garden wall and felt behind a dense evergreen shrub. He worked quickly, finding a phone wrapped in a black plastic bag taped to the wall. After checking the coast was clear, he ripped it off and left.

4

Zach passed the Greek food store that sold the marinated olives, and crossed Murder Mile, whose appearance at that hour of the day belied its name. Young mothers pushed buggies and walked slowly with their toddlers. A pensioner, pulling a bag on wheels, joined the queue at the greengrocers. The bookies was busy, the wine shop less so, and a couple of New Agers were looking through the window of the spiritual wellbeing shop. Lower Clapton Road looked just like any other inner-city street.

Over the road from Hackney Baths, Zach joined a crowd waiting for the bus into town. Half a dozen languages filled the air. When the 48 arrived, he peeled away from the pack with a group of teenagers talking in shrill east London accents. They flashed Oyster cards at the driver and piled up to the top deck. Downstairs, sad faces calculated how far the pennies would stretch at the market. Zach followed the teenagers up the stairs and stuck his earphones in, blotting out their jarring banter with a fusion of electronic music and punk.

He stared out at Mare Street, the business signs advertising fast food outlets, junk jewellers, opticians, bookies, and barbers. Zach spotted the Italian deli Abe always raved about and, further down, sandwiched by a pound stretcher shop and a launderette, the café with great coffee. The bus stopped at Ridley Road Market and the bottom deck emptied. Abe used to cycle there for his weekly fix of exotic fruit. Zach pictured him fingering a persimmon, a favourite, but soon all he could see was his brother slumped down dead, blood seeping out of cracks in his head.

At Liverpool Street Station he spent the last of Ester's money on a day return to Wivenhoe, a small university town on the Blackwater Estuary in Essex. Rachel, his three-year-old daughter, lived there with some guy he'd never met. This bloke saw his daughter all the time. That felt shit.

The house was on a hip street five minutes from the waterfront, populated by artists, writers, and university lecturers. He could hear Beth playing the piano, Ravel's second movement, the piece with a long trill at the end that she always got wrong, and perhaps still did. He rang the bell, and the music came to an abrupt stop. Zach braced himself for confrontation. The arrangement had not been easy. She'd offered him this four-hour window as her bloke was out giving a lecture on water problems in Sub-Saharan Africa.

Before the door was fully open, Bitz, an unintentional cross between a Welsh Sheepdog and a Springer Spaniel, squeezed out to greet Zach. Beth went through the ritual of telling the dog not to jump up and the hound ignoring her because he knew she wasn't being serious. Beth was wearing a classy summer dress. No doubt she bought it from a charity shop, made some adjustments on the sewing machine, and now it looked like a Givenchy. Surprisingly, she also wore a sympathetic expression, which was a relief. Her hair was short now, which suited her, but he didn't say.

Then he saw Rachel, hiding behind Beth. He could see little fingers tugging at a curl of hair. She was hidden, coming up no higher than her mother's waist. When she peeked at him, he blew her a kiss. But she didn't put out her little hand and catch it. Instead, she pulled Beth's dress round and his kiss disappeared into nowhere. Zach's heart sank.

'I'm so sorry about Abe,' Beth said. 'He was a really nice guy.'

'Yes, he was.'

Zach was not in the mood for conversation on the doorstep. He went straight up to the bathroom, brushing past them. Upstairs, in the cold light of day, he could see what he saw last night, barely two days' worth, and that was stretching it out. He checked his phone again. Still nothing. He separated out a smaller line than usual, rolled up a fiver and snorted the powder up his nose. He felt great in an instant. Earlier, he had been forlorn at Rachel's wary response. Now, he headed for the garden, not thinking for a second that she might not play with him. But Beth held him back. She had an indignant, haughty look on her face. Zach steadied himself for the inevitable poke. It would be drug-related, for sure. Beth thought he should feel bad having a line in his daughter's house. He didn't.

'Is cocaine your answer to everything, us splitting up, Abe's death?'

'I wasn't bothered about us splitting up. Only losing Rachel.'

He looked out at his daughter on the swing. Her pink dress ballooned in the breeze. Did it have to be pink? Who cared, she was a beauty. Every father thought his little girl beautiful, and Zach was no exception. She had his thick black curly hair, his dark skin, but Beth's nose, a small English number. He smiled at his three-year-old as she pushed as hard as she could. The swing wasn't going fast, nevertheless it was still a wonder Bitz wasn't getting his head knocked off. The dog was running back and forth with a lot of excitement and not much intelligence.

'She'll come round,' Beth said, picking at a jar of salted almonds. 'But your behaviour was pretty bad.'

'OK, I'd nicked your laptop, but you hit me in the face. That's not exactly great behaviour.'

Beth looked Zach up and down, all six feet of him, and flared her nostrils contemptuously. 'What, can't take a slap when you deserve one? You wanted to see Rachel, but I wanted to strangle you. I had a deadline for an article, and I missed it, because of you, never mind having to get a new laptop.'

Zach conceded the point silently, and stepped away into the warm midday sun. He grinned at Rachel as he walked round to the back of the swing. He caught its chain, bent down, and brought his cheek close to hers. Bitz panted in their faces. Zach pushed him away. The dog came back. Now Zach kept him at bay with one hand. With the other he held Rachel.

'I love you,' he whispered into her ear.

She said nothing, but stayed perfectly still. When he kissed her on the cheek, she accepted it by leaning on his lips.

He shoved Bitz out of the way. 'Want me to push you?'

'Yes pleeease,' she replied as she flew away. When she came back, she said: 'Really high!'

Zach thought about his own childhood. When he'd been a baby his mother hadn't been around. Later, when she was around, she didn't want to be. His response as a father was to over-compensate. He wanted Rachel with him all the time, making Beth feel both suffocated and rejected. They drifted apart. Her best friend pushed her to leave. So Beth left, taking Rachel with her. She was still a baby, not even able to walk. The best friend's interference still rankled.

He had a job then, working as an economic development officer, and was able to rent a flat where Rachel could come and stay. Now, two years later, he was lucky if he saw her more than three hours a week.

'Wheeeee! Higher! I want to go higher!'

He pushed a little harder. With his free hand he checked his phone. It was 12.30 and he still hadn't heard from Jake.

~~~

Three hours later, Zach was sitting in the sun on Hepzibah's front garden wall, his jacket on his lap, still waiting for a text or a call. He lifted his sunglasses. So far, there'd been nothing.

A group of teenage girls stopped at the front gate to flirt with him, sixth formers out of uniform. Zach turned bad boy in an instant and flirted right back.

'Get 'em off,' one of them said. The other girls looked at their friend in astonishment, then burst into laughter alongside her.

Whether meant or not, Zach obliged, happily, and began slowly to unbutton his shirt in the manner of a Chippendale. When he got to the last button he flashed his shirt open and closed in the blink of an eye.

'If there was a six-pack there you need to go back and point it out,' the same girl said, once again causing her friends to fall about laughing.

Zach laughed with them before the girls waved and walked away. He made himself decent once more and rang Jake, though he thought it fruitless. But the call was answered on the third ring. Zach's heart raced.

'Didn't you get my messages?'

'Yeah, I got your messages.'

'You never got back to me.'

'There was nothing to get back to you about.'

Now Zach's heart sank. 'Nothing at all?'

'Not what you're after.'

'So, what have you got?' he asked, breathing easier.

'Whizz, special k, if you're short. You usually are.'

'Got any tweak?'

'Yeah, but that baby's fifty a g.'

'You interested in a brand spanking new iPhone?'

'Might be.'

'How much?'

'Go on,' he said, like he was doing Zach a favour, 'I'll give you a couple of grams of the nice stuff for it.'

'I could get four hundred for the phone.'

'Sure,' Jake chuckled.

'How about throwing in some dope as well?'

'Yeah OK. An eighth, but that's it.'

'Make it a quarter.'

'I can't, man. It's black gold. You can have a quarter of some Moroccan I've got.'

'I'll stick with the nice stuff.'

'Cool. Six thirty, usual place. Don't be late.'

Two grams of tweak! And an eighth of an ounce of his favourite hash. *Nice.* In the end the price wasn't too bad. A hundred and twenty-five quid for Seth's phone. Zach ran up to the bathroom to celebrate. When he came down Hepzibah was rifling through the shopping he'd left at the bottom of the stairs. 'Been for a line?' she asked, without looking up. It didn't need an answer, and she didn't wait for one. 'Food looks nice. What are you making?'

'Sephardi pies.'

'Sounds great.' She took the bag into the kitchen and emptied it. At the bottom she found a computer cable.

'What's this?'

'A computer cable.'

'I can see it's a computer cable, but what's it for?'

'Just in case.' He took the cable from her.

'Just in case of what?'

'Might need it, you never know.'

Zach went into the living room. There, he opened Hepzibah's laptop and typed in her password. Then he connected Seth's SIM card to the computer using the cable he'd bought and clicked on 'download'.

~~~

It was almost eight o'clock when Zach let himself in with the spare key. Fawz was on Skype talking in Arabic. He got the gist. She was looking forward to seeing everyone back home but was anxious about the security situation. Hepzibah was in the kitchen, cooking. Her back was to him, and she was singing *You Know I'm No Good* along with Amy Winehouse. Oblivious to Zach's presence, Hepzibah moved her body to the slow beat. For a long moment Zach ogled the sway of her hips, only for the lure of drugs to drag him away. Up he went to the bathroom with his crystal methamphetamine, commonly known as tweak. Sensibly, he separated out a small line, otherwise he would have got well and truly tweaked and not slept a wink. He hoovered it up in the twinkling of an eye. A second later, the rush came.

Zach was on the edge of control, just how he liked it. He ran down the stairs, announcing his arrival at the bottom with a bounce.

Both Hepzibah and Fawz ran into the hall. Neither one of them had known he'd been in the house. Fawz, who was still on Skype, went back into the living room.

Hepzibah looked him up and down and snarled, 'You're completely out of it. I'm sick of it.'

Zach almost replied: 'And you've already polished off a bottle and are on to your second', but that would have caused a row. Zach felt stupidly happy, and he wanted to keep it that way. He ignored Hepzibah's aggression, grinned and said nothing. She was happy to fill the void. *'Obviously,* it's too late to cook your aubergines. I knew it would be when you left earlier. They're in the fridge wrapped in paper towels.'

'I did text to say I wouldn't be back in time to cook.'

Hepzibah grunted and called Fawz for dinner.

Zach picked at his meal. He was high as a kite. Food had become an irrelevance. But he did wonder what Fawz would make of a stir fry. He watched amazed as she ate everything, not just the chicken, but the noodles and tasteless strips of vegetables as well. She even said, 'That was very nice. Thank you.' Zach refrained from quizzing her on the veracity of this statement, not least because he knew Hepzibah would be incapable of seeing the funny side. She was already a bottle and a half in.

Hepzibah's moods set the tone for the space she shared with those around her. Zach hadn't discussed this matter with Fawz, but he imagined she felt the same. Abe certainly did. Hepzibah's moods dominated, whether they were good, bad, or indifferent, because the goal was always to avoid provoking the bad one – no mean task after ten o'clock in the evening. By that time, she was frequently on the slide. The trick was to keep her steady till she fell asleep.

She was looking ahead at nothing in particular when she claimed, with the certainty of an evangelical believer, 'We would have got back together for sure.' Fawz glanced at Zach. They both knew different. Hepzibah drank more wine and continued. 'We were getting on so well.' Who she was addressing wasn't clear. It didn't matter. All that was important was she uttered the words. They were sustenance to her alternative reality, where she and Abe would have rekindled their romance had he not died.

The landline rang, breaking Hepzibah's reverie, to Zach and Fawz's relief. But when Hepzibah answered the phone, she tensed.

'What do you want?' she snapped at the caller. 'You need to talk to me? And I should listen because?'

Despite her anger, Hepzibah was listening. She turned to Zach and Fawz, mouthed '*My sister,*' and left the room with the bottle.

Zach and Fawz were alone. Fawz was pretty, but Zach just couldn't see what caught Seth's interest. She wasn't about to jump in bed with the blond bombshell, no matter how good looking he was, and he didn't seem the type to hang about getting to know her before moving beyond a kiss. Perhaps Zach was doing him a disservice. Maybe it was her intelligence he was drawn to. After all, this was considerable. Fawz was in London studying for a PhD in modern European history at Queen Mary University. She had the ability to study at the highest level in a language different to her own.

'You're going back home soon,' he said, remembering the Skype conversation Fawz had earlier.

The sparkle disappeared from her big brown eyes. 'Yes, back to East Jerusalem, and the occupation.'

Zach put a log on the fire. 'There has to be peace,' he said, somewhat meaninglessly.

'And equality,' she added.

Zach didn't know how to respond to that. Israel was a Jewish state, a country for Jews, not Arabs. They could stay, if they wanted, with lesser status. He steered the conversation away from equality.

'I can't remember his name, the US Secretary of State, isn't he in Israel now trying to rescue the talks?'

Fawz took a moment to reply. Was she digesting what had just taken place? Zach had not been able to agree to a simple plea for equality.

'Yes,' she said, 'John Kerry. He has given Israel three days to release the last group of twenty-six prisoners and stop settlement expansion in the West Bank, otherwise the talks will end.'

Zach found himself saying, 'You never know.'

'You and Mahmoud Abbas must be the only people in the world who think Israel will come to its senses. Not even the Americans do.'

'Maybe not, but they can use their influence.'

'I was born in 1988, during the first intifada. I have been waiting twenty-six years for America to pressure Israel. I think I will be waiting another twenty-six years. Do you know what Fawz means? It means victory.' She managed a grim smile.

Silence filled the room. Zach reached for his tobacco and papers and rolled a cigarette. Victory? What did victory mean? The end of Israel? He went out for a smoke.

~~~

When he came back in, Fawz gave him a look that told him to be wary. Hepzibah was sitting by the fire in the rocking chair, drinking. Her mood hung heavy over the room. Had the call from her sister sent her mood crashing? Neither Fawz nor Zach asked. They sat quietly. Zach felt uncomfortable, and he imagined Fawz did as well.

'I want you out of here tomorrow,' Hepzibah said, out of the blue and without making eye contact. She continued to stare into the fire. 'You'll have to go back to yours.'

Zach assumed Hepzibah was talking to him, rather than Fawz. 'I don't have a mine anymore,' he replied. 'I've lost my flat.'

Hepzibah swung round. She glared at him, her words slurred and angry.

'You've lost it? Housing benefit paid your rent! I'm sure drugs are behind this somehow, so don't expect me to feel sorry for you. You're still leaving tomorrow, otherwise this will drag on. I want my living room back and I don't want a drug addict around anymore.'

Zach had seen this behaviour before. She was drunk and the phone call from her sister had tipped her over the edge. Now she was angry with Zach and unhappy with her lot. She would change her mind in the morning and let him stay. More likely, she wouldn't even remember the conversation had taken place. He was about to placate Hepzibah and say 'OK', when Fawz said,

'You can stay at the flat. Abe would have wished this.' It was said with no delight, but it was simple and obvious. Yet it hadn't occurred to Zach. He grinned at his good fortune. Mind you, they would argue.

Hamas are terrorists.

No, they're not.

Jerusalem is our capital.

It's ours too.

Israel is a Jewish state.

You made it one. You're a Zionist.

Is that such a bad thing?

Yes.

Why?

You stole our land.

But Jews need somewhere safe.

So do Palestinians, thanks to Israel.

Once Zach had prepared his bed for the night – a bed sheet over three cushions plus an old duvet – he rolled a juicy joint to counteract the effects of the amphetamine and help him sleep. He stepped outside to smoke. At first, when the dope mixed with the wine he felt dizzy. Later, when he lay down, he felt horny. Now that was the tweak talking.

5

Reports were coming in of a shootout near Rafah on the Israeli/ Gazan border and Fawz was glued to Al Jazeera TV, the Arabic channel. She was sitting bolt upright on a light grey Swedish two-seater with a back so low it didn't count.

'Shall I order pizza?' Zach asked, dangling her purse in front of her face. Fawz swatted it away, irritated, but she hadn't said no, so he took it as yes and ordered two. By the time they arrived half an hour later, there had been more news. Fawz was now agitated. She took a piece of pizza, but her attention was focused on the TV. Zach had to warn her on a couple of occasions that cheese was dripping onto her jeans.

It turned out there were now five dead men on Israel's southern border with Gaza, all Hamas fighters. Footage was shown of them arriving at the tunnel entrance. Fawz pointed at the screen with a slice of pizza.

'Look. They are not on a raid.'

Here came the argument he'd anticipated. Abe had died three days earlier and Zach had only been there a few hours. He didn't want confrontation, but he had to say something.

'They're carrying guns.'

'Yes of course they are, but they are lightly armed.'

'So, what are they doing?'

'Smuggling food or medical supplies, probably. You know Gaza has been under siege for the last seven years, since Hamas gained power in 2007. How would *you* manage living under those conditions? You would build tunnels as well.'

'You mean seized, not gained. Hamas seized power.'

'No, they were elected, whether you like them or not.'

'What about that little spat with Fatah? What was that all about?'

'If you knew anything you would know that was engineered by the US because they did not like the results of the elections in the Palestinian National Authority.'

'OK, OK, but these guys here,' he nodded at the TV. 'They're terrorists. They weren't found at a smuggling tunnel. They used a terror tunnel, what Al Jazeera is calling a *military* one. I understand some Arabic, remember?'

'*Terrorists?* The people of Gaza are defending themselves the only way they can. What would you do? Let the Israelis treat you no better than a caged animal? Take everything you have? You would fight back any way you could. As for Hamas, who I do not support, you should have talked to them seven years ago. Maybe the rise of Hamas is all your fault. Maybe, if Bill Clinton had forced Ehud Barak to negotiate with Yasser Arafat after the murder of Yitzhak Rabin by a Jewish terrorist, Hamas would never have become popular in Gaza and the occupied territories.'

Zach didn't pursue the argument. He stuck his earphones in, put on some electronic hip-hop and blotted out Al fucking Jazeera.

After five minutes, Fawz turned the sound down to make a call. She spoke in Arabic and discussed the five dead terrorists, or to put it more accurately, the 'Zionist killings'. She soon left, without saying goodbye or cleaning the greasy stain on her jeans. Zach unwound from their disagreement with a small line of coke. He'd had enough crystal meth for the day. Once he'd snorted up the last of the line, the doorbell went. He popped his wrap into his back pocket, left the flat door open and took the stairs down to the front door two at a time.

The moment he twisted the latch, the door flew open, hitting him full in the face. He fell back.

'Fuck! What's your problem?' Zach asked as he picked himself up and brushed down his chinos.

The voice brought him to attention. Four words, spoken with the menace of a samurai sword in the hands of a lunatic.

'*You, you are high.*'

Israeli accent. Looked like a heavyweight boxer on steroids, all pumped up. Wore a hood for effect. It worked, as did the sadistic smile. The stance, feet planted apart, was of someone ready to pounce in an instant. He was a soldier, or he'd been. What did he want? Zach tried to keep things cool.

'OK, your problem is that I'm high?' If it was, Zach did indeed have a problem.

'Perhaps you are too stupid to take me seriously. I can show you how serious I am if that is the case.'

'Don't worry, I'm taking you seriously. What do you want?'

'The SIM card.'

So, Zach had been right not to trust the Ashkenazi. 'How come Seth didn't come round to get it himself?'

'He is tough, but you would have fought back. We can do this easy or hard. SIM card or I hit you. Once will be enough, believe me.'

'Easy is fine. You can have it.'

But something did hit Zach. The man in front of him could be the bloke caught on CCTV. Similar build, white, hooded, shaved head. Was he looking at the man who chased Abe into the road?

'The SIM card!' The guy wasn't going to ask again.

'I almost threw it away,' Zach said, reaching into his back pocket. 'It's just a SIM card, hardly that important.'

'Yet you kept it. Funny that.' He took the tiny card and said nothing. But as a parting shot, he slapped Zach round the head.

'Hey! What was that for?'

'Being a junkie.'

'I'm not a junkie, I'm a cocaine addict.'

'*This* is for arguing.' His fist came so fast Zach didn't have time to move. 'You should learn when to shut up, junkie,' the man said as his knuckles smashed into the side of Zach's head. The punch sent Zach crashing to the ground. He was out for the count before his head hit the floor.

6

Finchley, North London

The brother got walloped tonight. I hope he's OK. I'm told the Israeli thought it hilarious, but it can't be funny being hit by him. You only have to look at the guy once to see how much damage he can do. Stupidly, the brother corrected him on the use of the word junkie. Now he's unconscious. I briefly considered calling 999 anonymously, but didn't for fear it could compromise me at some future point. He'll survive, with or without a call from me.

It's been three days since the professor was killed. How do I feel? Same as I did when I first heard, sick to the pit of my stomach. I'm off my food. I'm not sleeping. When the lights are out, and I'm trying to sleep, I'm tormented by my idiocy. The people I allowed to be involved, like the Israeli, the decisions I made, or rather didn't make. I let a genie out of the bottle then failed to take control. Given my day job, that is inexcusable. There are always consequences when you pay no attention. And now the professor is dead.

Ella and the girls can't make sense of my mood. Earlier in the evening Debbie asked, 'Why do they want to kill us?' She was looking at five dead Arab terrorists, their blood spooled out on the ground. I said nothing. I was looking at the television, but I wasn't watching it. I wasn't doing anything, not even responding to my daughter. Ella had to step in. 'They don't like us because we're Jews,' she'd said, and no doubt gave me a confused look. I've no idea. I didn't take my eyes off the TV I wasn't watching.

I'll have to tell them something soon, but I can't tell them the truth. For it's not grief I feel, but guilt. I am using the word in its literal sense. I didn't pull the trigger, but I am culpable. I'm guilty of an offence and I will forever fear the reach of the law. That is my life sentence. Every car I hear arriving on the drive, every knock on the door, I will always worry. Is it the police?

The truth is, it's my life rather than his death that is sickening me, knowing I could always be found out.

But it was an accident. He wasn't meant to be killed.

7

Albany Street was on the right side of town, a world away from Hackney. A period house on Nash Terrace would set you back five million, and for that you wouldn't even get a garden. But you would overlook Regent's Park, and there was a cop shop on the street, with police personnel on the spot to run round when you needed them.

It was outside this police station that Hepzibah was remonstrating with Zach. He'd stopped at the bottom of the steps, refusing to go any further. The squabble prompted the well-heeled locals to give them a wide berth. Zach wasn't the one doing the shouting. Nevertheless, it was him they stared at. His attire was passable – short-sleeved white cotton shirt and black linen trousers – but his look was wild, his crazed stare zipping about like a manic dragonfly chasing mosquitos.

Zach jammed his hands deep into his pockets and talked over Hepzibah's shrill wittering.

'For fuck's sake, Heps, what *is* the problem?'

'What's the problem? You, you lazy arsehole. Why should I be the one to do all the work? Honestly, you're ...'

Zach let her prattle on. He loosened another button on his shirt in an effort to cool down, wishing he'd worn shorts. It was unseasonably hot for early May. Twenty-four degrees, no wind, and a deep blue cloudless sky. Continuing to ignore Hepzibah, Zach pulled down his Wayfarers from the top of his head and looked up at the police station. It was bathed in sunshine. Not even that helped its cause. The building was brutal. The first tier of windows was twenty feet from the ground. No kidding. The police station, a rectangular block, sat on a fifteen-foot-high concrete platform, presumably as some sort of safety mechanism in case the residents of Albany Street stormed the station. Most criminal (pun intended), the station was built without regard for the elegant Georgian townhouses it was squeezed between. No surprise. It was put up in the 1950s when anything went, so long as it was functional.

Hepzibah was still blethering. '... So I don't see why you shouldn't wait with me.'

'But they're not actually going to do anything, and we're going to have to wait *ages*. It doesn't take two of us to tell them what's happened. You'll want to do all the talking anyway.'

'You've been whining all morning, Zach. It's understandable, but it's beginning to get on my nerves.'

'*Understandable?* Fawz found me lying face down in my own vomit.'

'Typical male. You were knocked out, so of course you suffered a concussion, and you're now left with a brain injury that will have you talking gibberish within three years.'

'Have you ever been knocked out?'

'No, but ....'

'Shall we give it a try?'

'Very funny. The doctor in A&E checked you over. I was there, remember? No memory loss, you're able to concentrate, and you're not sensitive to light or noise. OK, you're irritable. I guess that's to be expected, but he sent you away with painkillers which you combined with alcohol and drugs and slept like a log. Huh! *I* should be so lucky.'

'Wow, I'm the one who gets whacked, yet it's all about you and your lack of sleep. You're unbelievable, Heps.'

'I'm unbelievable? Everything is about you and your drugs. Look at you now, checking the time on your phone, wondering how long we're going to be. You've left your drugs behind. So what?'

So what? Zach tried to keep cool. 'Look Heps, I know you don't get it, but it's kind of important to me. I could nip home now. I'll be back in under an hour.'

'No you won't. It'll be nearer two with all the work they're doing on Essex Road. It'll take you ages to cross over at the lights. It took us nearly an hour to get here. I'll be waiting for you and that just isn't fair seeing as I'll have been the one at the police station.'

'You'll probably still be waiting to be seen when I get back.'

'Look Zach, you're really beginning to piss me off.'

'Does that mean you're not going to give me the car keys?'

'That's right.'

He tried to look on the bright side, but there wasn't one, not that he could find.

'Zach,' Hepzibah continued, taking the edge off her tone. 'You agree this is a lead, finding out Seth knows Abe's killer?'

'Of course. But he's gone, scarpered. There's nothing they can do.'

'We can at least tell them.'

'But it doesn't take two of us to do that and they're not going to do anything anyway. I'd planned to see Rachel today. Beth's bloke's out.'

'Yes, and I bet you were going to ask me for the train fare.'

'No, I was going to suggest I borrow your car, it's cheaper.'

'What if I said no?'

'You wouldn't, and if you did, you'd regret it. The guilt would get to you.'

'Don't take the piss, Zach. It doesn't sit well coming from you. And actually, it hurts, being constantly reminded I'm childless.'

'Yeah, sorry,' he said, relieved she hadn't told him once more he didn't deserve a child.

'So, coming in with me?'

He groaned in submission.

Hepzibah's hair was down today, and she swished it back over her shoulders. When Zach took her arm, tears came to her eyes. She fought them back. 'You're nothing like him, of course, but when you do that it reminds me of him.'

Zach could smell her perfume all the way up the steps.

'You even walk the same way. It really is unbearable.'

'Maybe I shouldn't see you for a while.' Like now. He could give her a break and go and get his gear.

'No. I have to see you, you're my connection to Abe. We have to find out what happened to him.' Hepzibah wiped her eyes and checked she had a business card for Murrell. 'I'm worried I'll forget to give him one.'

Zach held the door for Hepzibah, and she strode in, holding her head high.

'We're here to see Detective Inspector Murrell,' she told the desk sergeant. 'He's got the Abe Peretz case. I'm Hepzibah Peretz.'

The sergeant directed them to a waiting room where they sat under a poster urging ethnic minorities to join the police. Zach held the side of his head, his ear still ringing from the punch.

'What are you doing, Zach? Reminding me you're in pain?'

'For fuck's sake, Heps. Not everything is about you.'

For all the time he'd known her, thirteen years, from bad-boy eighteen-year-old to thirty-one-year-old drug addict, he'd annoyed her, and she sure annoyed him. Yes, she was hot, but she was also a pain in the arse. Somehow, they had to rub along if they wanted to find out what happened to Abe.

Two young white guys came in and sat opposite. They were puffed up, filled with testosterone, their posture insolent. They lounged, legs apart, and gawped at Hepzibah's low-cut summer top.

'They're staring at your tits,' Zach told her.

'I know.'

'Don't you mind?'

'Well yes, but please don't ...'

'Oi!' Zach called over. 'She doesn't want you staring at her tits.'

'What tits?' one of them said, and they both laughed.

Zach leant forward. 'So what's to stare at, funny guy?'

He felt an arm, Hepzibah's, urging him to relax. 'Do you want to get hit again? What's the matter with you? Calm down.'

'I'm in a bad mood.'

'This is about drugs, isn't it? It's only eleven o'clock in the morning. Do you normally snort at this time?'

'I've always had one by eleven thirty. It takes an hour to get back from here and we haven't even been seen.'

'Oh? I thought you could be there and back in an hour.'

'Yeah, well.'

'You're just going to have to cope.'

'It's not as easy as that.'

'Do you know what? I'm sick of hearing you say that.' Hepzibah kept her voice low, but their waiting room companions could hear every word. They were soon sniggering as Hepzibah revealed all. 'Go on, let drugs come before your brother. Why break the habit? Just don't embarrass me in there. Try not to make it *too* obvious.'

'This is better than EastEnders,' one of the white guys joked. They both burst into laughter. 'Yer a wanker mate, a sad wasteoid.'

'Fuckin crack 'ead,' the other chimed.

'I'm not a crack head. I'm a cocaine addict. OK?' Zach snapped. That was an important distinction.

'Ooooh, touchy ain't 'e? Fer a coke whore, a bag bitch.'

They both laughed out loud. Zach ignored his adversaries and sat in silence. But he fidgeted constantly, much to their amusement.

'Speed freak, psychonaut, pill popper!'

'Hahaha. He's perma-fried!'

'Wanker!' they said in unison and laughed their heads off.

The banter came to an end when a female detective constable came for Hepzibah and Zach. Before he left the room, Zach stuck his bum out, patted it, and said, 'Kiss it.'

The two white guys roared with laughter. 'When are you next here, mate? Not had this much fun in *years*.'

Zach couldn't help a smile. 'I'll let you know.'

He followed the detective up two flights of stairs and found himself in an open plan office. Desks were piled high with boxes, and the shelves were half empty. The police were closing shop. The DC knocked on a door off to the side.

'They're here, guv.'

'Come.'

Inside, the Venetian blinds were down against the sun, but not closed. Horizontal lines of sunlight broke through. A fan whirred in the corner.

DI Murrell stared at Hepzibah's top as well. She was used to unwanted male attention, receiving it every time she left the house, and the Inspector's interest was surely unsolicited. He was a scraggy, unshaven cop whose retirement party wasn't far off. The policeman put his hand out first to Hepzibah, then Zach. 'Good to see you both again.'

'Thank you for giving up your time,' Hepzibah said, sounding a tad obsequious.

'I'm busy, so I can't give you long. Please, sit down. There's nowhere out there, I'm afraid. We're in the process of moving. The station's closing next year, part of the Met's financial restructuring.'

'I hope they take the opportunity to demolish the building,' Zach said. 'It's an eyesore.'

The room went deathly quiet. Hepzibah glared at him. The detective constable appeared equally unamused. He'd hit the wrong note. The station was closing. Maybe she was thinking about job security, travel to the new station, changed conditions, working shifts.

The DC herself broke the silence. She addressed her boss. 'I'll get the coffee then, shall I?' Her tone suggested a routine was being played out, one she was tired of.

'If you don't mind,' Murrell said. She clearly did – not that he noticed.

Hepzibah fished out one of her cards and handed it to Murrell. 'Just in case I forget later and you need to get hold of me.'

'I know where to find you if I need you.'

The DI's comment, along with its tone, sent a shiver down Zach's spine. It also struck Hepzibah as creepy. 'Next you'll be telling me you know everything about me,' she said, hiding her distaste with a faux smile.

'I know the essentials. Hepzibah Peretz, freelance journalist, left-wing, Jewish, supporter of Palestinian rights. After you'd flirted with

Trotskyism for a few years, you joined the Labour Party, only to leave when Tony Blair became leader a little later. You were born Hepzibah Freida Belman in London, 1974. Your parents were members of the Communist Party and children of holocaust survivors. You have an elder sister. She lives in Israel.'

'Just so your records are straight,' Hepzibah said, giving the inspector a smile Zach knew to be fake, 'I left the Labour Party when Tony Blair ripped up Clause Four, a year after he became leader.'

Murrell ignored her. No doubt he had no idea what Clause Four was. He turned to Zach. 'Zach Peretz, born in Manchester, 1983, currently unemployed with no fixed abode. Aged seventeen you did a six-month stretch in Feltham.'

Hepzibah gasped.

'You intervened in a domestic taking place on the street, only you beat the guy so badly you were charged with grievous bodily harm.'

'Is this true?' Hepzibah asked Zach.

'Yes,' the Inspector said. 'Now let's get on with this.'

Zach agreed with the cop. 'Let's get on with this.'

'Shall *I* tell him the story?' Hepzibah suggested, to no surprise. Zach didn't care, so long as it was done quickly. But there was a delay. The DC came back with four coffees and made sure she handed the right one to each person. Then she dragged a chair in and sat down. Hepzibah finally began.

'Zach was attacked last night, probably by the man who killed Abe. He's Israeli. And Seth Laskowitz has gone missing. No one from Jews Against the Occupation has seen or heard from him for two days. We've been round. He's done a runner. Somehow, we've no idea how, Seth is connected to the killer.'

'Whoa, slow down. An Israeli, Seth someone or other, Jews against something, one at a time.' He turned to Zach. 'You were attacked last night. You say by the man who chased your brother?'

'Yeah, knocked me for six, for no reason.'

'*No reason?*' Hepzibah spluttered.

'Yeah. No reason.'

'Zach nicked Seth's phone,' she told the Inspector. 'So Seth sends this tough guy round for the SIM card. He looks like the guy who chased Abe into the road and now I'm beginning to wonder exactly who and what Seth is.'

'I downloaded his SIM card onto your computer, Heps. Maybe we'll find something on his contacts list.'

'When did you do that?'

'Two days ago, the day I bought the computer cable. Remember, just before I went out and didn't get back in time to cook? Then you told me to leave, so I left, and we didn't talk yesterday.'

'Have you two finished?'

Hepzibah turned to the DI. 'Sorry, but I had no idea about the SIM card.'

'Clearly.'

'Will you be able to check up on Seth Laskowitz?'

'Yes.'

'And that will take?'

'Can't say. It'll be done soon.'

Zach looked at his watch again. It was eleven-thirty. He twitched. He drummed

his fingers. He tapped his feet.

The DI ignored Zach's behaviour. 'Did Abe have any enemies?'

'The only one we can come up with is Juris Neilands. He's a PhD student and Abe was his examiner. They fell out over Israel.'

This interested Murrell. 'Juris Neilands is anti-Semitic?'

Hepzibah raised an eyebrow. 'Criticising Israel is not the same as criticising Jews. It isn't necessarily anti-Semitic. Anyway, it was Abe, a Jew, who was critical of Israel. Nobody was being anti-Semitic.'

'So the differences were ...'

'Ideological. Juris is a Christian Zionist. He believes Jews are the chosen people and their return to the Holy Land is in accordance with biblical prophecy.'

'And your husband didn't?'

'No, he didn't,' she replied with no explanation.

'And this was enough for Neilands to dislike the professor?'

'Juris saw him as an apostate. He'd shout at Abe in public and harangue him in the university grounds. Once, he followed Abe to his office to continue the argument. But he never threatened Abe with violence.'

'He's a squirt,' said Zach.

'Small people can improvise, Mr Peretz.'

'Fair point. He's in the frame for me anyway. What excuses did he give when you interviewed him?'

'We haven't yet.'

Even Hepzibah was surprised at that. 'But there's a history of harassment, recorded by the police.'

'And that's why he'll be interviewed.'

'When?' Zach asked. 'Abe died four days ago.'

'Yes, and we went round two days later. He wasn't in. We left a card.'

'And has he got back in touch?'

'Mr Peretz, I appreciate you're upset. But Juris Neilands looks nothing like the man who chased your brother the other night. We will interview him. Tell me, in the days before your brother's death, did he seem worried at all? How did he sound when you last spoke to him?'

'Fine, normal, upbeat, in a good mood.'

'Yes,' Hepzibah agreed. 'I spoke to him minutes before he left the pub. He was buzzing. Said public speaking beat lecturing hands down for thrills. Then he said, see you soon. Only I didn't.' She steeled herself, determined to keep the tears away.

'The husband from whom you were separated rings you to come round, after midnight?'

The question was there – whether she liked it or not.

'He was coming round with the recording of that night's meeting.'

'Couldn't it have waited?'

'He was excited. We were working on a book together, well, more a series of essays, and he wanted me to hear it.'

'A series of essays. It wasn't a novel, then.'

'No, it wasn't a novel.' Hepzibah's tone hinted at rising irritation.

'Something political?' the DI asked.

'Broadly speaking, but what has the book to do with Abe's death?'

'I don't know. Maybe nothing, maybe everything. The more information I have the better.'

'The book doesn't have a title yet, but in essence it seeks to get at what it means to be Jewish.'

'Doesn't sound very contentious to me.'

'That's because you're not Jewish.'

8

It was almost 12.25 – 12.22 to be exact – when they left the police station and crossed Albany Street, leaving Regents Park behind them. At the corner with the cathedral cemetery, they turned left, then right at the B&B for the super-rich, named after the royal park. Soon, the posh houses disappeared, replaced by an estate for those who were not rich. It was well-kept, with the odd tree but had no green space.

Zach walked briskly. He needed that line. Hepzibah was behind him, dragging her heels.

'Come on, Heps.'

'What's the hurry?'

What's the hurry? 'I can't imagine,' he answered sarcastically. 'Get a move on, will you?'

Hepzibah slowed even more, winding Zach up further. He reached the car and waited whilst she searched for her keys as if she had all the time in the world. This act continued whilst she climbed into her car. Once she'd belted herself in and started up the ignition, she checked all three mirrors twice. *Both* wing mirrors? Was she considering driving onto the pavement? Gripping the steering wheel with both hands, she edged out into the road, slow as a tortoise. It took her a minute to get up to twenty five miles an hour, and there she stayed, annoying every-one behind her. The speed limit was thirty.

Somehow, Zach kept quiet for ten minutes or so, then he offered to drive. The catalyst had been the guy behind them. He was gesticulating aggressively, telling Hepzibah to get a move on.

'Let's face it, Heps, negotiating busy London roundabouts is not your forte.' Zach said nothing of the missed opportunities to advance, nor anything about the guy behind. She must have known about him. After all, she looked in her mirror often enough.

All Zach had done was offer to drive. Nevertheless, an argument ensued, and they were still at it when Hepzibah pulled up at the flat half an hour later, bickering about each other's driving. *You're too slow. You're too fast.*

Zach breathed a sigh of relief. 'Thank fuck for that. We're here, *finally.*' He threw Hepzibah another look and undid his seat belt. 'I'll be back in a minute.'

He extracted keys from his pocket as he ran. At the door he poked hurriedly at the lock with no success. He slowed and the key slotted in. Once inside, Zach flew upstairs to the flat, opened that door, retrieved his gear, and prepared himself a line on the chest of drawers in the bedroom. The rush came in a second. No longer was he angry with Hepzibah.

Back in the car, Zach popped his earphones in and switched on his iPod. *Barra Grande* came on, kicking off an hour-long Electro House session. Zach turned to Hepzibah and grinned. 'Back to yours, Jeeves,' he said.

'*Back to yours, Jeeves?* Jesus, Zach.'

Hepzibah put the car in gear, checked her wing mirror, checked it again, and when she was doubly sure she drove away slowly, two hands on the wheel. Zach lived in Lower Clapton, Hepzibah in Upper Clapton. The journey wouldn't take long.

There was a suitable space outside the house, but Hepzibah was unable to park. She either started off wrong, went in too soon, or too sharply, or too late, or she straightened up too quickly, or a combination of any of those. The more she tried, the more flustered she got. A car was waiting. Another arrived.

'Do you want me to do it?'

She nodded and left the car in neutral with the handbrake on. When she reached for her bag Zach saw tears. Once she'd gone, he clambered across into the driver's seat, straightened the car up and parked an inch away from the curb.

When he joined Hepzibah she had already fired up her laptop and found the download of Seth's SIM card. She was immediately excited, grabbing his attention.

'I've found a name here that's more out of place than Sadiq Khan at a Welcome Trump party! Johnny Henderson. The leader of the Defenders of England.'

'You're joking.' Zach leant over her shoulder to look. There it was. Henderson's name and number. 'Fuck me.'

Hepzibah scrolled down the list. 'Your friend's here. Juris Neilands.'

'That is equally interesting.'

'Now why would Juris Neilands be a contact?'

'Why would Johnny Henderson be a contact? Go down some more.'

'Oh my god,' Hepzibah exclaimed. '*Ralph Maccabi*. He's been on my radar for a while. I've always got feelers out for him. He funds a movement here in the UK called Tahor Yisra'el, which means Pure or Clean Israel. They believe in an Israel free of Arabs. This Israel includes the Occupied Territories and is a Greater Israel.'

'What, all the Palestinians kicked out of the West Bank and East Jerusalem? That's a bit extreme. Can't have much support.'

'Tahor Yisra'el has sister parties all over the world, including Israel, where they have members in the Knesset. They are thriving.'

'Either the blond bombshell has got some nice friends or he's a fucking spy. I think I sized him up well.'

'Now the Johnny Henderson connection makes sense. About five years ago Maccabi helped establish a Jewish Division in the Defenders. It petered out last year. Lack of interest from the foot soldiers.'

'A *Jewish* Division of the Defenders of England? For fuck's sake.'

'They still work together when they can. My enemy's enemy is my friend. Maccabi and Henderson share the same Islamophobic views. They both hate Muslims. And presumably so does Seth.'

'I knew the blond bombshell wasn't kosher, but I'd rather not be the one to tell Fawz her boyfriend is a mortal enemy.'

'There's an Israeli name here. Tamir. Could he be the thug Seth sent round for the SIM card? And the man who chased Abe?'

'Could be,' Zach agreed. He checked the time again. 'Gotta go. See you later.'

'Where are you going?'

'I told you, I'm going to see Rachel.'

'You're high.'

'I'll be fine. I've just parked the car, haven't I?'

'That's different to driving to Wivenhoe.' She put out her hand for the car keys. Reluctantly, he handed them over. 'Honestly, you're like a child, Zach. The world doesn't revolve around you. You can have the keys back when you've sobered up.'

9

Zach didn't protest at the demand he come down. What choice did he have? But he could only come down a little, otherwise he wouldn't be able to drive at all. Timing was everything, and he knew he would be leaving in less than thirty minutes. In the meantime, he phoned Ester. They were worlds apart, Ester and he, yet they were close. They had a special bond. When he was young, she took the place of his mother. Yes, her tone when she was angry could remind him of Malka, but Ester was nothing like his mother. She loved Zach dearly.

The line was busy. The conversation, when he had it, would no doubt be a rerun of last night. They were still sitting shiva, after all. He'd ask how she was, and she'd echo the question before answering. 'How am I? I'm tired, Zach.'

He'd half-listen and get the gist. After three days she was tiring of the constant flow of well-wishers. Zach was sympathetic, but it was all so predictable. These people weren't friends of Abe's, they didn't even like him. They were following tradition and paying their respects to his father.

Zach dialled again. Still engaged. He went over last night's conversation once more. After he'd asked after Dov, he'd heard Ester close a door before telling him his father was fixed to his armchair. Dov was depressed. He stared into space. He barely talked. At night he sobbed.

When Zach pressed redial once more, Ester answered. For the first time in ages, happiness was evident in her voice.

'Dad's talking again!' she exclaimed. 'He's back to his normal self, better even. A letter arrived for him this morning. I put it on the table next to his armchair, but he ignored it. I kept telling him to open it. In the end, about an hour ago, I said I would if he didn't. That stirred him into action, although it took him an age to open the envelope. Nearly drove me mad. The letter changed his mood in an instant. He smiled, his face brightened, he was happy. He cried and opened his arms, and I hugged and squeezed him. He kept saying how sorry he was.'

'Es, that's fantastic! Did you ask about the letter?'

'No, it completely slipped my mind,' she replied with heavy sarcasm. 'Dad said it was about one of his investments, but it was handwritten, and he put it in his pocket before I could get a good look. It was post-marked Soho.'

'What could that mean?'

'I don't know.'

'Will he see me, do you think?'

'I'm not going to ask now. He's dozing. First time he isn't sitting with his eyes wide open staring into space.'

'Tell Dad he needs to stop being cross with me. He doesn't know how lucky he is, having children that continue to love him, despite everything.'

~~~

Ester was nineteen when Zach was born, living at home until marriage, which sadly had still not happened. Like all good Jewish daughters, she had no university education and only knew domestic work. When she wasn't baking pumpkin bread or savoury matzoh pie, or making sure Dov, their demanding father, had everything he needed, she would find time to pinch Zach's cheeks and tell him what a pretty boy he was.

His eldest brother, Nissim, was a distant figure. He was already working in the family business, young yet old, shuffling in and out of the house in his long black coat and black hat. He married and left when Zach was four. After that, Zach saw Nissim as much and as little as before. Abe, by contrast, figured massively in Zach's early childhood. Yes, he was nine years older, but that had its advantages. He never saw Zach as competition and was devoted to him. The first thing he did when he got home from school, even before a slice of Ester's baklava, was whizz Zach round the garden in a plastic car, round and round till Zach was dizzy and sick with laughter. His father would run him along the same track, if he was in a good mood and Zach badgered him enough. Although Dov couldn't push as fast as Abe, it was always special because afterwards he would beam, hug Zach like a bear, and call him 'my little Zachy Wachy'.

Zach was eight years old when Abe went off to university and left him with Ester and his parents, surrounded by exasperation, rage and violence. Dov and Malka were locked in a loveless, angry marriage and home was dominated by loud, irate voices. His father set the tone, barking out orders for the kosher cooking from an armchair in the living room.

Food and religion governed the house. Dov was a traditional Jew who believed food served as a magnet for holiness and acts of holiness, and that being kosher created a sanctified space within the home, thereby ensuring God was present. Yet Zach saw nothing holy in his father's behaviour. At table Dov could get into a rage in an instant. If Zach wasn't sitting quietly with a pious look on his face, Dov would shout at him and instruct him that prayer was the most important aspect of food, not eating it. God was watching him. Zach was a child who couldn't act like a child because he was in God's presence. But his father could yell at his mother, between blessings even, for handing him the salt cellar rather than placing it on the table before him.

Dov's temper was one thing, the Sabbath walk to synagogue quite another. Zach used to dread it. Dressed in heavy oversized black clothing and a black felt hat that fell over his ears, he felt as conspicuous as a Goth at a coming-out ball as he trudged the tree-lined suburban streets of Didsbury (often referred to as 'Yidsbury' in his youth). And he was filled with ennui at what was to come. Hours standing in a gaudy, brightly-lit, cavernous room watching old men in strange get-ups chanting in a language he didn't understand. The only words he could ever grasp were 'Eretz Y'israel' – The Land of Israel. He heard them over and over.

'The home of the Jews,' Dov would always tell him, his voice triumphant (this always puzzled Zach as there they were in Manchester). And then there were the festivals, almost one a month. The only one Zach enjoyed was Purim, a day for parties and celebrations, when everyone dressed up and ate pastries filled with poppy seeds, jam, and fruit.

The Ten Days of Repentance, ending with Yom Kippur, were the worst. Ten days on the trot, trudging to synagogue twice a day. On the High Holy Day, the last, he had to fast for twenty-five hours. Zach quickly learnt to hoard biscochos and heuvos haminadoes in the lead-up to The Day.

Meanwhile, when his mother wasn't arguing with his father, she was shouting at Zach. His mother always made him feel he was in the way, as though he wasn't meant to be there. She never did anything motherly (Ester took on that role). No hugs, bedtime stories or kisses goodnight. But she slapped him, regularly. When he was very young, she slapped him on his bottom or the back of his legs, but as he got older, she'd slap him across the face, hard.

Zach could remember the last time like it was yesterday. He'd finished his GCSEs and gone out partying. It was 1999. The Madchester music scene had fallen away, the Hacienda was no longer rocking, but that night the university union hosted the Chemical Brothers, pioneers of the big beat genre. Zach was only sixteen, but he could pass for a couple of years older. With a friend he slipped in, popped an ecstasy tab, and his love affair with rave began.

It was almost three in the morning when he got off the bus near home, four hours later than he said he'd be. He was looking out for his mother's bedroom light when three men confronted him. If he hadn't been on MDMA he might have been OK. He would have known he had to run. Instead, he said, 'Alright?' They didn't take too well to him being dead casual and matey. The nearest one jabbed Zach's cheekbone with his left fist then piled in with his right. Whilst Zach was off balance, a second man hit him in the stomach, and the third punched him in the head, sending him crashing to the ground. They kicked him over and over before searching his pockets, taking his phone and a few quid – all he had – and then kicked him again for having so little.

The street was deserted. No curtains twitched. Zach managed to stand. He was still high, thus partially anaesthetised to the pain, but the attack left him traumatised. Home was less than twenty yards away. He stumbled to the gate. Trembling, he opened the door and dragged himself up the stairs to Ester's bedroom. He tasted blood and wiped his mouth with the back of his hand. There was no sound from inside when he knocked. He walked in. The bed was empty. Ester was rarely away, today she happened to be on a trip with the League of Jewish Women. His mother's bedroom door was ajar. The light was on. His instinct was to make for his dad's room, but Malka headed him off.

'Zach!'

Surely his mother wouldn't be angry when she saw him. He staggered into her room. She was sitting upright in her single bed, arms folded.

'Mum,' he cried, and ran over. Zach didn't stop even though he saw no hint of a break in her ice-cold face. He was certain she would embrace him. How could she not? Up close, her face was a blur through his tears. And then it came. He didn't feel much, the MDMA saw to that, but the slap knocked him sideways.

To the day she died Malka never spoke of that night, not even the following morning when she drove him to hospital. On the journey she showed no concern, and dropped him off at A&E rather than wait with him. It turned out he had three cracked ribs, as well as bruising to his jaw and cheekbone.

Malka had never imagined she would fall pregnant with Abe aged thirty-eight, never mind forty-seven with Zach. She found it difficult to bond with Abe, but impossible with Zach. The circumstances didn't help. She stayed in hospital after the birth and didn't come home for a year. When he was old enough to ask, Zach was told she'd been ill.

It was uncanny the way unsavoury truths could be glossed over and, of course, a child would believe anything. In fact, his mother had suffered post-natal depression, and spent the time in Israel with her family, having been beaten by Dov during a pregnancy she had never wanted.

When Zach became a father, he tried to talk to his mother about the impact Dov's violence had on their relationship, but she still refused to engage. Zach shouldn't have been surprised given her cold attitude towards Rachel, but he was. Because despite everything, Zach was an optimist. He felt sure his mother would take the opportunity to finally forge a relationship with him.

10

After he was expelled from Jewish school aged fourteen, Zach got in with the right crowd and discovered he had a penchant for altering the state of his mind. Cannabis calmed him and gave him time to control the emotion in his responses, and so avoid arguments and slaps. It allowed him to drift into a world where he felt secure, one where he could push all anger and hurt to the back of his mind.

Drugs became Zach's escape from himself.

And now he was hooked on cocaine.

One night, a couple of months after Rachel had been taken from him, some friends took him out. They figured he needed a pick-me-up and gave him a line of coke. He felt good for the first time in a long time. In fact, he felt fantastic. In his bereft state, Zach quickly became dependent on the feelings of euphoria cocaine gave him, the grandiose sense of power, the increased energy, the mental alertness. Now he could function. Now he could get by at work. But Zach soon began taking it more and more frequently and in larger and larger doses, until he needed a good few big hits a day. It wasn't long before he was ignoring the demands of his job and failing to turn up for Rachel. Getting hold of cocaine had taken priority.

Zach lost his job and his friends as he descended into a semi-nocturnal life, a world of dealers, addicts, and thieves. His habit was costing him a fortune. So Zach stole whatever he could whenever he could, no matter who it belonged to. He even raided his dying mother's jewellery box.

And he was still letting drugs come before Rachel. When he pulled up outside Beth's he prepared a big fat line. In Wivenhoe you didn't get mugged for your stash, but he was still discreet. Seconds later he was buzzing, prepared for anything, even Beth. Or so he thought. She answered the door holding Bitz by the collar and looked Zach up and down. Then she eyed Hepzibah's car. Her jaw dropped. 'Did you drive like that?'

'No, I've just had a line.'

'Oh, that's OK then. You didn't drive here on drugs, but it's OK to be off your head when you take your daughter out.'

'I thought we'd walk to the woods with Bitz. It's a beautiful day.'

Beth pushed the dog into the house, put the door on the latch and pulled it to. 'I don't want you taking her out when you're high anymore. She's three. Anything could happen to her.'

'You can't be serious.'

'I'm deadly serious.'

Beth's tone rocked Zach. 'What, not even a walk in the woods?'

The door opened slowly and Bitz came out, followed by a bemused Rachel. Beth positioned herself between Rachel and Zach and told her daughter to go back inside. She pushed Bitz in once again and said, 'Not even a walk in the woods.'

'But you have to let me see her.'

'No, I don't.'

'Yes, you do, I'm her father.'

'So go to the Family Court. I'm sure they'll be very impressed with you being a drug addict.'

'Come on Beth, you've got to do the right thing by me and Rachel.'

'I am doing the right thing, for Rachel. You need to clean yourself up.' She went into the house and slammed the door in Zach's face.

~~~

Zach hit the A12 westbound mid-afternoon, driving into the sun. The car visor was down and his Wayfarers were on, but he had no music playing. He wasn't in the mood. The traffic was light, and just over an hour later he was parking the car outside Hepzibah's. Fortunately, she wasn't in, and he didn't have to explain why he was back early. He headed up to the bathroom, needing a little something.

Once that was taken care of, he convinced himself everything would be fine with Rachel. He dropped the car keys into a bowl on the work-top, sent Hepzibah a text to thank her, and headed for the bus stop opposite Hackney Baths.

Fifteen minutes later he was walking down Homerton High Street, having just got off the bus. His phone rang. It was Hepzibah. He paused his iPod and took an earphone out.

'You're back earlier than I thought you'd be.' She didn't sound displeased.

'Yeah, well.'

'Murrell's been in touch. Seth Laskowitz doesn't appear anywhere, social security, DVLA, Inland Revenue, nowhere. It's a made-up name. They're going to look into it.'

'Give him Seth's phone number. That should help. Gotta go.'

At Star Pizza & Kebab, Zach went round the back. There, just as the doctor had said, was the drop-in centre. A sign on a dirty red door said so. Zach stepped inside. That was a start. The corridor down to reception was uninviting but he persevered, urged on by the rocking slamming beat pumping through his earphones. A woman behind the desk gave him a form. Once he'd filled it out, she directed him to a busy waiting area. To pass the time, Zach played 'guess the addiction', but the game was futile, because addicts didn't walk into a clinic when they were high or drunk. They walked in when they were edgy, agitated, and paranoid. Zach bucked the trend.

A while later, Zach was called to see a drugs worker named Alan. Zach switched his iPod off, bringing an abrupt end to another funky gem, and walked into interview room three.

'I'm a cocaine addict,' he told Alan.

Alan was in his fifties. He had one of those craggy been-there-done-it-all-faces, with wild silver-grey hair reminiscent of Billy Connolly. Unlike the legendary comedian, Alan wasn't laughing. He wasn't even smiling.

'And?' he said, the tough Geordie present in every word.

'And what? I'm here because I'm a cocaine addict.'

Alan made an effort to tone down his Newcastle accent. He wanted Zach to understand every word. 'And what do you expect us to do about it?'

'Help me?' Zach suggested.

'I know it's a cliché, son, but you can only help yourself. If you'd come in here and said you wanted to kick your habit, I might have been impressed. Do you?'

'Of course.'

'Really? You're high now. You'd be happy never to have another line, would you? You're not going to have one later when you get home?'

Zach hung his head.

'Good. No bullshit. So, you're a cocaine addict. Do you smoke crack?'

'No.'

'Inject cocaine?'

'Never.'

'Canny, lad. OK, you can go cold turkey with support. We could do residential. It won't work long term unless the commitment's there, but it's always good to detox. You'll only get referred to the unit once, so if you want to detox after that you'll have to pay. People who walk in here usually can't.'

Zach was on the edge of his seat, ready to leave. '*Detox?* You're joking. I'm not detoxing, I'm not crashing, I'm not going cold turkey, with or without 24/7 medical supervision.'

'Ok, you've made that clear.'

'Is that my only option? Surely there are other more civilised ones.'

Alan was inscrutable. He gave nothing away. Perhaps there were, perhaps not. He continued. 'Have you managed to keep your job?'

'No, but I've got my eye on an MSc at UCL. I want to get back into my old career.'

'That's good. You have a goal. Have you got somewhere to live?'

'My brother's,' he replied with a lump in his throat.

'You're lucky to have his support.'

'I was lucky to have his support,' Zach replied quietly. There was no reproach in his voice, only sorrow. He felt a tear in the corner of his eye. 'He's dead, killed four days ago.'

Alan's hard guy persona melted away. He was lost for words. 'Killed?' he said in a low voice.

'Abe was killed in a road accident, only it wasn't straightforward. The police are involved, but ...' Zach trailed off and shrugged.

'It sounds like you don't think there's much the police can do.'

Zach agreed. After all, what did he expect? A manhunt combing the streets of London looking for an Israeli built like a brick shithouse and Seth whatever his name was?

'And how are you coping generally? Have you anybody ...' He left the question hanging.

'I've got family in Manchester, but I don't see them much. Abe's ex is close by, we see a lot of each other, and I live with a friend of Abe's, a mature student. She's Palestinian.'

'Is that your heritage as well?'

With his dark skin, black curly hair and strong Middle Eastern features, Zach was frequently mistaken for an Arab. When he was younger, the suggestion almost drove him to dress in black (with a white shirt), grow long sideburns and wear a Homburg. Nowadays, he met it with a weary shrug.

'I'm a Jew,' he replied, 'a *Sephardi* Jew, that's why you thought I might be Palestinian. Bagels are not part of my culture, nor is chopped liver or gefilte fish.' It was a bitter pill for Zach to swallow, but he shared more culture with an Arab than an Ashkenazi Jew.

'I didn't mean to offend you.'

'You didn't offend me.'

'Good, well let's get on. We need to talk about how you're going to deal with your habit.'

'Deal with my habit, that's an interesting phrase.'

'It's a realistic one. You're a cocaine addict. An option other than detoxing is to manage your habit downwards, so you're gradually coming off it. That way your body has time to adjust. You'll have to commit to a twelve-week programme with us, by which time we hope you'll be cocaine-free.'

'The gradual approach sounds more my style.'

'You'll *have* to commit to the twelve-week programme,' he said, repeating himself. Zach was tempted to ask what would happen if he withdrew part way. Would they send law enforcement officers round? Bailiffs? Would Alan come round personally and demand monies with menace, or force Zach to attend the programme? Alan was giving the process an air of importance and formality. This was weighty stuff. Zach had to conquer his addiction.

'I'm serious,' Zach replied. 'I have to give it up. I just need help.'

'I'll be your key worker, unless ...'

'No, that's fine.'

'OK, on a typical day, when would you take your first hit?'

'In the morning. I try to make it as late as possible, but it's rarely later than eleven thirty.'

'OK, so your first target, starting tomorrow, is to push that time back, as close to twelve as you can, and then as soon as you've managed that, try to push it back to twelve thirty, and so on.'

'How am I going to do that without any help? I struggle to keep it as late as eleven thirty as it is.'

'You'll be seeing a therapist in a moment. He'll prescribe something for you. Try and see how you get on. I'd like you to keep a diary and mark the times you take a hit. There's no point not being accurate. You'll just be wasting everybody's time. OK?'

'OK.'

'How many lines would you normally make out of a gram?'

'If I'm flush, no more than five. If not, eight, tops.'

Alan looked aghast. 'Well. We've certainly got room to work with there. I want to get that up to at least ten, quickly, more if you can. As from today I want you to make your lines progressively smaller. We'll be able to see how many lines you're making from each gram through your record of when you've had a hit. OK, I'll take you through to meet your psychotherapist.'

They both rose from their seats. 'Tell me,' Alan asked, 'was it your brother's death that brought you here?'

The question rocked Zach. Abe's death had played no role in getting him into interview room three on the other side of a table from Alan.

'No,' he replied, blushing. 'I have a three-year-old daughter. If I don't give up cocaine, I'm going to lose her as well.'

11

It's after four in the morning. I gave up trying to sleep five hours ago. Been drinking and watching action movies with the sound turned down ever since. Boy, did I need calming. It's been four days, but I just can't move on from the mistakes I've made. They clearly led to the professor's death.

I've had to lie to Ella and the girls to explain my mood. I told them I lost money on one of my investments. Ella has accepted the explanation at face value, bless her heart. I said we'd be fine, not to worry, and that's it. We haven't spoken about it again. There are many things I love about my wife. Her easy-going trusting nature is up there with the best of them.

I take advantage of Ella, of course. Who wouldn't? The girls do. They're just like me. In temperament, in intellect, they're me to a T. My eldest, Izabel, is eleven. She was suspicious from the off. She said to me, out of Ella's earshot, 'I don't believe a word of your story.' She'll go far, that one. Typically, she's convinced her younger sister that 'this lost money business', as she calls it, is about as kosher as pork and shellfish.

Debora's pretty smart too, for a nine-year-old. Before bed she said, 'Normally you get angry when you lose money, Dad. This time you've gone all weird.'

*'Yeah,' Izzie agreed, 'you're like reading the **Bible** Dad, in **Hebrew**, I mean, I know we go to synagogue on Sabbath and stuff, but we're not like **religious**, are we?'*

Of course not, I assured her. We go through the motions for the sake of appearance, and not just the tedious trips to synagogue. We have two kitchens, but we eat and cook anything in either of them.

An important caveat, which explains my disagreement with the professor. Whilst I am no longer religious, I still believe in Judaism. Judaism is important symbolically, for what it means, what it represents. It is more than a religion, it's a nationality as well. And Zionism, the belief in a Jewish state for the Jewish people, is Israel's national ideology.

On that note I will say good night. I feel quite tired now.

PART TWO

Heatwave

12

Zach was lying on the Swedish two-seater, his head resting on its low arm. He and Fawz were watching TV. A celebrity was in a tent somewhere God-forsaken with a torch on his head, recording a diary about how miserable and lonely he was. Zach had no idea where the riveting action was taking place, and he found it hard to believe Fawz did either, but she was sitting in the other retro armchair with a back so low it was useless, so she must have been paying attention. Unless she'd fallen asleep upright.

'Fawz, you awake?'

These were the first words spoken between them since a furious row two hours earlier. Fawz had called the new Labour leader a breath of fresh air. That really got Zach going. He didn't tell her he used to like Labour before *he* took over. Of course, Fawz thought the new leader was great, for the very reason Zach didn't. He was anti-Israel. He said he was anti-racist, but he was an anti-Semite. Why else did he support terrorist groups calling for the destruction of Israel? And why did he refuse to sign the international declaration on anti-Semitism?

'I am awake, of course,' Fawz replied, over-pronouncing every word as always. 'What do you want?'

'You watching this crap?'

'You can watch what you want. I am going to bed.' She got up and left the room without saying good night.

Zach watched Fawz mount the stairs, then flicked through the channels, keeping an ear out for her movements. The moment he heard the bathroom door close, he tiptoed into the kitchen, opened her bag and took out her purse. Fawz had sixty quid in three twenty-pound notes. He took one, found his keys, and quietly left the flat.

Ten minutes later Zach was in a queue at the kebab house on Stamford Hill, which was unusually busy for that time of night. There were five people in front of him and a couple behind. After some time, the queue shortened and someone loud came in, a stocky guy with an oversized neck. He pushed into second place, the next to be served. Zach looked at the guy whose position had now been taken. He was clearly miffed but wasn't going to say anything. Zach, however, now third in line, took umbrage.

'What do you think you're doing?'

The man turned and glared at Zach. He reeked of beer. 'Bargin' in. What's it look like? Now fuck off.'

'Why can't you queue like everyone else?'

'I said, *fuck off.*'

'No, I won't *fuck off.*'

'You wanna make somethin' of it? OK.' The drunk jerked a thumb. 'Outside.'

Why not here, now? Because he had mates out there? Zach bet a zillion to one. Sure enough, he could see two guys over the road about to cross. If he hit the drunk now, he'd be trapped. Zach made sure he stepped outside first. The moment he did, he turned and lashed out, connecting with bone twice. Then he legged it. The drunk got up and was joined by his two mates. A chase was on. They swore loudly as they ran. Zach was a cunt, he was a twat, and they were going to rip his fucking head off when they caught up with him.

Zach was determined to make sure that didn't happen. He put on a spurt as he headed north on Stamford Hill. They kept up. They were drunk, but showed no signs of slowing down. Perhaps Zach smoked too many cigarettes. He shot right, down Lampard Grove. They followed, hot on his heels, threatening to chop his balls off. People came to their windows and looked out at the commotion. Zach swung left, away from his home, onto Kyverdale Road, then left again. They were catching up. He went right when he hit Stamford Hill once more and headed north towards Tottenham. He shot past a series of independent shops and a Shell petrol station, propelled by adrenalin. He glanced over his shoulder. The gap was narrowing further.

The community centre was up ahead. He could see no lights. The shops were shut tight. There were no police and the people he passed were too scared to help. His assailants were now promising to rip his eyes out of his skull. Their threats carried on the wind. Windows opened. People stared. A man in the doorway of Scope, the disability charity, got up from a sleeping bag. He held back a staffie with a jaw the size of a melon. The dog snarled and pulled, desperate to sink its teeth into a human leg. Its owner lowered his free hand and signalled for a grateful, out-of-breath Zach to get alongside. Then he shouted:

'Stop! Or you'll face the three of us.'

The dog slavered at the thought of being let off the leash. Its front legs were off the ground as it strained on the lead. Wary, the three guys pulled up. They swore, they cursed, they waved their arms, they jabbed their fingers, before retreating and swearing vengeance when they next saw Zach without the fucking dog.

Zach's saviour, Neil, had a beard and walked with a limp. He was around Zach's age, with a strong estuary accent and a sparkle in his eye. Zach put out a hand to say thank you to Neil's dog. Just minutes earlier it looked ferocious. Now it was super friendly.

'She saved yer bacon.'

Zach had no doubt that was true. He felt for the folded twenty-pound note in his side pocket and said, 'Fortunately, I'm flush enough to buy you both some food, if you fancy.'

'Yes mate, we do.'

13

Zach opened the front door, turned to Neil, and put a finger to his lips. 'Shush. We don't want to wake Fawz.' They tiptoed up, the dog included, and spoke in whispers. Zach pointed to a grubby winter jacket Neil was carrying. 'Leave it here at the top of the stairs.'

'What?'

'It's not coming in.'

'Why not?'

'Do I have to tell you? Just leave it there. I'll put the food in the oven while you shower. Remember, be as quiet as you can.' He opened the door to the flat and walked in.

'Why can't I shower after I've eaten?'

'I'm going to tire myself telling you why. Now give me your clothes.'

'Me clothes?'

'Yes, your clothes, all of them.'

He began undressing. 'Nellie'll whine if the bathroom door's closed.'

Nellie? Neil and Nellie? Zach suppressed a laugh. 'It's OK, you can leave the door open.'

Zach held his nose as he stuffed Neil's clothes into the washing machine and put them on a quick cycle. He gathered Neil's shoes and put them outside to air, washed his hands, then went to his bedroom and brought out underwear, socks, a T-shirt and jogging bottoms. These he left by the bathroom door, next to the dog. Then he dug out a Boss jacket of Abe's. It fit Zach perfectly, but it was padded and he feared arrest by the style police. Finally, he found a clean sleeping bag and put Neil's outside to de-fumigate.

Zach heard a scream of surprise down the hall, and went to investigate, though he knew what it was. Fawz, in her dressing gown, was standing outside the bathroom looking bemused. 'There is a naked man in the bathroom,' she said.

'That's Neil.'

'And the door is open.'

'For Nellie, the dog.'

'Why are they here?'

Zach explained, leaving out the bit where he stole twenty quid from her purse to pay for the food they were about to eat. Meanwhile, Neil showed his clean face at the bathroom door in a T-shirt and jogging bottoms.

'Sorry if I offended ya.' He was embarrassed, yes, but there was still that twinkle in his eye Zach had noticed. In a different life, not on the streets, Neil would be a catch. He was lean, muscular, and good looking in a rugged way.

Fawz put up a hand. 'Please do not worry. You and your dog are most welcome.'

'I'm starving,' Zach said. 'Why don't you join us Fawz, I'm sure there's enough.'

'It is bad to eat so late.'

'Not if you're hungry.'

Zach found a suitable bowl and Neil fed Nellie with dog food bought from the garage on Lea Bridge Road. Meanwhile, Fawz put on some clothes to sit with them. She said she wouldn't eat. Nevertheless, she picked at Zach's chicken biryani and his sag aloo. Fawz came across Asian food when she arrived in London and was beginning to acquire a taste for it. She kept picking and approved when Zach added a squeeze of lemon to the sag aloo. He poured wine for the three of them.

'You're not much of a Muslim, are you?' he said.

'Why? Because I drink alcohol? Many Muslims do.'

'What, in Islamist Gaza they let you drink?'

'I do not live in Gaza. I live in East Jerusalem.'

'Well, I'm sure there are restrictions there too.'

'You cannot drink in the street, but why would you want to? You can drink alcohol at a restaurant, a café, in your own home, in other peoples' homes, at parties, in clubs.'

Neil pushed his plate towards Fawz. 'Like ta try some rogan josh? It's very popular.'

'Is it hot?' She prepared to take a small mouthful.

"Ave it with some yoghurt,' he advised. She did as he said and liked it so much, she took a few more mouthfuls. Meanwhile, Zach was washing down his meal with a very decent red. He refilled all three glasses (his was empty; theirs were half full) and left for the bathroom to prepare his smallest line of the day, the last.

Fawz whispered 'cocaine' to Neil. At the doorway Zach turned and said, 'Can't offer you one. I've not got enough.'

'Don't want one, mate.'

Zach heard disapproval. From a homeless person. He didn't dwell on the irony. Instead, he snorted a line with a rolled-up fiver. *Whoosh*, all his cares disappeared. Told off by a homeless person? That was history. Or maybe he'd imagined the disapproval. Look at Neil now: no longer hungry, rosy-cheeked from a large glass of red, and looking forward to that joint Zach had just rolled.

'Mate, you gonna light that?'

Zach could have stood at the open back door, but instead he led the way into the living room. All the windows in the bay were fully open. He leant out of the middle one, lit up and sucked greedily on the joint. Fawz sat down in one of the retro armchairs whilst Neil and Nellie joined him on the floor at the window. He handed the spliff over and watched Neil. He smoked like a pro, long and deep.

'So, how did you end up on the streets?'

Fawz leant forward and echoed the question. 'Yes, how?'

'Got kicked out of the army. Couldn't get a job. Lost me house, me wife an' me kids. That simple.'

Zach could easily see how that could happen. 'What did you get kicked out of the army for?'

Neil took a long toke and pushed out smoke with his words. 'Attackin' a senior officer. It's a long story, goes back to an incident in Basra when we was withdrawin' to base.'

'Tell us,' said Fawz, leaning forward.

'Down by the palace there was a bunch of clerics. They were jeerin' us an wavin' bye bye. It was our last time out an' we were mad man. All that death, what the fuck was it for? Just to leave Iraq to the Mullahs? We pulled up and it got heated.' He faltered and glanced at Fawz.

'Go on,' she said.

'Let's just say a guy in me unit broke the rules of the Geneva Convention. It was shockin' what 'e did. I refused to re-write me report. I was ostracised, got no support from above. I was hung out to dry, an' one day I snapped.' He toked on the joint and handed it back.

Zach checked Fawz had understood everything. She had. He turned back to Neil. 'Is that when you hit a senior officer?'

Neil nodded. 'They were all part of it. 'E just happened to be there, anna it 'im more than once.' His grin soon disappeared. 'It didn't take 'em long to get there. Anna knew I'd get a beatin'. Left me with permanent damage to me back an me knee, an they got what they wanted. Me dismissal.'

'But what did they do?'

'There was this cat I fed. We'd meet same spot every day. I'd bang a tin with a fork, and he'd come. Only that day 'e didn't come. I found 'im later, strung up in me locker.' He bent down and stroked his dog. 'Come on Nellie, you must need a pee.' They left the room together.

'He has no one, his family have left him,' said Fawz, barely believing they could. 'We must invite him to stay. It is what Abe would have done.'

14

The next morning Zach's mobile rang at nine, waking him. He considered ignoring it, then saw it was Hepzibah and answered.

'I'm looking at an email from the solicitors,' she told him. 'Abe changed his will two days before he died.'

The news hit Zach like a brick. Did Abe think something might happen? Why didn't he say? He'd had endless opportunities. Three nights before he died, the evening before he changed his will, they met for a drink. Abe paid, of course. He seemed just like he always did. Optimistic, happy. He loved life. Now he was dead, and all Zach could see of him was blood seeping out of cracks in his head.

'What do you think, Zach? Did Abe seem worried to you?'

'Not at all. I didn't see any change in his behaviour. I'll check with Fawz when she gets back, but I'm sure she would have said already if she'd seen anything.'

'I saw no change either. Could be a coincidence.'

'Yeah, spooky though.'

'Want to know the contents of the will? They're typically Abe.'

Zach was waking up. 'Go on then.'

'I'm just going through it now. He's left Fawz thirty thousand, though some of that will pay for the renovation of their family house in East Jerusalem. He's left me sixty thousand, but again, more than half of that is to pay the council tax on his flat for the next forty years. And he's leaving the Palestine Solidarity Movement fifteen thousand. He hasn't left you a penny. Instead, something far more important: his mortgage-free, council tax-free flat, on two conditions. First, Fawz gets to keep her room, free of rent. Second, you can only sell up if you're buying somewhere else.'

Zach was speechless. The flat was his.

'Look, I need to get a move on. I've got a work call to make. There's something else. I've had another email from Murrell. Seth, his name is Seth Silberman and his phone is owned by Ralph Maccabi. He works for Maccabi and was presumably spying for Maccabi. I gave Murrell Tamir's number to see what he comes up with.'

'It's handy, Murrell fancying you.'

She ended the call saying nothing. Zach got up, slipped a pair of boxers on, and surveyed his home. In the large living room, a staffie of considerable size lay on a Persian rug Abe had bought in Istanbul fifteen years earlier, and a homeless bloke was asleep on a blow-up bed in front of the Edwardian fireplace. The two bedrooms were bigger than average, the bathroom had a power shower, and the kitchen, which was a decent size, gave access to a garden via wrought iron steps. At the moment, it was a fusion of purple allium, bluebells, and white apple blossom.

~~~

An hour later Fawz got back with the shopping, which included the ingredients for baklava. She also brought in Neil's old jacket, which she held with her fingertips and kept as far away from her body as possible.

'Out!' Zach shouted at the smelly garment and pointed to the door. '*That* is *not* coming in. It's going in the bin outside. I've got a jacket of Abe's for him.' He watched her leave the smelly item on the other side of the flat door and let her wash her hands before saying anything more. Then he probed.

'I need to ask you. Do you think Abe's behaviour changed in any way in the days leading up to his death?'

'Changed? How?'

'Do you think he seemed worried, or anxious about anything?'

'No, he seemed normal. Why?'

Zach was about to explain when Fawz's phone rang. She took the call.

Woken by the activity around him, Neil tried to prop himself up on the blow-up bed, but his elbow wouldn't stay still. He sat up and said, 'Mornin' mate.'

'Morning. Breakfast?'

He put his thumb up. 'Nice one mate. Quick wash an' am with yer.'

Zach made tea and began scrambling eggs. Fawz, who was now off the phone, had something to say.

'Hepzibah has just this minute received evidence that a Zionist she is investigating has links to the Jewish Liberation Army. She is very excited. She told me to tell you. It is important.'

Fawz's liberal use of the word Zionist irked Zach, but he said nothing of his feelings.

'The Jewish Liberation Army? They sound weird.'

'They are terrorists.'

'Says who? You?'

'Shin Bet, Israel's security services.'

That shut Zach up. He served the scrambled eggs on toast. Neil tore off the end of his and handed it to Nellie who was under the table, by his feet.

'So, what's this guy's name?' Zach asked, 'this *Zionist?*'

'Ralph Maccabi.'

15

Hepzibah's front door was ajar when Zach arrived the next morning. He went through to the study, where a forensic officer was lifting fingerprints for analysis. Another was examining the burglar's handiwork. The entire windowpane had been taken out.

'Jeez,' Zach whistled. He pushed his Wayfarers on top of his head. The arms caught in his thick curls and held. He wore shorts, a T-shirt, and flip flops. The policemen weren't so lucky. He left them to their work and approached the living room, where Hepzibah was on the phone to DI Murrell. She waved him in and put the inspector on speakerphone.

'Mrs Peretz, you've been burgled. You should leave it with the investigating officers.'

'I will. The thing is, it's what they took that will interest you. My laptop, my external hard drive, and a hard copy of the last essay Abe and I worked on. You wondered whether the book might be involved in Abe's death, and now a chapter has been nicked. Maybe it means something, maybe it doesn't.'

'If it meant something, what could that be?'

'I don't know. It's bothering me. It doesn't fit the profile of the guy who ordered the break-in. He'd hate it. The chapter is called 'Jews are a people, not a race or a nation.'

'And who do you think ordered it?'

'A guy called Ralph Maccabi. I received important evidence against him yesterday. He stole it when he stole my laptop and everything else.'

'This important evidence, is it backed up?'

'Yes.'

'Well then, not too bad. By the way, we interviewed Juris Neilands a couple of days ago.'

Zach leaned into the phone. 'And you never thought to tell us?'

Murrell took in a sharp breath. He hadn't expected to hear Zach's voice. When he replied he was short and to the point.

'There's nothing to tell, otherwise I *may* have been in touch. Neilands has an alibi. Goodbye, Mr Peretz,' he said, and ended the call.

'I don't think he likes you,' Hepzibah pointed out.

The two forensic officers appeared in the hallway and Hepzibah left to talk with them. Zach pulled his Wayfarers down and walked through the open bi-folding doors to the garden. It was picture book tidy. The gardener had just been, leaving the grass short, the edges neat, and the borders weed-free. Zach sat under the rose arch and listened to the chatter of birds congregated in the large evergreen shrubs next to the feeders.

Hepzibah came out with fresh coffee in a cafetiere and called him to the patio table. He watched her as he walked over. She'd lost none of the grace and poise of a ballet dancer and was looking very sexy in a low-cut sleeveless top and loose shorts. He smiled at her. She smiled back. When she looked away to pour the coffee the smile was still there.

'You're looking very pleased with yourself,' Zach said.

'I ordered a coffee maker before Maccabi stole my PC. It should arrive tomorrow.'

'Fantastic.' Zach was excited. 'Can I use your phone later so I can YouTube making a flat white?'

'Tomorrow, maybe.'

Hepzibah's cafetiere coffee frequently came with a redeeming feature: cream, sometimes double, if that was all she had. Today it was single. Zach finished his quickly and poured himself another.

'Maccabi, he's been in the news recently. Can't think what for,' he mused.

'It's ironic he's called Maccabi, don't you think?'

'Why?'

'You know, Maccabi and the Maccabees, the Jewish national liberation movement, circa 165 BC.'

Zach looked at her blankly.

'Never mind. The family firm, Maccabi Facilities Services, has been in the news. They've just won a huge contract to repair housing for yet another London borough, their sixth.'

Now Zach remembered the interview he'd seen on the local news. 'How old's Ralph?'

'Thirty-nine. Born June the sixth, 1975.'

'That's very precise. Are you his wife?'

'I'm a *journalist.*'

'Well, that's not the guy I saw on TV. He was mid-sixties. Loaded, they said.'

'That's the father, Benjamin. He's loaded, all right. Owns the company. Ralph's a director.'

'OK, so you reckon that the son, who funds an extremist movement and supports a terrorist organisation, nicked your stuff. I assume he gets rough.'

'Very rough. Only he doesn't get his hands dirty. He delegates violence to a bunch of thugs called the Jewish Volunteer Force, who he helps fund. They call themselves a self-defence group but they go on training exercises at Israeli army camps, paid for by Maccabi. He makes out he's a real family man, always smiling and posing with his wife and kids, but he's a nasty piece of work.'

She disappeared into the house and came back a minute later with a piece of card. 'Here, look at this. It was left where my computer used to be.' A note, printed in capital letters.

YOU HAVE BEEN WARNED

'He'll know I'll have everything backed up.'

'I think I'd put that article on hold for the moment.'

16

Mrs Peretz needs to be careful. The Israeli doesn't distinguish between the sexes. If someone needs hitting, they're hit. Man or woman. My worry is, she hasn't heard of him, though that would be a surprise. He has, after all, developed quite a reputation amongst anti-Zionist activists since he arrived. The professor had certainly heard of him. That's why he ran that night.

It's been seven days since he died and there's been no sign of the police. Thing is, I need seven months without incident before I can start to relax. It's killing me, the wait. I'm drinking way too much and I'm not sleeping. I don't look good. Even Ella said. The girls have been saying for days. At work eyebrows have been raised at the number of meetings I've missed.

Because Ella and I are sleeping in separate bedrooms the girls are convinced we've had an argument. They tell us again at bedtime.

'Of course we haven't, darlings,' Ella assures them. 'It's just that your father isn't sleeping well at the moment. Now get into your pyjamas, both of you.'

'You've fallen out,' Izzie says, 'I can tell.'

'Your father isn't at his best right now.' Ella looks at me while she says this. She is wearing an incongruous half-smile which I can't make out.

'Is that why you've fallen out, Mummy? Because Daddy isn't at his best? That's what me and Iz think.'

Before I have a chance to defend myself Ella says, 'Izzie and I, darling, Izzie and I. Anyway, we haven't fallen out. It really is no more complicated than your father not wanting to keep me awake all night, and frankly darling, I don't want him to either. Now get ready for bed.'

'I think Dad's been better today.' Izzie looks at me and is hopeful. 'Don't you, Mum?'

Ella nods in agreement. 'Yes, I do.'

*I **have** been better today. I had to be if I wanted to meet my future PA, never mind have any say in who they may be. I drank less last night, got up early and walked the dog. Would you believe it was twenty-seven degrees centigrade at six thirty in the morning? When I got back, I shaved and showered. Ella said I looked presentable, and I left. I am determined to keep it together for Ella and the girls. I must be positive. The chances of being found out are slim. And the more each day passes the slimmer they become.*

'Come on darlings, bedtime.' I usher them off the sofa. The dog is on Izzie's lap, looking up at her. She strokes it and gets her face licked in return.

*'Can Poppy come up? **Please**.'*

Normally I'd say no, but I want another drink. 'Course she can,' I reply to the girls' amazement. But not to Ella's, who watches me refill my glass once I see the girls are at the top of the stairs.

17

At one o'clock the next day, the mercury hit thirty-four. In the evening it cooled, but the temperature at 8pm was still an eye-popping twenty-seven degrees centigrade. That was outside. In Zach's kitchen, where the oven was on, it was undoubtedly hotter. Every window in the flat was fully open, as was the back door. The fan in the kitchen was going as fast as it could.

Zach had nothing on but a pair of shorts, yet every pore in his body oozed sweat. He turned the cooker off and knelt down. The moisture on the back of his legs squelched as upper and lower parts met. When he opened the oven, he was hit by a blast of hot air. The sweat on his forehead mushroomed. He wiped it away and brought out a baking tray.

'Hmmm, that smell, it reminds me of home,' said Fawz to the others around the table. Zach's family food reminded a Palestinian of home. It no longer shocked him to hear that. He'd always known he ate the same food; his family had lived with Arabs for long enough. Now he was learning to embrace the fact. He smiled at Fawz though she didn't see. She was sampling a tasty dry white and sharing a laugh with Neil and Hepzibah. Neil looked relaxed, not fazed by the company of two super-intelligent women. Cleverly, he didn't try to hold his own, though he kept up and brought welcome banter into the conversation. He was wearing Abe's clothes, a pair of Rohan shorts and a dapper summer shirt. Hepzibah had the good grace to welcome their use.

Zach had finally cooked Sephardi pies. He favoured the non-meat recipes, and tonight he'd made four aubergine and cheese pies, and a large spinach one which Sephardis called a pie but was more like a soufflé. He put two large green salads on the table and mixed a lemon-based dressing in one bowl, and a white wine vinegar one in the other. The latter was for Hepzibah and Neil. Then he opened another bottle of that nice white Hepzibah had brought and filled everyone's glass.

In stark contrast to everyone else, Neil approached his meal gingerly, poking it with a fork. He pushed the aubergine pie aside and brought the spinach and egg one into the middle of his plate, cut off a small slice and put it warily in his mouth. His frown soon turned to a smile. He liked the pie, and cut off another larger piece, and another, finishing it with salad. Nellie stirred by his feet, perhaps aware of her master's satisfaction.

'That was great,' he said, pushing his plate away.

'Aren't you going to try my aubergine pie? It's got cheese in it, feta and parmesan.'

'Nah, 'onestly mate, I'm full.'

Fawz said, 'Try it, you may like it.'

Hepzibah joined in, goading him to taste the pie. He cut off the smallest amount, swallowed and realised he'd cut off mostly pastry. He gave it another try, this time with a larger piece, and found to his surprise that he did like it, but not enough to eat it all. Zach divided what was left between himself and Fawz (Hepzibah said she was full). He ate his share standing, in three bites, and went to the fridge for baklava. Now he opened a Portuguese red as dark as night, bought with Fawz's money and her blessing.

'The baklava looks good,' Hepzibah said. 'Where did you buy it?'

'Fawz made it, and I have to say, it's every bit as good as Ester's.'

'That's praise indeed,' said Hepzibah and took a piece. She turned to Neil. 'Ever had this before? It's delicious.'

'No, but I like sweet things.' He took a bite. Turned out he loved it. 'On the streets people often give us cake, but never anything like this.'

'A bit like Marie Antoinette,' Hepzibah said.

'Huh?'

'Nothing, I was being silly. On a serious note, how do you cope during the really bad times, when it's absolutely freezing and you've got nothing, no food at all?'

'Nellie,' he answered, without hesitation, 'best thing I ever did, get Nellie.'

'Even though it's meant an extra mouth to feed?'

'There 'ave been times when she's gone a couple of days without food an yer think, is it fair?' He didn't answer the question, and nobody asked him to.

'The homeless need a Labour government as well as a dog,' Hepzibah said.

'Yeah, Heps,' Neil was already shortening her name. 'Totally agree. I like what I hear about them now.'

As the conversation turned to the new Labour leader, Zach's mood soured. Fawz called him a breath of fresh air, again. He wasn't like other politicians. This was true. He wore authority like it was a disease. When the (Jewish) Labour Dame, a leading light in Labour Supporters of Israel, called him 'a fucking anti-Semite' behind the speaker's chair, Zach didn't know whether to applaud the slanderous attack or cringe when the Labour leader didn't slap the Dame down for humiliating him in public. He should have held a press conference and demanded she repeat the allegation outside the House of Commons or retract it. What did he do? Hide in a corner and feel sorry for himself.

Zach could take the eulogies no longer. He drank more red, which went down smooth as velvet, and readied himself to intervene. As it happened, he agreed with much that had been said, but he wasn't going to say. Instead, his comment was:

'He's an existential threat to Jews.'

Fawz and Hepzibah turned to him, fury in their eyes. He'd made a promise. No arguments.

Neil looked confused. 'Whadaya mean?'

Zach reached for the bottle and topped up everyone's glasses.

'I mean he's a threat to the very existence of Jews.'

'What are you saying, Zach?' Hepzibah asked, barely able to contain her anger. 'He wants to kill Jews?'

'His views are a threat to Jews. He's an anti-Semite. Why else would he refuse to sign the declaration on anti-Semitism?'

'OK Zach, you want an argument, you got one. The declaration just wants to shut debate down. Want to criticise Israel after unarmed Palestinian demonstrators are shot dead? Better not, you'll be labelled an anti-Semite. I've heard you use the tactic numerous times.'

That was true; more often than not it worked. Anything to defend Israel. Zach didn't want to think about the consequences for Jews if Israel fell. They would be catastrophic.

He took a drink from his glass and said 'OK, but what's-his-face, the Labour leader, he thinks it's OK for Palestinians to have a state but not Jews. In fact, he says Jews are racist for wanting one.'

'You're distorting things. He said that Israel is racist. Jews have an exclusive right to self-determination in the country. It will always be racist until it affords Arabs the same rights. How can there be independence for one at the expense of the other and that not be racist?'

Out of the corner of his eye Zach saw Neil nod in agreement. No doubt, under the table, Nellie was nodding as well. What had Zach done to be surrounded by anti-Zionists? Been closer to Abe than the rest of his family, that was what. When Hepzibah came along, Zach was always a minority, having to constantly argue his corner.

'Yeah, but he still doesn't want Israel to exist. He doesn't support Jewish self-determination because it means recognising Israel's right to exist.'

'You don't get it. What he says is Israel was made at the expense of the Palestinians, that it continues to exist at their expense and must change. Jews have to move on and accept the Arab as equal. Arabs have to move on and accept that Israel is here to stay.'

'Anything else? Apple pie and cream forever?'

'Jews and Arabs have to learn to live together, but for that to happen, Israel must cease to be an exclusively Jewish state.'

'But Israel *has* to be a Jewish state. It *has* to be a refuge for Jews. Look at our history. Look at *your* history, Heps. Think about what happened to your own family, for fuck's sake. It could happen again, you know. Anti-Semitism is on the rise throughout Europe and America. Jews are gunned down in synagogues, on the streets, sometimes by white nationalists, sometimes by Islamists. We *need* a refuge.'

Hepzibah softened her tone. 'You're right, anti-Semitism is on the rise worldwide, but Netanyahu doesn't care. Quite the reverse. The more anti-Semitism there is, the better. It increases the raison d'être for a Jewish state.'

18

For the third day in a row, Zach had borrowed Hepzibah's car and gone to Kingston University looking for Juris Neilands. It was a long shot, as PhD students didn't attend lectures. If Neilands turned up, he'd go to the history department where he'd have a meeting, use the printer and the photocopier and chat to friends. Or he may have occasion to visit the library. Most likely it would be the former, but Zach couldn't hang around the department without attracting attention. So the library it was, an ideal place to be inconspicuous. To pass the time, Zach read a book he'd pulled off Abe's shelf the night before. It was written by one of Israel's best-known authors and was a droll reflection on the argumentative condition of the Jewish people. They'd argue with anyone, even God.

Officially, the heatwave began six days ago, but there'd been blue skies for well over a week. During that time the temperature had risen steadily. It was still rising. Today, the mercury hit thirty-six, and Zach's bare legs stuck uncomfortably to the chair seat.

Spread out in front of him were books on the crises of the late Middle Ages, all open, with a notepad and pen. Paraphernalia so Zach didn't look out of place. The environment took him back to his graduate days and forward to a post-grad to come, he hoped. The room was spacious. One side was glass with a view onto silver birches and an older part of the university. The desks were on that side, in an open sunny space, well away from the bookshelves. He could see the advantages if you wanted to use the library for what it was intended, a place for peaceful learning, but it made his job difficult. Fortunately, the desk Zach had used for the previous two days was free again. It was as near to the medieval history section as you could get. Neilands' PhD was on some aspect of the Crusades, a period on which Abe was considered an expert.

If his picture was anything to go by, Neilands was unremarkable. Small, thin, with a pinched face and beady eyes. Zach wanted to meet him in the flesh. He checked the time. Ten minutes later than when he last looked. He leant back and glanced down the medieval history aisle once again. There, he saw a woman leaning against the shelves, reading. She was in her early sixties, Zach guessed, with grey hair pulled back from an open, eager face.

Zach left his desk and walked to the aisle, staying at the end. He pulled out a book and pretended to be interested in the fall of the Western Roman Empire. The woman, who was near the letter P, looked at the inside flap of her book and stared at Zach in astonishment. After a moment, and perhaps some deliberation, she went over. In her hand she had a book of Abe's. It detailed the massacre of over a hundred thousand Jews in the Rhineland as the first crusade was readying itself to leave.

'Excuse me, are you Professor Peretz?'

'No, I'm his brother.'

'I'm sorry.'

'It's OK, an easy mistake to make.'

'I think your brother's work is great. If you want to know what happened to Jews during the crusades, he's your guy.'

'And what did happen to them?'

'You don't keep up with your brother's work? In Jerusalem, my speciality, they were slaughtered alongside Muslims, but there were exceptions. Some crusader orders had Jewish physicians working in their hospitals.'

'Are you a post-grad student?'

'Yep, finally doing that PhD.'

Zach worked hard not to look excited. 'Do you know what the coffee's like here?'

'My friends say it's dreadful.'

~~~

Zach shuffled with the line towards the cashier carrying a tray with their drinks. His was a sparkling elderflower, Ruth's a green tea. The bill came to the best part of a fiver. A fiver Zach didn't have. He patted his back pocket and pretended to feel for a wallet. 'Oh dear, I've invited you for a coffee, but I've come out without any money.'

'That's OK, I'll get it.'

She paid and they found somewhere to sit in the busy cafeteria. Zach looked at Ruth, dreading the news he had to deliver. A tear formed in the corner of his eye.

'There's no easy way of telling you this. Abe's dead.'

Ruth brought a hand to her mouth. Her eyes widened. 'Oh my god,' she said.

'Eleven days ago.'

'May I ask?' She left the unfinished question hanging.

'It was an accident, nobody's fault. I'm sorry, I've given you distressing news. The least I can do is help you. Have you heard of Hepzibah Peretz?'

'His wife? Of course. She's a well-known journalist.'

'I can put you in direct contact with her. She'll be delighted to help you in any way she can. If you want to know anything about the Middle East today, she's your woman.'

'You'll give me her number?'

'Yep.' Zach found Hepzibah's number in his phone and gave it to Ruth. Maybe you could do something for me,' he said.

'If I can.'

'Do you know someone called Juris Neilands?'

'Sure, I was talking to him half an hour ago.'

'He's here?' Once again, Zach had to sit on his excitement.

She nodded. 'Having a meeting with his supervisor.'

'I've got something that belongs to Juris. Abe was one of his external examiners. Do you mind taking me to him?'

"Course not. He should be finishing soon.'

'Back in a sec.' Zach hurried to the toilets. There, he found an empty cubicle, locked it, and prepared a line on top of the toilet cistern after he'd put the lid down, just in case. Then he rolled up a fiver and hoovered up the cocaine. Up his nose it went, straight to the top of his head. He felt great. Neilands would be putty in his hands. At the sink he smiled at his reflection in the mirror, pleased with what he saw. Cool, confident, in control.

'You OK?' Ruth asked once he got back.

'Tip top. Let's go.'

'It's just that you look a bit strange and you're chewing your lip.'

'I'm good. Let's go.'

Ruth finished what was left of her green tea and they left. She weaved her way through the crowded corridors. Zach followed. She said nothing. Had she twigged he was on something? Probably. Did he care? Not really. Only one thing mattered. *Neilands.*

'Is it far?'

She shot him a glance. 'No.'

Soon, they turned off the main corridor. Here, Zach was able to walk alongside Ruth. He was buzzing now, itching to see Neilands. They turned right. Ahead was a set of double doors, the words 'History Department' above them. Ruth led the way through. Inside was another corridor with rooms off to the side.

'There he is,' Ruth said. Neilands was about twenty yards away talking to a tall bloke in an open doorway.

Zach brushed past her. Over his shoulder he said, 'Thanks,' and marched towards Neilands. His movement alerted the Latvian, who hightailed it. Zach chased after him. The bloke in the doorway made a half-hearted attempt to stop Zach that was more akin to a blind swipe. He missed entirely. 'Call security!' he yelled.

The game was on. Zach pelted down the corridor, catching up on Neilands with every stride. He was flying. Neilands cut right. Zach followed, on his heels now. He could hear the ragged breath of his prey. He put on a spurt, reached out and grabbed hold of the back of Neilands' shirt. He reined the Latvian in.

'Whoa, no need to run. I just want to talk.' Neilands didn't seem convinced. He flinched whenever Zach moved a muscle. There was fear in his eyes and Zach was pleased.

'What do you want?' Neilands asked.

'Like I said, I just want to talk. Let's walk.' They headed back. 'Why did you run just then?'

Neilands didn't answer. He heard something, boots, security, and his pace quickened. Zach didn't have long. He pulled at Neilands' arm. 'Look at me,' he said. Neilands turned, convinced he'd be hit. 'Who's Seth Silberman?'

'I have no idea,' Neilands said, and walked on quickly. He was lying. He knew Seth. He was a contact on Seth's phone. The swing doors pushed open and two beefy security guys marched towards them. Suddenly, Neilands was all tough. He leant into Zach and whispered, 'Fuck you.' Then he said to the security officers, 'This man has been harassing me.' They grabbed Zach and escorted him from the university premises.

20

The brother needs to watch his step. Juris now has contacts, including the Israeli. If I cared enough, I'd warn him, but I don't. Not anymore. His persistence is annoying me now. It's dangerous. I'm still worried the police will widen the horizon of their CCTV coverage. If they were to look further up Eversholt Street to Mornington Crescent they'd see people with the professor that would finish me. I wasn't there. I knew nothing of the attack. Yet I can't claim innocence.

It's the children's bedtime. I've had a couple of glasses of wine and already secured Ella's disapproval. But I'm going to have another one. I'm only waiting for the kids to go up. I'll tell Ella it's the last glass, but once she's gone to bed, I'll crack open the whiskey.

Is my relationship with my wife suffering? Without question. And with my daughters? Certainly. But we'll get over this tricky period, I'm sure. My ordeal can't last forever.

'Dad, can Poppy come up again? Please.'

I'd set a rod for my own back. 'I suppose so, darling.'

19

Two police cars were parked opposite Hepzibah's, their blue lights flashing silently in the daylight. After a few moments, a black guy was led out of an open front door, handcuffed and held by two cops. His distressed white girlfriend came running out after them and pulled unsuccessfully at one of the policemen's arms. All she could do was blow her boyfriend a kiss before they put him in the back seat of one of the pandas.

'Love ya babe,' she shouted.

Over the road, Hepzibah was oblivious to the commotion. Somewhere in the kitchen, probably near the open bi-folding doors, her MP3 player was belting out Regina Spektor. Zach rang the bell to announce his arrival but let himself in with the spare key. She was expecting him.

Hepzibah was on the patio, lounging in sunglasses and a skimpy bikini under the shade of an umbrella. An empty wine glass lay on the stone beside her.

'Hi Heps,' Zach said, his gaze focusing on what was showing of Hepzibah's breasts.

She opened her eyes and realised what he was doing. 'Jesus, Zach, you never stop. I'd be a millionaire ten times over if I had a pound for every time you've stared at some part of my body.' Her words were not quite slurred, but her voice was thick with alcohol. His eyes turned again to the empty glass, and this time she noticed.

'Are you trying to make a point, Zach?' She sat up on the lounger, ready for a fight. 'I've had a glass of wine. How many lines have you blasted through today?'

One glass? He doubted that. 'OK, OK,' he said instead, conceding defeat. He sat down at the patio table and rolled a fag, wishing he'd been more circumspect. It wasn't as though he hadn't known Hepzibah long enough.

'And don't you dare lecture me.'

'I wasn't.'

'No, but you wanted to.'

'When have you ever heard me lecture anyone? You're mistaking me for Abe.'

She considered the point. Her drinking had been the Achilles heel of their marriage. And yes, Abe used to lecture her. He lectured Zach too, only Zach took the lectures on the chin. Hepzibah, in contrast, lashed out in denial.

Zach lit the fag he'd rolled.

'Keep that away from me,' she said, waving her hand in front of her face. Zach moved to the far end of the table and drew on his cigarette. The late afternoon sun beat down on him.

After a prolonged silence, Hepzibah said 'Well? Are you going to tell me? Did you see Juris Neilands this time, or was it another wasted day?'

'Yes, to both those questions. I saw him but he ran off. I caught up with him ...'

Hepzibah interrupted. 'You didn't hit him, did you, Zach?'

She was so predictable. 'No.'

'So what did you do?'

'Asked him a couple of questions, but security arrived and he decided not to answer.'

'So you wasted your time. What did I tell you?'

'He did say something. He said fuck you, like it was a message.'

'What sort of message?'

'I don't know. Maybe there'll be repercussions.'

'Great,' she said, grabbing her empty glass and getting up from the lounger in one flowing movement. Zach couldn't resist a lingering look at Hepzibah's fit body before she disappeared into the house.

A few minutes later, she was back with a full glass. Hepzibah couldn't help defending her drinking, though no-one had challenged it. 'Unlike some people, I worked hard today. I wrote two articles, one on the growth of ISIS, and another on why the plug was pulled on nine months of US-mediated peace talks between Israel and the Palestinian Authority. I deserve a drink.'

'OK, calm down.' He dropped his cigarette butt onto the patio and stepped on it.

'Pick that up. And don't tell me to calm down. If I'm not calm, is that such a surprise? You've quite unnecessarily unleashed the hounds of hell.'

'That's a bit dramatic.'

'The point's there,' she grunted, and took a large swig of wine. 'What do you think's going to happen?'

'I don't know. Nothing, probably.'

'What did you do to make him so cross?'

Zach shrugged. 'I told you. He hightailed it as soon as he saw me. I ran after him, that's all.'

'Did you not think that chasing him might scare him?'

That consideration had been at the forefront of Zach's mind. He'd *wanted* Neilands to be scared, but he didn't let on to Hepzibah. 'What was I supposed to do? Let him run off?'

'Look Zach, I never wanted you to bother with him in the first place. Neilands wasn't there. He's got an alibi.'

'Huh! His 'girlfriend'. Pull the other one. He's up to something. What's he doing on Seth's contact list? And why did he run if he's not involved? What did he think I'd do if he'd stayed where he was? He was talking with some bloke and there were other people around. He was scared, but that wasn't why he ran. He ran because he's guilty.'

'He had every reason to be scared of you. He'd been harassing your brother.'

'Yes, but what did he think I'd do with all those people around? Anyway, I better get off.' Zach got up to leave.

'Stay, if you want. I've got enough left-over moussaka for two. It's a vegetarian one, with lentils.'

'Sounds great, but you'll only get narky when I have a line and complain that I'm always drinking your wine.'

'I'll put up with it.'

The proof of the pudding, Zach thought. He was sure she'd forget her promise, but the lure of food and wine was too great.

'Let's hope Neilands doesn't know Maccabi.' Hepzibah said, moving into the kitchen to put the oven on.

Zach followed. 'So you *are* suspicious of him.'

'No, I'm not. These are two separate things. Whether I'm right or you're right, he could still know Maccabi. He is a Christian Zionist, after all.'

21

The next day, while Alan read that week's drug diary, Zach was wondering how he'd get his hands on some money. He'd finished the crystal meth bought with Seth's phone and was almost through a gram of cocaine paid for by changing Abe's euros into pounds. He had enough for two days. Then what?

Alan could see a pattern emerging. Zach had only managed to delay his first line of the day by half an hour, but was managing to cut out at least one every evening. It was also evident he was working hard to shorten the lines, particularly his first of the day, making a dozen hits from a gram now, double the number of a week ago.

Alan was slow to congratulate him. In fact, he never did. Finally, he said, 'Why is it so hard for you to push it back in the morning?'

'I can't do it without benzos.'

'That's what they're there for, Zach.'

'I don't want to take benzos in the morning.'

Alan waited.

'Because I can't do fuck all on benzos and I stuff myself full of them in the evening, OK?'

Alan took a moment, then moved on. 'How come you manage to cut out two lines on some evenings and only one on others?'

'It'll depend if I go out. If I do, I'll only skip one.'

'You can't go out without having a line?'

'Well, I'm hardly likely to go out partying on benzos.'

'You could try going out on nothing.'

The two men stared at each other. They were at an impasse. On this point, Zach was not going to move. Alan pushed from a different angle, suggesting Zach could stay in more often.

'You're going out more often than not.'

'Yeah, well, Fawz watches a lot of Al Jazeera TV. Drives me mad, *endless* anti-Israel propaganda. So I go out. If I don't, we argue.'

Her words rang in his ears. *Israel's actions give Israel less security, not more. The children of Gaza and the Occupied Territories will be bent on revenge, more so than their parents.*

Alan looked at his watch. 'Time to go in. Can't keep your therapist waiting.'

Zach didn't agree. Kevin wore a suit and tie and was both old enough and young enough to know better. And he was a behavioural psychologist, which didn't suit Zach at all. Kevin liked structure, whereas all Zach wanted to do was talk about his crap relationships and have someone nod sympathetically at the right moments. Like when he was expelled from Jewish school a month after his bar mitzvah for kissing Rachel Shabas behind the school building. His father was furious. He burst into Zach's bedroom, eyes blazing, and whipped Zach's bare bottom with a leather belt.

At least the sessions with Kevin were short.

'How are you finding him?'

'Yeah, good.' He didn't tell Alan he was only seeing Kevin for the benzos. 'By the way, my dad rang this morning.' Zach preferred to tell Alan this momentous news, not least because Alan dressed casually and didn't feel superior.

'I'm guessing that was a surprise.'

'Yeah. He said he loved me, and I did too. He cried and so did I. He even said sorry, and I apologised for nicking Malka's jewellery whilst she lay there dying.'

'So, all good.'

'Yep, I'm going up tomorrow. I checked with Fawz and she's cool about being left with Neil and Nellie.'

'Who are they?'

'A friend and his dog. They're staying at the moment.'

'Great. Now get in there.' Alan pointed to Kevin's door.

~~~

Today's session sailed by because, as Zach found out, Kevin stopped on time, no matter how late his client. When he walked out of the building Zach noticed an unchained mountain bike leaning against a wall. He could get at least a gram for that, maybe more. He checked nobody was about, hopped on and made sure he cycled slowly while passing Star Pizza & Kebab. No one looked out. He turned left onto Homerton High Street and sped off. After some moments, he swung round to see if anybody was following. He saw no one.

'Hah!' he shouted and punched the air.

22

Zach's family home was a semi-detached three-storied Victorian house in Didsbury, South Manchester. The posh residential street was off the more affluent end of Palatine Road, below Barlow Moor down near the River Mersey. It was midday when Zach arrived. The gardener was there, mowing the front lawn in the boiling sun. He wore a floppy green hat, green T-shirt, and shorts. It was a uniform of sorts, each item stitched with the firm's bright yellow logo.

The smell of a beef tagine bubbling away on the stove wafted through the open door, bringing back mixed memories. Mealtimes were the only occasions Malka agreed to sit down with Dov. She never hid the deep hatred she felt towards him. When Malka had an audience, she talked *to* him and *about* him with complete disdain. She criticised the way he hunched over his food and shovelled it into his mouth, and broke wind so loudly she could hear him wherever he was in the house. She was never interested in anything Dov had to say, but he would persevere, because he was anxious to communicate, further irritating Malka. Cue argument.

Malka's behaviour needed perspective. She was sixteen in 1946 when she arrived as a refugee in the nascent Israel. Those desperate times were seared into the Sephardi psyche, as Jews across the Middle East came under attack from Arab nationalists, enraged by Jewish emigration into Palestine. Peace had been declared in the world, but in the Middle East a regional war loomed. For the first time in at least two thousand years, Jews weren't safe in an Arab country.

But the times were also a personal disaster for Malka. The moment she stepped off the boat in Haifa, she was separated from her poorer family and put on another boat with Dov and his family. She was to live more than three thousand miles away from her own. Malka's marriage to Dov had been arranged between the two families over Malka's head. Seventeen-year-old Dov was looking forward to a large family but had to wait thirteen years for his first child. Malka's revenge? No one knew.

Perhaps she wanted a divorce? Zach had always thought this highly likely. Dov could have both broken free of his loveless marriage *and* kept the children. Malka would have gone to Israel. But Dov's views on divorce were legion. He believed it brought shame upon the family, even if the divorce had the rabbi's blessing. So they lived together for sixty-seven years, hating each other for all that time. Dov could be violent, and no doubt Zach was not the product of consensual sex, but unlike Malka he was an affectionate and loving parent.

And Ester, always a great cook, was now an even better one.

She was attending to the tagine, her back to Zach. Dressed inappropriately for the weather but traditionally, she wore a white headscarf, a dark blue dress with the form of an overall, and dark blue tights.

'Smells lovely,' he said, by way of announcing his presence.

'Zach!' Ester turned and opened her arms. Her embrace was followed by a big smacker on each cheek.

'The tagine for tonight?'

She nodded.

'Can I taste?'

Ester handed him a spoon. The sauce was sizzling hot. He blew on it before tasting. 'Nice Es, just right.'

'Not too sweet?'

'Nope,' he replied, having another taste.

Beads of sweat broke out on Zach's forehead. He looked at Ester and could see no sign she was sweating. But Zach stepped back from the cooker and pulled a tissue from the pocket in his shorts to mop his brow. He was wearing as little as he could get away with, yet every centimetre of his sister was clothed from the neck down, and not lightly either. People said drugs ruined lives, but they never said tradition did as well. For fifty years Ester had adhered to each and every aspect of orthodoxy without letting up an inch, not even during a heatwave. A life wasted, if not ruined.

On his way out to join his father, behind Ester's back, Zach dipped his finger into a bowl of homemade humus and took just a little, so it wouldn't be noticed. Dov was sitting at a garden table under the shade of an umbrella, wearing a thawb, a white cotton tunic worn by men in the Middle East, ideal for the current weather.

'Zachy!' his father called when he saw his youngest son. Dov rose from the bench, his eyes sparkling. He was leaning on a stick, prompting Zach to run over. Zach wrapped his father in his arms, and when Dov whispered, 'I love you, Zachy,' Zach forgave him everything.

'I love you too, Dad.'

'I should have welcomed you at Abe's funeral. I am sorry.'

Zach couldn't say, "it's okay", but he wanted to. He did the next best thing. He said, 'I'm sorry too.'

'But my behaviour? What would Abe have thought?' At that, Dov began to sob, uncontrollably. He was crying for Abe over Zach's shoulder. Zach was comforting his father at last, thirteen days after Abe died. It wasn't long before Zach joined him in tears.

Ester came out with a tray of food. She smiled at the scene, prompting them to smile back and dry their eyes. She laid the table with green and black olives, a bowl of *baba ganoush,* the humus, some pitta bread and three small pies made with spinach, feta, and ricotta.

'Let's eat,' Dov said, sitting back down. He patted the space next to him, encouraging Zach to join him. Once Zach was sitting, Dov squeezed his son's thigh affectionately. 'You are right. I am lucky. I miss Abe terribly, but I have the rest of my family to enjoy.' He put his arm round Zach, pulling him close, and kissed him on the cheek. Zach could feel his father's moist eyes on his skin.

'No prayers?' Zach asked.

'Just for Abe.' Dov closed his eyes and prayed silently, leaving Zach and Ester to their own thoughts.

After a few moments he said, 'Now, eat and enjoy.' He patted Zach's knee. 'I've made mistakes. No more. Nothing is more important than family.'

Zach popped an olive into his mouth and worked around the stone. Once he'd eaten all the flesh, he announced, 'I have to stop taking cocaine.'

He turned to his sister and said, 'You're right, Es. It'll kill me or end my relationship with Rachel, or both. I've made a promise to her, not that she knows. I'm giving up.'

'I knew you would see sense,' Ester said, as if she never had a doubt.

'Wonderful, Zach!' said Dov.

There were lots of Thank Gods and prayers that he would be cured.

As they settled into their light meal, Zach told them about his twelve-week programme with the drugs counsellor.

'Twelve weeks?' Ester echoed. 'That's three months. So, in three months you won't be taking it anymore?'

'That's right,' Zach replied, not quite sure he meant it.

'That's my boy,' Dov said and patted him on the back, again.

'Also, I've got an interview for a post-grad course. It'll help me get back into work.' This news was greeted with more bravos and pats on the back.

'So,' Dov said, squeezing Zach's knee affectionately, 'when am I going to see my beautiful granddaughter?'

Dov had met Rachel only once and hadn't taken much interest in her. After all, Rachel's mother was a goy and so was she.

Zach was pleasantly touched. 'I'll organise something, soon.'

~~~

In the middle of the afternoon, when Dov was dozing in the shade and Ester was resting upstairs, Zach sneaked into his father's study. It was tucked away between the dining room and the downstairs toilet. The door was always closed, but never locked.

As a child Zach knew he wasn't allowed in. Nevertheless, one day, aged six, he opened the door. The room was dark with a small window. There was a leather-topped desk jammed against the wall. It took up most of the space, the captain's chair the rest. The carpet was brown, and the walls were a dirty cream colour. There was a large photograph of a rabbi, and shelving that contained religious texts. He had walked straight out. It was not a room to interest a child.

Nor an adult with any sense, but Zach was looking for a hand-written letter postmarked Soho.

The room hadn't changed much, only it looked lighter than he re-membered. The walls had been given a fresh lick of paint in the not too distant past. No sunlight came through the small north-facing window, though the day was bright enough to dispense with the desk lamp. He worked quickly, not allowing the framed black and white family photo-graphs from Syria to distract him. The side drawers were filled with bank statements, financial papers detailing his father's investments, insurance documents and minutes of family company meetings. Zach rifled through them, but he could find no letter. He opened the slim middle drawer, but found nothing that could explain the profound shift in Dov's mood. Just Sellotape, rubber bands, paper clips, a stapler and a 'Dear Donor' newsletter from Tahor Yisra'el, the organisation Hepzibah was investigating. Dov had taken out a family membership that included not just Ester, but every adult in Nissim's family. Zach was the only one missing.

Quietly, Zach closed the study door and tip-toed up the stairs to his father's bedroom, careful not to wake Ester. It was stuffy, as if it had been undisturbed for some time. Zach searched the obvious places. The bedside table drawers, the chest of drawers, the pockets of his jackets, his dressing gown. He could find no letter. Zach had drawn a blank.

But what he had discovered disturbed him. His family donated money to expel Palestinians from the land in which they were born. Zach had no idea their views were so extreme. Or perhaps he'd never stopped to think.

23

Late afternoon the next day, the moment Zach opened the door to the flat, Nellie's head appeared at his feet. Zach walked through to the kitchen, where he could smell something rich and tasty cooking. The dog followed, her nose attached to his ankles.

Hepzibah was sitting at the table on her phone. They kissed on the cheek. The backdoor was open, and Neil was sitting on the first step down to the garden, smoking. He took a last drag on his fag, put it out in an ashtray full of dead butts and got up. They were both unsure how to behave. Should they hug? They settled on a close handshake, patting each other on the back in a comradely manner.

'Hiya mate.'

'Hi Neil.' Nellie was still at Zach's heels. Zach bent down and patted the dog's head once more. 'She'll get bored of this, right?'

'Payer no attention an' she'll soon give up.'

'Dogs,' Hepzibah said, with barely disguised contempt. 'Who'd have 'em?'

Zach slugged on a beer from the fridge, and said, 'Lovely smell. What's cooking?'

'Shepherd's pie.'

'That rules Fawz out. So unless you've come here to cook, Heps, which is very unlikely, I'd say Neil is responsible for that lovely smell.'

'Yeah well, saves yer time tonight.'

Hepzibah was chairing a debate between a Jewish Labour MP under threat of deselection because of his support for Israel, and a Labour councillor, a member of Jews Against the Occupation. Zach had said he'd go. He was just going to say that he'd decided to give it a miss when Fawz walked into the kitchen. She had come from the bathroom and had a towel wrapped round her hair. They kissed on the cheek.

'How's it been without me?'

'Peaceful,' she replied. 'How did it go with the family?'

'Mixed. Everything was fine, only I found out the entire family are members of Tahor Yisra'el. I had no idea they were so extreme.'

'Really? *I* did,' Hepzibah said. 'So did Abe.'

Hepzibah was probably right, but she was *definitely* a pain in the arse. 'Think they'll be at the meeting tonight?' he asked Ms Know-It-All.

'Tahor Yisra'el? Unlikely. The meeting's too Labour-specific.'

'I hope you are right,' Fawz said, looking at Hepzibah. 'Remember what happened the last time?'

'What happened?' Zach asked.

'They sat behind me, pulled at my keffiya and called me a terrorist. I am hoping the Zionists there tonight are a little more civilised.'

'*The Zionists.* What do you mean, apart from being derogatory about Jews?'

'That is exactly what they are Zach, Zionists. They believe in the Jewish state, a state that was born out of violent robbery, that flouts UN resolutions, squeezes so-called independent Gaza, and invades it every two years. Do you want me to go on? I could.'

'No Fawz, I don't. But Israel doesn't invade Gaza every two years. Don't exaggerate.'

'It is not an exaggeration. Four years ago, Operation Cast Lead. Two years ago, Operations Returning Echo and Pillar of Defence. And you do not have to live in Gaza to know there is another invasion coming soon.'

'But how do you deal with Hamas?'

'You talk to them, Zach.'

'Talk to Hamas? They're either terrorists, or anti-Semitic, or both.'

'I am tired of this conversation. What do you want to do, Zach? Leave it until everyone in Gaza is dead before you come to a solution because you think Hamas are anti-Semitic terrorists?' Fawz left, drying her hair as she went.

Neil shouted after her, 'Dinner in five, Fawz,' then he grinned at Zach. 'That's you told mate.'

'I must say, Zach, I find your attitude towards Hamas irritating as well.' Hepzibah put her phone down. 'We don't like them any more than you do, but they're not terrorists. And it's difficult for a Palestinian to hear when they see the death and destruction Israel inflicts on Gaza and the Occupied Territories.'

~~~

At the meeting that evening, security was tight. Bags were searched, bodies patted down, but Zach wasn't worried. They were looking for knives and bombs. Not a wrap of cocaine.

'Fawz, keep a seat for me.'

'Do you have to?' Hepzibah asked.

He shrugged dismissively and headed for the toilets. Luckily, there was a free cubicle, and he was done in a minute. He sniffed up the flecks of cocaine that had remained at the bottom of his nostril and closed the door behind him.

The meeting room was full, a large minority wearing kippahs. The audience appeared middle class and Zach could see no sign of trouble-makers. He felt ten feet tall as he strode through the hall, high as a wallaby on a poppy farm. He scanned the room and located Fawz towards the back. She was small, but her keffiya marked her out.

'Zach, you are chewing the inside of your mouth,' Fawz whispered. 'People are staring.' Zach shrugged and sat down. A couple of min-utes later the room quietened. Hepzibah, on the platform with the speakers, introduced the debate. The MP, David something or other, kicked it off.

'Under the current leadership, the Labour party has lost the con-fidence of the Jewish community.' A significant number in the crowd murmured their agreement.

David continued, emboldened. 'No wonder over the last year, ac-cording to the official figures, there were almost a thousand complaints of anti-Semitism made against party members. The real figure is undoubtedly higher.'

Again, David had struck a chord with a section of the audience. People nodded in union. 'Of course it is!' someone shouted.

'It is surely not coincidental that this spike in anti-Semitism has taken place since the election of a new leader. And it is surely no coincidence that very little action has taken place under his watch.'

David was cranking up the rhetoric, splitting the hall in two. Those who supported his position and those who didn't. There was no persuasion, no leeway, no give. No explanation, only rhetoric. Nothing to entice those in the middle of the argument.

'He said he'd eradicate anti-Semitism in the party, but in fact it's got worse. The culture is now bullying, bigoted, and intimidating.' This last comment drew boos. He ignored them. 'Jewish MPs are targeted for abuse and deselection because they are Jewish.'

'That's a lie!' someone shouted to applause.

David was not put off. 'I am being hounded out of the Party, a Party I joined over forty years ago because it was the natural home for Jews with its proud tradition of fighting racism, promoting equality, and fostering tolerance. How things have changed. It's so bad now that some constituencies are not just calling for the deselection of Jewish MPs, but for our Party to reject the International Holocaust Remembrance Alliance code on anti-Semitism. These constituencies should be shut down. They bring disgrace on the Labour party.' He sat down to applause from half the audience.

The Labour councillor stood up. She looked familiar and Zach remembered seeing her at Abe's, several times. Her name was Ruth. How would the waverers in the audience take to her views, given she was Jewish?

'The elephant in the room here is Israel,' Ruth began. There were murmurs of agreement and nodding of heads. 'David doesn't mention it because it undermines his narrative. The Party is moving to a pro-Palestinian position under the new leader, so what better thing to do than accuse the left of anti-Semitism?'

'Well said!' someone shouted. Most nodded.

'The social democratic wing, of which David is a proud member, has lost control of the Party. Dirty language is their fightback. The Party has been "hijacked by the hard left." It is now "institutionally anti-Semitic." The new culture is "bullying." Here, Ruth turned to her opponent. 'There is nothing new about bullying in the Labour party. More than a touch disingenuous, that point, David. And, you're not being targeted for deselection because you're Jewish, but because you consistently voted both for the Iraq war and against any investigations into it, consistently voted for replacing Trident with a new nuclear weapons system, and because you're a member of Labour Supporters of Israel which is leading the campaign to undermine the new leader.'

This drew applause from many in the hall. Zach was as much in the middle of the argument as anyone in that room, and he was listening to Ruth more than he had David.

'As a general rule, the left tends to be pro-Palestinian, the right pro-Israel. This is a political battle, not a racist one. I'm not saying there are no anti-Semites on the left, but the idea that anti-Semitism is institutionalised there is ludicrous. But it's become part of the narrative. Say it enough times. It's no surprise the party has lost the confidence of the Jewish community. The campaign that you are part of, David, led by the venerable Dame, has made sure of that,' Ruth said, prompting applause. She was persuasive. Zach understood how the narrative worked. No doubt her allegations were true.

The noisy audience did nothing to put the councillor out of her stride. Indeed, she appeared to thrive on it. Turning to David she said, 'You are beating the leader with the stick of anti-Semitism, whilst simultaneously kicking the cause of Palestine into the dust.' Now she faced her audience. 'The same tactic is being used to silence a group of young, female, left-wing, pro-Palestinian Democrats recently elected in America. Coincidence? I'll leave you to reflect on whether that's Israel's long arm at play. Israel calls itself a Jewish state. It purports to speak for all Jews. But it doesn't speak for me, nor countless other Jews worldwide.'

Ruth sat down to loud applause. Fawz was on her feet whooping and cheering. Zach wasn't sure what to do, what to think. If the Dame and her gang did have it in for the leader, he knew how easy it was to lob the anti-Semitism grenade into the mix. He did it all the time and it usually worked to great effect. Finally, he gave Ruth a polite clap. It was more than he'd given the MP.

A flurry of hands went up in the audience. After a couple of friendly points had been addressed to the MP, Hepzibah picked out a woman. She addressed the councillor.

'Even if you're right, there's still anti-Semitism in the Labour party. What's happened to the hundreds of complaints?'

'I agree with you. The leadership's response to this crisis has been woeful. It's been ham-fisted, it's been slow. Although, to be fair, he doesn't have control of the Party machinery. His enemies do. As for what's happened to hundreds of complaints, I don't know, is the answer.'

Hepzibah took a young man with a kippah. He had a question for Ruth. 'Do you think Israel is behind the attack on your leader?'

'If not behind, then part of the attack. Israel pours huge amounts of money and resources into fighting the negative image it attracts around the world, but its main areas of concern are London and Washington. What do you think?'

'I think Israel is a democratic state. I asked you that question because I knew your views. Now we all know. She is suggesting there is a worldwide conspiracy by Israel to meddle in other countries' affairs. Is there not a whiff of anti-Semitism here?'

'No,' someone shouted to applause.

Hepzibah took a question from a woman near the front, perhaps on the basis that she was small and had to work harder to be seen. Immediately, Hepzibah must have wished she hadn't.

'Call yourself a Jew?' the woman asked the councillor. 'You're a *traitor!* There was a smattering of applause. 'Jews are under attack everywhere and you side with the anti-Semites.'

Ruth stood firm. 'I've turned my back on both religion and Israel, but I can't turn my back on being Jewish. It's who I am, and I don't put up with any anti-Semitism.'

'Rubbish!' the woman shouted. 'You support terrorists who want to kill Jews. Shame on you.' More applause. 'And the leader of the Labour Party? He's a racist. You support a racist.'

This angered many in the crowd, Fawz included, prompting the other side to defend the accusations. Tempers rose. The situation was beginning to turn ugly.

Ruth lost her cool. 'The irony in this whole debate is that anti-racists are being called racist by racists.'

There were gasps in the audience.

'Who are you calling racist?' the woman demanded to know.

'Not you, of course. The newspapers, I won't name them. You all know who I mean. But I can see how supporting the oppression of Palestinians can be construed as racist.'

It started with sniggers, as it took the hall as well as the woman a moment to digest Ruth's last sentence.

'You *are* calling me racist, and you're calling Israel racist.' She shouted abuse, and was joined by the group around her.

'Traitor, scum, terrorist,' they shouted, and intimidated those around them when asked to be quiet. Where was security?

'I think we should move on,' Hepzibah said. The group quietened down, but their anger could be heard bubbling under the surface.

Zach turned to Fawz. 'I can't quite see them, but I can hear them. There's going to be trouble tonight. Why the fuck couldn't Neil have left Nellie and come?'

'Because she would have peed all over the kitchen floor. Or worse, Abe's lovely Persian rug.'

'He should have just brought her. She'd have been useful.'

There were more questions, accusations, and points from the floor, before Hepzibah brought the meeting to a close. Zach kept his eyes peeled on the group near the front. He could see the tops of their heads. As the crowd began dispersing, they rushed the platform, half a dozen of them. He heard shouting and hurried down, pushing against the flow of people. Two security guards were preventing the young woman and five athletic men from getting onto the stage. The woman was shouting up at the Labour councillor.

'Call me a racist? I'll show you, you scumbag!'

The MP told them to calm down and go home, finding it difficult to keep a straight face and sound convincing. He left, passing Zach on his way.

A big guy at the back of the group pressed up against the two guards became aware of Zach's presence. He turned.

'What's going on?' Zach asked him.

'What's it to you?'

The woman started up a chant: 'Judas! Judas!' which was picked up by her group, including the big guy confronting Zach. The bloke was now off-guard. If Zach had needed to hit him, he would have done it then. Fortunately, he didn't. If these guys had wanted violence, it would have already kicked off.

'I'm a friend of theirs,' he replied, looking up at Hepzibah and the Labour councillor. The big guy stopped chanting and steadied himself so he was able to land more than one blow at a time.

'Calm down,' Zach said. 'Just because they're my friends doesn't mean I have to agree with what they say. I've spent more than ten years arguing with them over Israel.' Zach gestured toward Hepzibah again, and said, 'She's my dead brother's ex-wife. The Labour councillor's my dead brother's best friend.'

'And who's *she?*' the big guy asked, looking suspiciously at Fawz, who had joined Zach. 'Is she your friend too?'

'Yep.' Zach said.

'And do you disagree with her too?' the big man sneered.

Zach saw three more security guards rushing to the scene. 'I've disagreed with her all my life,' Zach replied, 'but I'm beginning to understand her. As for the Labour councillor, I'm beginning to understand her, too.'

The woman called her posse away. The big guy snarled before he left. They met with the guards on the way, but they'd done nothing, and anyway, there were six of them.

Ruth showed her appreciation of the two guards by jumping down and hugging them. She turned to Zach, a big smile on her face. 'That was great, what you said. And thank you for coming to our rescue.'

'I made no difference. Believe me, and I'm sure those two security guys behind you would agree, if that group had wanted to rush the platform to get to you, they would have done it. They had ample opportunity. It was all posture, frightening posture, intimidation. But maybe you shouldn't have called her a racist. What do you think?'

'Yeah, you're right. Heat of the moment. It was stupid.'

'So, were they Tahor Yisra'el?'

'Yes,' admitted Hepzibah. 'I'm surprised they were here. Even more alarming, I recognised three as JVF. The big guy at the back confronting you and the two guys either side of the woman. I bet she's JVF, I've just never seen her before.'

'And they are? Remind me.'

'The Jewish Volunteer Force. They're a self-defence group, but think of them more as the military wing of Tahor Yisra'el. If there's any physical damage to be done, it's done by the JVF.'

24

After the meeting, Hepzibah invited Ruth, Fawz and Zach back to her place. They stopped by Zach's to scoop up Neil. When Hepzibah realised this meant Nellie too, she said it was fine. To give Hepzibah some credit, it *was* fine, for a while. Ruth and Fawz left as soon as the wine had loosened Hepzibah's tongue. Zach, Neil and Nellie should have left with them, but they stayed and listened to Hepzibah go on about the dog. It was smelly, dirty and left hair everywhere.

'What's the point of a dog anyway?' she'd asked as she went up to the bathroom. 'They just lie about the place doing nothing.'

Zach threw back the dredges of his wine glass and, instead of re-filling it, raised his eyebrows at Neil. Along with the dog, they glanced towards the door, and the three of them left while Hepzibah was up-stairs having a pee. Zach knew she would be furious and hurt, and he was running the risk of her still being angry when he knocked on her door in twelve hours' time. Hepzibah had a rendezvous with Solly Benayoun, president of the Association of British Zionists. Zach was tagging along, at the beginning of a steep learning curve.

~~~

Waiting in front of her house the next day, under a sky of unbroken blue, Zach was prepared to move on, as was ever his way. But when Hepzibah finally opened the door, it was clear she was not. She didn't utter a word as she flashed past in a white linen jumpsuit with an open back, tied loosely at the waist; a smart choice as the mercury had already hit thirty-four. On the way to the bus stop she walked three metres ahead, and once there she stood as far from Zach as was possible.

They sat separately on the bus. When they were walking again, Hepzibah made sure she was ahead of him. Zach couldn't care less how far behind he was. He knew where they were going, and it was far too hot to comfortably walk at her pace. They were on Horseferry Road, heading south towards Lambeth Bridge. At St John's Gardens, Zach saw Hepzibah cut in, and he knew in an instant what she was up to. The square was shaded, and sure enough, when he arrived Hepzibah was waiting under the trees by the fountain. She took the next exit out and Zach carried on, continuing at his leisurely pace.

He soon noticed Hepzibah had slowed hers. She passed MI5 head-quarters and turned right at Millbank, crossing the road to walk along-side the river. Zach followed suit, even though the air was too still for the water to make an impact on the heat. He began to dream of the light, air-conditioned atmosphere of the Tate Britain Café.

Hepzibah continued with her slow pace, and it wasn't long before Zach had almost caught up with her. Hepzibah noticed, stopped and turned. When Zach arrived, she didn't walk on. She took his hands and searched his face with her big brown eyes. What was she looking for? Not forgiveness, that wasn't her style. She rarely said sorry and wasn't about to now, but her softened features and gentle touch said she was. Her hair was up in a bun and she flicked stray hairs off her forehead.

'It's not easy, you know. Even now, looking at you, I can't stop thinking about Abe. I miss him so much. And the meeting last night? Impossible not to think about Abe, and later, when I was with you and Neil, I was struggling. I mean, I struggle all the time but last night was really difficult. You annoyed me. I can't remember why. Other than you look like Abe, but are nothing like him. And Neil. Was I very rude about his dog?'

'Very. And you were rude to him.'

'Was I? Oh dear.'

'Your tone with him was condescending. It was like you were talk-ing down to him.'

'Oh dear,' she said again, and blushed. 'I must apologise to him.'

'Yes.'

'Why don't you come back to mine after we've finished and get Neil round? I'll make us a late lunch.'

'We'll try not to annoy you. But it's hard work.'

Hepzibah checked to see if he was joking. He was, but there was always at least a scintilla of truth in a joke. Here, there was a bucketful.

They left the riverside, crossed back over the road, and walked up the steps to the gallery. Inside, the building was cool and airy. Zach followed Hepzibah across the lobby to the bar, where they queued for drinks before joining Solly Benayoun, who was sitting at a table in the corner. Zach had no idea what the president of the Association of British Zionists might look like, but he had not expected a handsome man in his late thirties, urbane, sophisticated even, wearing just a touch of cologne and a well-tailored suit.

Zach approached Benayoun first, as Hepzibah was at the till. Benayoun stood and met Zach's extended hand with his own, but his grip was noncommittal and he didn't make eye contact. Having paid, Hepzibah joined them, placing the tray on the table. Whilst she introduced herself, Zach tasted his flat white, and thought he could do better.

Benayoun wore an air of displeasure, and though polite, was curt. Hepzibah had warned Zach she wouldn't get a warm welcome and, by association, he wouldn't either. Benayoun found her views on Israel loathsome. His position was simple, but no less effective for that. Criticism of Israel was anti-Semitic. Why? Because Israel was a Jewish state. The accusation shut the debate down. Who wanted to be accused of being anti-Semitic?

But what if the critic were a Jew, like Abe or Hepzibah? How to make sense of a Jewish anti-Zionist? Zach knew the idea was difficult for a mind that had embraced Zionism to rationalise, so it turned to irrationality and anger. These people were traitors, working with the anti-Semitic enemy to destroy Israel. Zach said it all the time.

It was beginning to sound hollow.

Benayoun brought a bite of carrot cake to his mouth, chewed deliberately, and finally swallowed before speaking to Hepzibah.

'You know I don't like you, people like you.'

'Yes, but I also know you don't like people like Maccabi, otherwise I wouldn't be here. He is dangerous. His views are dangerous, and the people around him are dangerous.'

Although cool and remote, Benayoun was listening, and he showed no sign of disagreement. Tahor Yisra'el was an embarrassment to the Association of British Zionists, a predominantly mainstream organisation that accepted the idea of compromise with the Palestinians. They were pragmatists who didn't believe it sustainable for Israel to remain perpetually at war.

Benayoun nodded when Hepzibah finished.

'I agree. Far too many people now believe in a Greater Israel with no Arabs. Last year, my cousin, an army commander, was carrying out orders to pull down some illegal settler homes on the West Bank. He was spat at and called a *kapo*. Can you imagine? These people are extreme, for sure, but don't make the mistake of thinking they don't have much support.'

'I wouldn't,' Hepzibah replied. 'There are a lot of extreme people in Israel. The settler movement as a whole is extreme.'

'What's a 'kapo'?' Zach asked.

Benayoun turned to him in surprise. 'You are Jewish, aren't you?'

After a moment Zach realised Benayoun wasn't being rhetorical. It was a question, requiring an answer.

Zach could have been very rude at this point. Never before had anyone demanded he confirm he was Jewish. A Jew always knew when they were in the company of another Jew.

'Of course I am.' Zach's response was indignant more than rude.

'He's a Sephardi,' Hepzibah said, by way of explanation. 'His family didn't go through the holocaust.'

'That's no excuse. I'm a Sephardi too.' Benayoun addressed Zach. 'This is *Jewish* history, Ashkenazi or Sephardi. 'Kapo' is the term used for Jews who worked for the Nazis in the concentration camps.'

A silence fell, broken by Hepzibah in a positive voice. 'Let's get back to Maccabi. We're agreed, this man is dangerous. The guy's so extreme he's calling you and your organisation anti-Zionist.'

Benayoun produced a grim smile. 'He's not just dangerous, he's mad, which makes him doubly dangerous.'

Hepzibah relaxed, looking confident. And why not? After all, Benayoun contacted her. She put her cup of tea down with surprising care and said, 'When we spoke, you told me there had been a plan to attack worshippers at the Al-Aqsa mosque.'

'Worse than that. They'd planned to set off explosives. God knows what the fall-out would have been. Blowing up the Al-Aqsa mosque? Can you imagine?'

'And how was it foiled?'

'Shin Bet has a Jewish terrorist department. It infiltrated the gang.'

'And just to be clear, we're talking about the JLA?'

He nodded.

'And you know this how?'

'I have contacts in the Israeli security services.'

The aim of the Jewish Liberation Army, Zach found out later, was to 'liberate' Israel of anything Islamic or Arab, including the Al-Aqsa mosque, the third holiest site in Islam.

As she didn't trust Benayoun, Hepzibah asked him a question to which she knew the answer. 'I've often wondered whether Maccabi has any links to the JLA. What do you think?'

'Of course he has. He's in regular contact with them.'

'How do you know?'

He gave her a withering stare. 'Their calls are monitored. At the moment there's no evidence linking him to any criminal or terrorist activity, but it'll come, and when it does it will finish him. In the meantime I'm chipping away at my contacts. I'll find something on him, and when I do, I'll be in touch.'

Looking Hepzibah squarely in the eyes for the first time, Benayoun continued. 'It'll be sweet coming from you. He *hates* you.'

'More than you do?'

'I don't hate you. I just don't like you.'

~~~

When they got back to the house, Zach went straight up to the bathroom for a line.

'That's how it is with addicts,' Hepzibah said when he returned. 'As soon as you walk in.'

'That's my first line of the day, at three pm. I've come a long way. Three and half hours, to be precise.' He'd also continued to shorten the lines, but he didn't say. He wanted a bit of peace, and to continue crafting the perfect flat white on Hepzibah's new coffee machine.

She huffed, rolled her eyes and moved on. 'So, our late lunch. Better be something quick and easy. I hear we're now having a big slap-up meal at yours tonight. Neil, who can't come for obvious reasons, is helping Fawz as we speak.'

'I wonder, is Fawz keen on this guy?'

'I don't know, but he's certainly keen on her. He's driving from Cambridge and can't leave before seven, and knows he'll be driving back a few hours later.'

'How did they meet?'

'A PSM meeting. So, what shall I make? Spaghetti alla carbonara sound good?' Zach put a thumb up.

'OK, beat three eggs, grate the cheeses, wash and chop the parsley.' She brought out all the ingredients they needed, including a tub of single cream.

Before she put the spaghetti on, she read an email she'd received. It was from Murrell. It must have been good news because Hepzibah was smiling from ear to ear.

'Guess what?' she said. 'The bill for number 05219587229 is paid by Mr Ralph Maccabi.'

Zach got it straightaway. 'Tamir works for Maccabi. So that's Seth and Tamir. I wonder if Juris Neilands does as well. What about sending Murrell Neilands' number? Does he like you that much?'

'I don't want to push my luck. Anyway, I think we have our proof.'

Zach finished her thought. 'Maccabi was behind the attack on Abe.'

25

The next morning, Zach got up early. Beth had agreed to let him see Rachel, albeit supervised, and Hepzibah had lent him her car on the condition that Zach had no cocaine till he got back. For Zach this was an opportunity to see if he could last till late afternoon. He showered, had breakfast, let Nellie out, and left, all done quietly so as not to wake Neil.

On the journey Zach paid constant attention to the speedometer. He had nine points on his licence. But the sun was shining, making everything all right. He put his shades on and wound the windows down. Zach was a fan of rock and roll as well as rave, and whilst he kept to the speed limit, the Allman Brothers belted out *Statesboro Blues*.

~~~

The car scrunched to a halt on the unmade road outside Beth's house. She was playing the piano, a jazz piece he didn't recognise. It stopped abruptly when he rang the bell, which was a shame. Beth answered the door in a sleeveless white vest and shorts. She was flanked by Rachel on one side and Bitz on the other. Beth had Rachel dressed in another little pink number, accompanied by a floppy pink hat to ward off the sun. Zach bent down and kissed and hugged his daughter whilst the dog joined in.

'I see you don't mind catching the sun yourself,' he said to Beth, once he was up.

'She's three years old, Zach.'

'So? She's got my skin colour.'

'She can still get skin cancer. It's less likely, but if she does get it, it's more likely to … you know.'

'Does that mean she'll be wearing a floppy pink hat every summer for the next ten years?'

'What's skin cancer, Mummy?'

'It's a complicated thing darling, but whatever it is, you don't want it. Now let's go, you and your Dad in the lead.'

Zach swung Rachel's hand whilst Beth took the dog and the four of them walked through town down to the river. He tried not to think about how it felt, the three of them out together with the family dog. It was too painful. Once they were past the sailing club, Beth let Bitz off the lead. He ran down to the marshes and disappeared, the movement of the bulrushes the only indication he was there. When he scrambled up the bank, he was covered in fairy moss. Rachel laughed her head off as the dog shook himself. Bits of green weed were thrown in all directions from his long coat. Beth called him and he came, swerving at the last second to dash off into the distance. Rachel squealed in delight. Bitz was dashing for water up ahead. Beth shouted for him to come back, but he ignored her. He climbed down the shallow bank and lowered himself into knee-high mud, thinking he could plough his way through to the water a hundred yards away. But the tide was at its lowest of the day and Bitz soon gave up. When he came back, his legs were black from the knee down and his look was sheepish. Indeed, he looked very much like a sheep. Rachel laughed and laughed and laughed.

Soon, they arrived at what locals called 'the beach', a piece of scrubland stretching out into the mud, large enough to host two family barbeques. Beth laid a rug on the ground and brought out a picnic she'd made. The dog forgot about water for a moment. It helped that he was given Rachel's sandwiches as she'd suddenly gone off Dairylea cheese.

Zach put his arm around Rachel and pulled her close. 'You know, if you carry on following the river you get to the sea in an hour or two.'

'Can we go?'

'When you're older. We'd need a rope.'

'It's easier and quicker in the car. And a lot less dangerous,' Beth told Rachel. 'Now have this.' She handed Rachel a strawberry petit filous, who wolfed it down and ran off with Bitz to the edge of the beach.

'So, how are you doing?' Beth asked. The question wasn't general. It was very specific.

'I'm on track,' he replied, which was true.

'What does that mean?'

'It means I'm on track,' he said, irritated that he had to explain himself. 'The last time I saw you, which wasn't long ago, I would have had a line by now. My first will be when I get back. Search me, nothing on me.' He emptied his pockets. 'Search the car. You won't find anything. I'd say I'm on track.'

Zach saw Rachel slip and fall. He got there first, picked her up and she cried in his ear. He gave Rachel to Beth so she could cry in her ear instead. Meanwhile, he examined Rachel's wound. A graze on her knee. He poured water onto a tissue and cleaned it, intensifying Rachel's crying momentarily, partly because he had to hold her leg still.

Rachel dried her eyes with the back of her hand and hugged Bitz, who was by her side. She wanted to go home.

'Want me to carry you on my shoulders?' Zach suggested.

'Yes please!'

Rather than return through the woods, which had been the plan, they turned back on themselves and took the quicker river walk back to the sailing club. Once there, Beth fixed Bitz on a lead and Zach put Rachel down. She limped the rest of the way home. A brave soldier returning from battle.

'I think it's better not to come in, Zach. Say goodbye to your father, darling.'

'Bye Dad,' she said, hugging him.

'Bye darling,' he said, and kissed her on the cheek. He watched her leave him and walk into the house.

~~~

Zach parked the car outside Hepzibah's and popped the keys through the letterbox. There was no point ringing the bell, as she was at a yoga class. He sent her a text and walked home along the river in the burning mid-afternoon sun.

When he got back to the flat there was no one in. A note had been left on the kitchen table.

Dear Zach and Fawz,

Thank you for making us so welcome. I am sorry I didn't say goodbye, but I'm not sure I could have faced it. I became so comfortable with you I could have stayed forever. But I can't. So it's best I go now. I wish the best for both of you. Fawz, I hope you and your people get the freedom you deserve. Zach mate, good luck on that journey, and keep your eyes on the prize: Rachel.

Neil and Nellie, forever your friends.

Zach felt surprisingly disappointed they'd gone, and mooched around the flat till Faz got home.

26

At nine o'clock that evening, it was a balmy twenty-six degrees centigrade. Once again, Zach walked by the river where it was cooler, taking the long way round through Millfields Park down to Lea Bridge Road. He had his iPod on and was rocking to Sander Van Doorn's *Neon*, the original mix.

That time of night, it was dark and quiet down by the water. The only people he passed were a man in a high viz jacket with a small dog on an extendable lead and a couple walking slowly, close to each other, deep in conversation. That was it in twenty minutes.

Zach left the river and veered toward the main road. On his way, at the edge of the recreation ground, he came across some youths smoking a joint. The only white in the group, little more than a kid, looked up as he was toking. Zach grinned at him.

The kid nudged the teenager next to him and said, 'Look at dat chief man, finkin he's all bad!' His mate laughed. The kid pointed at Zach and said, 'You bait, blud!'

The teenager was telling Zach he was simple. He'd been called worse. He turned right at the main road and picked up his pace. By the time Vesuvio's was in sight, Zach had chosen the wood-fired pizza he wanted. A thin and crispy Napoletana. Zach was a sucker for anchovies.

Soon he was on the move again. He bit into the pizza. Turning into Lower Clapton Road, A.K.A. Murder Mile, Zach noticed a young man sitting up in a sleeping bag in the chemist's doorway. As Zach got closer, he saw that the guy was hugging a young staffie. The man held the puppy like a small child, whilst the little dog rested its head against the young man's cheek. It was a beautiful tableau, but heart-breaking.

Zach stopped under a streetlamp and studied his pizza. He'd only had a couple of bites, most of it was there. For a second he thought about taking an anchovy but that would have been mean. He was sure to have another sometime soon, maybe even at Hepzibah's. He put his pizza down on the pavement in front of the man. The puppy, catching a whiff of the offering, squirmed and whimpered. Zach looked over his shoulder as he walked away. He saw the man flip the box open and tear off a bite for his hungry, young companion first.

'Thanks mate,' the man shouted and stuffed his mouth.

Zach carried on before he gave them the shirt off his back or burst into tears. He was sure two pairs of baleful eyes followed him. In time, he would forget about the man and his dog. But they'd still be on the streets.

Turning into Hepzibah's road, he saw her neighbour from across the street hanging out on his front steps, smoking. Zach hadn't seen him since he happened to come across his arrest the other day. He walked over.

'You look happy. Police give you your weed back?'

The neighbour laughed out loud, his dreadlocks swinging wildly.

'Tieves man, dem tieves.' He raised his hand, the one with the joint. Zach accepted the invitation and walked through the gate. All the houses had small front gardens, with a short path. A couple of strides was all he needed to get to the joint. He took a long toke; too long. He spluttered, then coughed. They both laughed. He toked again, a shorter one this time, and was fine. So he toked one more time.

'That's *nice*,' he said, and handed the spliff back.

'Anytime, man.'

They bumped fists and Zach went over the road to Hepzibah's. He could hear Dido playing. He let himself in, but rang the bell out of courtesy. The music lowered and Hepzibah appeared, swaying. They went through the ritual of a peck on the cheek, neither saying anything about the other stinking of alcohol or tobacco. He went straight through to the kitchen and cut himself a slice of bread.

'Help yourself to cheese, why don't you?'

'I was going to ask whether you had any anchovies. I fancy them in a sandwich with a tomato'.

'I thought you said you'd eat before you got here. You're always eating my food.'

'I gave my pizza away.' He was so hungry he ate the bread as it was and cut himself another slice.

'You're dropping crumbs on the floor.'

'So have you got any anchovies?'

'No, and I haven't got any tomatoes either.'

Zach got cheese from the fridge and ate over the worktop, clearing away the debris with his hands and sweeping it into the sink. Hepzibah gave him a dirty look but said nothing. She took a bottle from the fridge, went outside, and plonked it on the patio table. Zach brought out two glasses and poured for them both.

'And you're always drinking my wine.'

'I'll pour it back if you like.'

'Don't be silly. I was just pointing out a fact.'

'You asked me round, which meant your wine would get drunk.'

'Yes I know, Zach. But it would be nice if every once in a while, it was your wine.' Her tone had not been aggressive. He noticed an unexpected touch of sorrow, perhaps wondering when Zach was going to sort himself out.

'Nice wine, Heps.' The poignancy of him liking Hepzibah's wine did not escape him. He ignored it. 'You wanted to see me.'

'I always want to see you. Until I do.'

'That's nice.'

'Well. You are a pain.'

'Unlike my brother.'

'Unlike your brother. For one thing you like hitting people, whereas Abe never hit anything in his life.'

'What are you talking about, Heps? Apart from wanting me to be Abe.'

'You almost beat a man to death.'

What on earth made her say that, or even think it?

'If that had been the case I'd have been done for attempted murder, not grievous bodily harm.'

Hepzibah refilled their glasses. 'What happened that night? Why did you beat him so badly? Was it because you were high?'

'Probably. I blacked out, because of the drugs I'd taken. I wasn't aware of anything until I'd been pulled off him and I saw the state of my fists, and his face.'

'Blacked out?'

'I was on acid, having a bad trip. To get home I had to cross Princess Parkway, a dual carriageway, because at that time of night there were always youths hanging about in the tunnel looking for trouble, which if you're on acid you want to avoid like the plague. By the time I'd negotiated the speeding cars and crossed the road my bad trip had worsened. I turned off Princess Parkway, leaving the noise of the traffic behind, and heard screams. I knew they were real and I moved quickly in their direction. Around the corner a woman was on the ground, in the foetal position, being kicked over and over.'

'Then what happened?'

Zach shook his head. 'All I can remember is running straight at him. Everything else is a blank.'

'How could you have hit him if you blacked out?'

'I don't mean I wasn't conscious. I just mean I wasn't aware of what I was doing. I wasn't doing it consciously. I know I hit him because I could see the evidence, but the event isn't stored in my conscious memory.'

'But you *still* take this acid.'

'No, I don't. I haven't taken any since then.'

'So what do you have when you go to raves?'

'MDMA, ecstasy, that's different.'

'Oh, and they're OK, are they?'

'Yeah, they are. They don't send you on a bad trip.'

'They're still dangerous. People die from them.'

The numbers were small. And compared to alcohol? He wasn't going to make the point. 'You're right, Heps, they do.'

'You said drugs were only partly the reason.'

'I'm no psychologist, but the sight of him kicking her must have triggered something in me.'

'What?'

'I've no idea. Dov was violent towards Malka, but that's not it. Too simplistic. As you know, just like Abe, I had a crap relationship with my mother, and was always closer to Dad. It triggered something, but I don't know what.'

'You have a violent streak. In that respect, you're nothing like Abe.'

'And what would Abe have done to stop him kicking that poor woman in the head? Talked to him?'

'Why not?'

It was time Zach left. In a different world, one where he could buy his own wine, he sometimes wondered if he'd bother with Hepzibah. Sure, they were close (in a thrown-together way), and would always look out for each other, but they just didn't get on.

Even now, with the shared purpose of finding out what happened to Abe, she had to carp and criticise. There were reasons. Depression, alcoholism. The combination made Hepzibah hard work.

Zach went back over the road to get stoned.

27

Zach woke after a fitful few hours' sleep. All night, he kept going over his petty comment to Hepzibah. *And what would Abe have done? Talked to him?* Of course, Abe would have tried to stop the attack, in whatever way he could. He would have understood straight away that talking wouldn't be enough. Zach had no idea what his brother would have done, but he would have done something.

A glance at the clock by the bed told Zach it was 7.29. He adjusted his pillow and put his head down for a bit more kip. Fawz, who was flying home today, wasn't leaving for the airport for two hours. But he tossed and turned thinking about Abe, and was soon plagued by the unsettling image of Abe's cracked head seeping blood. He got up rather than fight it.

The moment he opened his bedroom door, Zach smelled coffee. Fawz was up. He went to the bathroom in his birthday suit and yawned in the mirror. While he was having a pee, he thought about the line of cocaine he would have at the end of the day, and salivated.

Zach went back to the bedroom for a T-shirt and shorts. There were many things he loved about a heatwave. Top of the list? Suddenly, attire became dead simple.

Fawz was sitting at the kitchen table staring out of the window, a small glass of Turkish coffee in her hands. The morning sun streamed in, illuminating her face, which was framed by a headscarf, the first time Zach had seen Fawz in full traditional dress. She turned her head toward the door and their eyes met. He saw sadness. Now was not the time to fiddle about with the kettle. Turkish coffee would have to do.

'May I?' he asked, lifting the copper pot of coffee.

'Of course.' He heard sadness as well.

'You'll be back soon,' he pointed out, to comfort her.

'Quds Day is three days away,' she said, by way of reply, and looked down at her cup. 'With the blessing of the Israeli government the 'ultras' will march through East Jerusalem and wave the Israeli flag. The ultra-nationalist and the ultra-religious, led by tens of thousands of football ultras. They will shout abuse and attack our shops and homes. If you are out on the street, you will be beaten. My family say tension is mounting.'

Zach took a sip of coffee, still hot, and digested her words. Fawz was referring to June 23, which Zach had always known as Jerusalem Day, the day in 1967 when Israel captured East Jerusalem and gained control of the whole of the city. In the Peretz home, it had always been a day of celebration.

Fawz's phone, on the table next to her cup, began to vibrate. Zach saw it was Hepzibah and left the room. He wanted to be alone with his thoughts on Jews smashing windows and beating people because they were Arab. He winced, recalling Fawz's words. Her face. He'd seen fear. Yes, Israel's might was frightening. But did it ensure safety? No, it created hatred.

Fawz found Zach in the living room and handed him her phone. 'Hepzibah wants to speak to you.'

Was she going to apologise for the night before?

No, she was not. Instead, she said, 'It's about time we visited Maccabi.'

Zach refilled his glass with coffee from the pot. 'I agree. But we need to make an appointment, we can't just knock on his door. I thought you knew this guy better than me.'

'He won't agree to see me.'

'So, you think an unannounced visit is a good idea? You're going to have to accept you can't come.'

'What makes you so sure he'll see you?'

'I'll ask nicely.'

~~~

The next day they headed for Maccabi's house in Finchley. Hepzibah kept well below the speed limit, infuriating any driver unfortunate enough to find themselves behind her. Zach distracted himself, alternating between looking out of the window and stealing glances at Hepzibah's suntanned legs.

'I know what you're doing Zach,' she finally said, taking her eyes off the road just long enough to roll them.

'You should be flattered, you look gorgeous.' Tucking his chin and pushing his sunglasses down the bridge of his nose, he gave her cleavage an exaggerated appraisal.

'Zach! Stop it. Jesus.'

He sat back and said nothing, leaning his elbow out of the open window and looking out on another glorious day.

For a while they drove in silence, until Hepzibah asked, 'How come he agreed to see you so quickly?'

Zach was looking in his wing mirror, aware that the car behind was so close it might as well have been in the boot. The driver's face was a mixture of fury and desperation. Hepzibah's confidence behind the wheel was already low, so Zach said nothing of the man behind. Instead, he answered her question.

'Maccabi? I got lucky on that one. He was free.'

Hepzibah was in the left-hand lane at the bottom of Great Cambridge Road. The roundabout was busy, so she'd have to push in, like everyone else. She was nervous and agitated, missing several opportunities. In the wing mirror Zach could see the guy behind wave his arms about in frustration, watching car after car pass him in the right-hand lane.

'Heps, there's a gap coming up. Take it.'

'You're making things worse,' she hissed without looking at him, and Zach realised he had, although he hadn't thought that possible. Hepzibah put the car in gear but brought the clutch up too high, and they jumped forward onto the roundabout. They weren't in lane. She dragged the steering wheel down, overcorrecting. They swerved left and almost hit the curb. She straightened up and left enough space for an articulated lorry between her and the car in front. Everyone else was nose to tail.

She turned left and kept to the inside lane on the North Circular, relaxing a little. Zach smiled in empathy, but her expression remained fixed on what was in front of her.

'I still don't understand why you wanted to come,' Zach said. 'You're only going to have to sit in the car.'

'Keeps me close, alright?'

He shrugged and phoned Ester. His sister sounded down.

'Is Dad OK?' Zach asked, worried he'd relapsed.

At the other end of the line Zach heard a door close, and expected the worst. 'He's fine,' she replied.

'You don't sound great Es, is everything OK?'

'I'm just tired. It's a lot of work looking after Dad.'

Zach felt for Ester. Her whole life had been devoted to looking after other people. First Zach, when he was young, then their mother when she was dying, and now their father in his old age. She had spent a lifetime of unpaid domestic service, no holidays, no days off. And to rub salt into the wound, no husband to look after, cherish, share a life with. Poor Ester: lonely, yet never alone.

'Don't know how you do it, Es.'

'I just have to get on with it, don't I? My life could be worse. I'm comfortable, at least. Enough about me. Tell me your news. How are you getting on with stopping drugs?'

'Good, but I can't quit overnight. It doesn't work like that. It's gradual.' Hepzibah threw him a look.

Ester sighed. 'I just want you to get better, Zach.'

'I will. Focusing on Abe helps. It's good to have a project. I'm on my way to talk to someone now, actually.'

He heard a door open and the brush of Ester's skirts against a surface. She was on the move, having had enough of the conversation. Perhaps it was for the best. If she'd been interested, and asked who it was Zach was meeting, he'd have had to have told her it was someone she knew.

Abruptly, she said, 'Dad's here now.'

'See you soon, Es. I could come up again in a few days if you want.'

'You mean if I pay.'

'Well, I can't come otherwise. Anyway, Dad's paying. He just doesn't know he is.'

'It comes out of my allowance, Zach.'

'OK, don't worry, Es. Pass me to dad.' A moment later, he heard his father's voice. Dov was on good form.

'Zachy! When are you going to visit with my beautiful grand-daughter?'

'We could come up in a few days, I guess.'

'Wonderful!'

'I'm going to need the train fare.'

'Of course. I'll get Ester to transfer the money.'

~~~

The late afternoon sun bathed a magnificent wisteria that stretched the length of Maccabi's detached mock-Georgian house. Clusters of light blue flowers hung like lanterns, softening horizontal lines. On the immaculately trimmed front lawn a blackbird listened for worms before pecking at the grass. Zach, who was walking up the drive, stopped and watched. He could hear the bird's long yellow beak twitching, the only audible sound in this quiet suburban neighbourhood. It hopped a few feet away and eyed Zach from there. Unimpressed, the bird flew off.

The beds in the front garden were planted in a low maintenance, no nonsense style, filled with clipped evergreen shrubs and bordered by a six-inch high hedging of box. There wasn't a weed to be seen in the gravelled drive that swept past the entrance to the house. Two square terracotta pots flanked the porch, each planted with identically sized box shrubs.

Zach pressed the bell. If he played it straight, perhaps he could come away knowing more than when he arrived. That didn't mean he didn't expect Maccabi to lie. His biggest worry, though, was Maccabi's reaction, because Zach's strategy was risky. It had to be. If he played it cautiously, he wouldn't learn a thing.

Mrs Maccabi answered the door. She was young and conventionally attractive, with a big meaningless smile. Accompanying her was a small dog that sniffed at Zach's feet.

'Mr Peretz, please come in,' she said and showed him into a large study. 'Would you like tea? Coffee?'

Zach put up a hand. 'I'm fine, thanks.'

'I'll let my husband know you're here. He's in the back garden snipping and spraying the roses. Apparently, it's something you do at this time of year.' She smiled and left. The dog gave Zach a look that could have meant anything, then scampered after her.

Sunlight streamed in through two arched windows, lighting up a wall lined with black and white photographs of victorious soldiers waving the Israeli flag. On a leather-topped desk by the windows there were pictures of the family, Maccabi, his wife and the two girls. A calendar for June 2014 lay in the centre. Most days were circled, with notes. A small Israeli flag was planted in a wooden holder, and to the side was a sepia-tinted black and white photograph of two soldiers, rifles at their sides, posing for the camera.

Ralph Maccabi entered the room smiling. Like his wife, he was small and svelte. Unlike his wife, his hair was slicked back, and he wasn't pretty. One point in his favour, he was as under-dressed as Zach in a cotton shirt and shorts.

Maccabi took off his gardening gloves and held out a hand. Neither of them liked the other. Nevertheless, they gripped and shook and smiled.

'The soldiers in the photograph,' Maccabi said, gesturing toward the desk, 'are two of the greatest men in history. The man on the left is Ze'ev Jabotinsky, a hero of Jewish resistance in the Russian pogroms. The younger man on the right is Menachem Begin. I'm sure you've heard of him. They are wearing the battle fatigues of the Irgun which they set up in 1931 to fight for a Jewish state. My wife's grandfather served under them. He took that picture, and the ones on the wall.'

'They're good,' Zach said, feeling a response was expected.

'Yes, they are. Please, sit down.' Maccabi directed Zach toward a low-slung armchair, one of two facing each other. They both sat down.

'Now, how may I help?'

'My family, they're all supporters of Tahor Yisra'el,' Zach began.

'And you're not. Still, you're not on the other side by all accounts.' Big smile.

'I am not. It's true I'm working with my mad sister-in-law, and believe me she is mad, but obviously we both want to find out what happened the night Abe was killed. It's about the only common ground we have. I'm nothing like her, I can assure you.'

'Killed?' he said, still smiling. 'Did someone kill your brother?'

'Yes, the unfortunate driver of the car.'

Two could play that game. The man with the smile knew more about Abe's death than Zach. Indeed, the two main suspects worked for him. Zach was mulling over the situation when Maccabi replied.

'Yes, it must have been awful for him.'

That was one thing they could agree on.

'But how may I help you?'

Zach had thought long and hard. Maccabi was unlikely to tell the truth. He'd deny knowing them. Then what? A chat about the weather and possibly the football, before saying cheerio? What if Zach told the truth, or a version of it? They might get some movement, or it could bomb.

'I was hoping you would help me with Seth Silberman and a man called Tamir.'

Maccabi's smile was still there. He said nothing.

'I need to talk to them about Abe's death, Tamir specifically.'

'And how may I help?'

'By contacting them for me.'

'But I don't know them.'

Zach was at the point where he packed up and went home, or he took the plunge. 'Look,' he said, his tone sympathetic, 'they work for you. I know you know them.'

Maccabi's smile got even bigger. He laughed. 'Zach – do you mind if I call you Zach?'

'Not at all.'

'Zach, there are literally hundreds of people who work for me. I can't know them all.'

'Do you give them all a mobile phone?'

The smile was still there. 'Excuse me?'

'The mobile phones used by Seth and Tamir, they're in your name. You pay the bills.'

Now Maccabi's smile disappeared. He stared at Zach, stony-eyed.

'And where did you get that information?'

'The police.'

Maccabi said nothing.

After a moment, Zach continued. 'Look, it's like this. Seth really got my goat that night, the night of my brother's funeral, wearing a fucking *'Free Palestine Now'* badge. So I nicked the traitor's phone to buy cocaine. But after he sent Tamir round for the SIM card I hated the turncoat even more. I told the police he was involved in Abe's death and gave them his number. Turns out there's no Seth Laskowitz and the phone belongs to you.'

'Your time's up,' Maccabi said sharply. He got up and waited for Zach to do the same. Clearly, Zach's strategy had backfired. Maccabi had gone off the deep end. Reluctantly, Zach rose to his feet and left the room. He closed the front door behind him and walked back along the drive down to the street.

The news was on in Hepzibah's car. A shooter had killed six and wounded thirteen in a small town near Santa Barbara, targeting students in a crazed murderous spree. Hepzibah turned the volume down.

'Well? You weren't in there long. Good? Bad?'

'Bad. He denied knowing Seth and Tamir and when I told him I knew he paid the bills for their phones, he terminated the conversation.'

'Why did you tell him?'

'Because otherwise we'd have sat there and had a nice chat over tea. It was a long shot. It didn't work.'

'So you didn't get very far.'

'I didn't get anywhere.' From the back pocket of his shorts Zach took out a loyalty card, a fiver and a wrap. It was time for a toot.

'Do you have to do that now?'

'Yes.'

28

At dusk, it was still warm enough for shorts and a T-shirt, so Zach detoured along the river Lea rather than go directly through the park. He'd just done a line and was flying. He had his iPod on and was rocking to the big beat of *Summertime Sadness* (the Cedric Gervais remix). The lyrics to the trip hop ballad were sad, depicting a young woman's suicide alongside her lover's, but Lana Del Rey's voice took you everywhere: high, low, she had it all.

In the distance groups of youths sat around in the large grassy area between the trees and the recreation ground. Getting stoned no doubt. By the river it was quiet. The odd dog walker. The occasional lovers. Zach didn't have a dog or a lover, but he was rocking, and singing along.

Alert to danger he was not.

Bang!

A fist connected with the side of his head. Zach's earphones soared then descended, hitting the ground before he did. A boot flew at Zach's head. He rolled. His back took the kick. The next time the boot came, it hit him flush on the side of his head. Thud! Before Zach could move, another came, catching him on the back of the head, followed quickly by a couple of kicks in the ribs. The pain would come later, but for the moment, luckily, Zach was high. Otherwise, he would have been dead and buried.

Zach heard muffled shouts and made out figures running across the field towards them. His assailant was distracted. This was Zach's chance. He was up in a cocaine-fuelled flash, his earphones flying around his head like crazed satellites gone into overdrive. He kicked his attacker in the testicles, hard, and the man doubled over. Zach wasted no time. He leaned in to give the man's jaw an uppercut. He heard a crack. When the man fell backwards, Zach went with him, pinning him to the ground, where he continued his furious assault. He heard shouts but that didn't stop him. He punched the man's head again and again.

'Hey man, enough!'

They were the same guys from the other night. Four of them black and one white trying to sound black. They came near and stared. His assailant wasn't moving. Zach gave the man a good look for the first time, but couldn't tell much from his bloodied face. Dark hair, short on the sides. It wasn't ringing any bells.

'What the *fuck*, man?' The teenager waited for an answer, but Zach hadn't realised there'd been a question.

'And how the fuck did you get up from that kickin'?' The kid looked closer. 'What the *fuck* are you on man?'

'Cocaine.'

'You OK?'

'I am now. I won't be later.' He checked for a pulse on the guy lying on the ground. 'He's breathing.'

Zach stuck his earphones back in. The Bingo Players were on. *Get Up (Rattle)*. Pump the volume, feel the base. Simple lyrics, great remix, crazy feat.

'Thanks for interrupting this guy here.' He bumped fists with the kid who'd been asking questions and left their curious looks behind.

Now Zach was pissed, in the American sense. He made his way smartly to Hepzibah's. He rang the bell and waited; he wasn't expected. When Hepzibah opened the door, she looked at him curiously.

'You OK? You look as though you've been in a fight. And your eyes are wild. What's happened?'

'You're right. I've just been attacked. Funny that, seeing as I went to see Maccabi earlier.'

'JVF,' she said, letting him in. The Jewish Volunteer Force.

Zach went to the kitchen and put his hand under running water. Blood washed away. Hepzibah came over as he was studying his knuckles. The skin was red and raw.

'You hit him?'

'A few times.'

'What happened?'

'I got knocked to the ground and kicked in the head and ribs.' He saw Hepzibah wince. 'I need to get to A&E. I was flying at the time, so didn't feel much. I'm starting to come down now. Pain is setting in.'

'I'll get you a taxi. I can't take you, I've been drinking.'

'That's silly, seeing as you'll have to give me the money to get there and back. It won't be long before I can drive.'

~~~

Zach drove to Homerton Hospital, a mile south-east, via Finchley, nine miles to the north. He passed Maccabi's house and pulled over. It was quiet, like last time. He pulled out his wrap, prepared a small line and snorted it up. Wham! The effect was instantaneous. In the time it took the cocaine to travel up his nose, Zach was repaired. No more aches and pains. *Come on Maccabi.*

The light in the porch illuminated the two sentinel box shrubs. He pressed the bell and kept his thumb there. No one came to the door. Through the stained glass he could see a dim light at the end of the hall. The curtains were drawn. He rang again. Nothing.

He went back to the car and rummaged in the glove compartment till he found pen and paper. He wrote a note which he posted through the house letterbox. It said:

FUCK YOU MACCABI

29

It was midday when Zach woke. Sleepily, he made his way downstairs in boxers and bare feet. It was another gloriously hot day and the bi-folding doors at the end of the kitchen were fully open. He put the kettle on and went to see Hepzibah in her study. The leaves of a small palm hung gracefully over her laptop, softening the edges. Zach stood in the doorway and smiled.

'Morning.' He fought back a yawn. 'Did you mind me sleeping here?'

'I guessed you might. What time did you get back?' As she spoke, Hepzibah tried not to ogle his bare chest.

'You're staring at my body,' he pointed out with a wicked smile.

'You're half naked.'

'The important bit's covered up.'

'So, what time did you get back?'

'About five.'

'Blimey, you were a long time. What did they say?'

'I've got bruising to my head and ribs. Nothing serious. They've given me painkillers and stuff. So, what do you think? Was I being told to back off?'

'I think that's a fair assumption.'

'Well fuck 'em.' He turned and headed for the kitchen. 'I need a drink.'

'Wait a minute, wait a minute,' she said following. 'What do you mean?'

'Fancy a coffee?' Zach ignored the kettle and headed for the coffee maker he'd forgotten about.

'What? Yes,' she replied, and quickly returned to her question. 'What do you mean?'

'What do you mean what do I mean? Fuck 'em. Can't be clearer.' He made coffee as they talked.

'Yes, but that's what I mean. What do you mean when you say that?'

'I mean *fuck them*. I sent a message saying just that.'

'What do you mean you sent a message? What did it say?'

'The guy that attacked me, I gave him a message to take back,' he replied, being economical with the truth.

'What did you say? What was the message?'

'Explicitly?'

'Get on with it, Zach.'

'Fuck you Maccabi.'

'*Fuck you Maccabi?*' She followed him from breadboard to toaster. '*Fuck you Maccabi?* What's that supposed to achieve?'

Zach finished making the two flat whites just as his toast popped up. 'It was to let him know I'm not giving in.'

'And how is that clever?'

Zach got Manchego and a bowl of olives from the fridge and sat down to eat. 'I wasn't trying to be clever,' he said, buttering his toast. 'I was just letting him know...'

'Yes, yes, I know, that you're not giving in. Jesus Zach. Maybe you should try being clever occasionally, rather than an idiot all the time.'

30

That evening, on his way home, Zach looked for the spot where the attack took place. He may have passed it, or not arrived at it, but it was somewhere nearby. Fuck Maccabi, wherever it was.

The weather was still crazy. Lea Valley Park with Seville temperatures. But instead of La Giralda and the best tapas in Spain, there was the Coppermill Lane Water Works and a couple of fast-food outlets everyone agreed were shite.

Zach shivered, despite the heat. He had well and truly come down from his last hit, almost five hours earlier, and was denying himself another. Benzos when he got in, benzos again later, and a bottle of Hepzibah's wine in between that hadn't been asked for and hadn't been offered. The big, rich, dark red from Portugal had been taken, without authorisation. He'd need it. On top of that, he'd have a big fat spliff and forget about cocaine. Until tomorrow.

But he wasn't home yet, and paranoia had set in. A group of youths were coming towards him. Could be perfectly innocent – probably was, he kept telling himself. He didn't want trouble, not now. The kids looked weird, or maybe it was him. Were they scowling? He couldn't tell in the dark.

In the event, they ignored him completely. He passed the sports ground and turned left into Watermint Quay. The key to the name quay was that it sounded so much cleaner than dock, which was what it used to be called. What had been industrial was now residential. The houses were all mock something or other, and dock just wouldn't do. So, quay it became.

Zach walked quickly and crossed the road diagonally to gain time. There wasn't a soul on the street. The only cars were stationary. Nevertheless, he kept his eyes peeled coming up to the corner. Nobody around. Only a man and his dog, walking the other way. Zach turned right into Leadale Road. About half-way along, there was a semi-detached Edwardian house. Although probate hadn't yet gone through, the upstairs flat was now his.

Zach was home. He mounted the stairs to the flat, opened up, and headed for the kitchen down the hall where his benzos were. A loud bang made him flinch. Something hit the door behind him. A cricket bat? He swung round. A well-built guy dressed in black, wearing boots, a balaclava and leather gloves, stood in front of the door to the flat. In one hand he held a baseball bat with which he tapped the palm of the other. Zach was shaken by another bang, this time on the kitchen door. He swivelled sharply. Another tough guy, dressed identically to the other, also armed with a bat. One of them blocked his escape, the other the way to his benzos. But right now, it was a line of cocaine Zach needed.

By his feet, a photograph of Fawz in front of the Al-Aqsa mosque lay smashed, along with one of the mosque itself. Bent frames and broken glass littered the floor. The living room door was open; he was level with it now. Same in there. Pictures shattered and pulled apart. Much of Abe's academic and political writings had been torn to shreds and scattered all over the room.

The tapping of batons quickened. These guys meant business. And if they weren't there to kill him, they were there to do him serious damage. They weren't there to punch him with gloved hands. They were there to batter him with wooden bats, and Zach didn't want to live in a wheelchair for the rest of his life, or worse, a bed. They were moving towards him now. Frantically, he sought a way out. There was only one. He'd take his chances. He dropped the very expensive bottle of red and turned into the living room. There, he headed for the single-paned sash windows in the bay at speed. He was soaring now, his feet way off the ground. He put his arms up to protect his face and take the brunt of the impact, along with his feet and legs. Zach's speed sent him crashing through. The glass broke and the timber frame shattered. Shards cut Zach everywhere.

He landed on a hedge and was stabbed by a twig in his upper cheekbone, not far from his left eye. His scream was so loud it was probably heard in West London. Then he fell five feet onto the pavement. A golden retriever licked his face whilst its owner dialled 999.

~~~

The pain was almost tolerable now Zach was in hospital and drugged up to the eyeballs. The journey was over. No more travelling, lifting, or wheeling. He could keep perfectly still. His eyelids fluttered to a close. The sedatives, as well as the pain relief, were beginning to work.

Later, seemingly from another world, Zach heard a voice he recognised. Was he dreaming?

'You have to let us see him! We are family. I am his sister.'

'It's much too late. It's the middle of the night.'

'I insist!' Ester said, and rushed over. 'Zach!' she cried, 'what were you thinking?' He pulled himself awake and turned his head, gritting his teeth at the shot of pain he felt. 'You could have been killed!' she said.

Looming over him he saw Dov as well as Ester. His father was elated. 'Thank God you're alive, Zachy! You should be dead, but you're not. You're alive. Thank God. I nearly lost two boys in three weeks.'

Zach smiled sleepily at his father's exuberance. But he was about to shatter it. 'JVF attacked me and Abe.'

His father and sister recoiled in horror. Shock registered on their faces. Dov looked utterly shattered at the news.

'Don't worry, Dad,' Zach said, closed his eyes and let himself go.

31

To control the pain, Zach was on enough fentanyl to send most people into a state of euphoria. He'd told the medics he was a cocaine addict, so they put him on triazolam as well, used for insomnia, during the day as well as the night. The hospital tranquilised him.

Zach was quite a sight, covered in deep cuts and scratches. He looked like he'd been mauled by a tiger. His arms and legs were torn to shreds, having led the charge through the window. His left wrist was heavily bandaged. But it was Zach's right arm and leg, the first to go through, which were cut up the worst. He could move his left arm slowly, but the pain in his shoulder was too much when he tried to move his right arm. He suffered wounds to his neck, his face, and the top of his head. And a centimetre below a severely bruised eye, a deep bloody gouge had been stitched up and left to heal. Though heavily sedated, Zach was awake, scratching at open wounds on his lacerated chest with a bandaged left hand.

A bloke stood at the end of his bed looking at him with a bemused smile. He was middle-aged and a touch overweight. With an innate belief in himself, he wore a bright red bow tie with a light blue suit. When he spoke, his accent betrayed his privileged roots. He sounded like a 1950s advert for an exceedingly good mint.

'Well, well, Mr Peretz, you are a very lucky man.'

'I am?' Zach queried, grimacing at the slightest movement.

'Jumped through a first-floor window? I'd say so. According to your case notes you sustained no injuries to your internal organs or your neurovascular structures. I think we can safely say you have been extremely lucky. You have soft tissue damage to your skin and muscles, but that'll heal, and you nearly lost an eye when a twig dug into your upper cheekbone on impact with the hedge. That's what saved you. The hedge. Would have been curtains otherwise. It meant you only fell five feet to the ground. Enough to sustain serious injuries though. I'm going to be busy with that shoulder and pelvis.'

'Tell me.'

'Apart from half a dozen fractured ribs, you have a fractured pelvis and a broken shoulder, both requiring rapid surgical treatment. The broken shoulder is the less serious injury, though it could take two months to heal once I've moved the pieces of bone back into place. With the pelvic fracture, the operation is more complex because it's difficult to get inside to manipulate the bones.'

The surgeon prattled on about open reductions and incisions. He sounded like he was positively looking forward to cutting Zach open later that day. Zach couldn't concentrate, but he got the gist. The guy with the bow tie was going to cut holes in him big enough to stick his hands inside and move bones back into position, before using plates and screws to hold them in place. Zach would have bits of metal inside him for the rest of his life.

~~~

Later, he had no idea how much later, Zach heard Rachel and opened his eyes.

'Daddy!'

Rachel climbed onto the bed to hug him. It hurt, but he said nothing. He couldn't say much anyway, dosed up as he was on sleeping pills.

'Careful, darling,' Beth said. Hepzibah was there as well. Both adults were dismayed to see the extent of Zach's injuries, but Rachel appeared intrigued. She traced her fingers along the cuts on his cheek.

'Does that hurt, Daddy?'

'No,' he replied truthfully.

Beth raised the head end of his bed and Rachel curled up next to him. He relished the feel of her. Just like when she was a baby: soft, small, and part of him. Beth and Hepzibah asked how he was, what his pain levels were, about surgery and rehabilitation. Their behaviour was guarded, their conversation limited around Rachel.

'Don't worry about the flat,' Hepzibah assured him. 'Everything's being fixed as we speak.'

Beth leaned in. 'Do they know you're a ...?' She put a finger to her nose and sniffed.

'Course,' he said. Keeping his neck as still as possible, he lifted an arm, pointed to clothing, and said, 'Trousers.'

They were on top of a cabinet with his shirt. Beth looked at them in horror. They were covered in blood. She composed herself and handed the trousers over.

'They're ripped to pieces.'

If there was a point there, he ignored it. He took the trousers with his good arm, the one around Rachel, and gently passed them to his right hand, with which he could at least hold the material steady. Using his left hand, he searched the back pocket. No wrap. He checked it again. Still no wrap. He searched the other back pocket, but all it held was his wallet. Then his side pockets. His keys were in one, his iPod in the other. But no wrap.

'Shit!'

'What, Daddy?'

'*Shit!*'

'*What, Daddy?*' Rachel moved sharply. Pain shot through his body.

'It's OK, darling, it's nothing.'

Fuck! No cocaine.

It must have fallen out. His wallet was still there and somehow his iPod was undamaged.

Fuck! No cocaine.

He'd had less than half a gram. Its value couldn't have been much more than twenty quid, but that wasn't the point.

He didn't have any cocaine.

That was the point. The only fucking point.

Beth leant forward. 'Zach, you OK?'

No, I'm not fucking OK. But he couldn't say, not in front of Rachel. His only consolation was that the hospital staff were willing to pump him full of triazolam rather than tie him to the bed. He'd be doing a lot of sleeping over the next few days. He'd cope, but only because of the fentanyl. It definitely took the edge off. And then there was the triazolam.

'Lost your stuff?' Hepzibah wasn't waiting for an answer. 'Well, you're trying to give up. Here's your ideal place to start.' Then she nodded at Rachel. 'For her.'

Rachel, who was under Zach's good arm, looked up at him, her eyes wide with excitement.

'What for me, Daddy?'

'A hot chocolate, what do you think?'

'Yes, please!'

'Go with your mum.'

'When will you be better, Daddy?'

'Soon, darling.' She reached up and kissed him on the cheek.

'Remember,' Zach said, 'get off slowly.'

Ever so carefully, Rachel slid down the bed and left with Beth. Once they were out of earshot, Zach turned to Hepzibah and said,

'You're not safe at your place.'

'I guess you're right,' she agreed, grim-faced.

32

With each passing day I unwind a little more. I still get anxious when I hear a car coming up the drive, or when the landline rings, but I'm functioning normally now, working long days when I need to. No one at work has asked me anything about anything. I didn't expect anybody to probe my odd behaviour or my absence, but it does seem strange that nobody has inquired about my health. They're all being super nice and treating me with kid gloves, so I think it's just embarrassment.

I'm glad the professor's brother is alive, but he jumped out of a first-floor window! He must have thought they were going to kill him. They wanted revenge for their beaten comrade, but nothing too serious. The talk was of damaging his knee so he couldn't kick anyone in the testicles, but now, he's lucky he's going to be walking again. He lucky he's alive, for god's sake. Whatever lessons he draws from this saga, I hope he's finally realised what he's up against. These people mean business, and I guess I should be grateful for that. I don't want anybody hurt, but I do want both him and her to stop investigating. Because if the chain unravels, the police will find me at the end of it.

Today, I'm home before four. Ella is frying on the patio where the thermostat records thirty-five degrees. Her head is under the umbrella. The rest of her tanned body glistens in the sun, arousing me. It's been a while since I took the time to appreciate my wife.

If I tell you the girls are out, I think you can imagine what happens next. It starts with a bottle of dry white from the fridge, and moves quickly on to a kiss, where it lingers. Then my hands begin to roam.

Ella gives me free reign for some moments, then she pulls away, and asks, 'Do you know how long it's been?'

'Since I kissed you?' I have no idea and hazard a guess based on how long it's been since the professor died. 'Fifty-five days.'

'It's been fifty-six, but who's counting?'

33

Zach heard the familiar estuary accent, somewhere between received pronunciation and cockney.

'Zach Peretz? This the right ward, yeah?'

It was Neil, but Zach barely recognised him at first. He was clean-shaven and his hair was neat. He also looked freshly showered, and his clothes were clean.

'Zach mate! I won't ask how you are. You look crap.' Neil grinned at his friend and pulled up a chair. 'Mate, you're on the front page of the Standard! I couldn't believe it when I read it was you. What were ya finkin? You could've killed yourself. They said it was a first-floor window. Were you high?'

Zach shook his head. 'They had *baseball bats* for fuck's sake.' He involuntarily jerked his right arm. Pain shot through his shoulder. He gritted his teeth and said, 'You talk.'

Neil got the message. 'Me and Nellie have a room above a pub in Kentish Town. We're security at night and I help out with the pots and stuff. I've fallen on me feet mate. No bills, free grub, the odd pint.' He grinned. 'Life's good. Been to see me mum and dad, they're getting on now. I've even seen me kids.'

'Great.' Zach was delighted at the turn of events in Neil's life, but he didn't have long to chat. The nurse could arrive any minute with the last of his pre-meds.

'Pass me my phone and wallet.' They were on a shelf inside the open plywood wardrobe next to the bed. Zach turned his phone on, went to contacts and scrolled down to Jake. He showed Neil his dealer's number and gave him fifty quid. Neil hesitated, realising what he was being asked to do. Zach pleaded with him, waking his elderly ward mates. They were staring now.

But that didn't stop Zach. '*Please.*'

Eventually Neil gave in, but made his displeasure clear. Zach really didn't care how Neil felt.

~~~

Hours after surgery, whilst Zach drifted in and out of consciousness, he felt a new pain, alternately throbbing and acute. He was also aware of a noise, snoring, and Zach remembered he was in a small ward with four old geezers. It was night time.

In the dark he sensed someone's presence. Once his sight had adjusted, he saw Ester sitting by his bed glaring at him.

For a moment he saw his mother. He heard her too, through Ester, who spat her words out.

'You spiteful, *nasty* boy.'

Never before had he heard Ester use that tone. Zach was shocked. His head began to ache.

'Did you stop and think for one second about your father? He's traumatised. Traumatised! He's not sleeping, he doesn't talk or do anything. He's gone into such a deep depression I don't think he'll ever get over this. Abe killed by the Jewish Volunteer Force? Why would you say such a thing?'

'Because it's true.'

'It's a wicked lie. Those boys protect us. They don't kill Jews, you fool.'

He saw malice in Ester's eyes. This was a side to his sister he'd not seen in his thirty-one years.

She got up from the chair and loomed over him. 'This is worse than when you stole Mum's jewellery while she was dying. This could kill Dad.'

Was she right? Zach couldn't think straight. He was drugged up to the eyeballs, in pain, and now his head hurt.

Ester straightened up. 'I won't be coming to see you. I won't be ringing, and I certainly won't be taking any calls from you. And when you get out, don't come to the house. You are not welcome. And don't bother with Nissim. He'd spit on the ground you were standing on.'

With that, Ester turned and left.

34

When Zach next opened his eyes, it was daylight. Now Hepzibah was sitting by his bed. She was studying him with a smile filled with sorrow. He saw tears in the corners of her eyes. Once she saw he was awake, she spoke, without so much as a 'good morning' or 'how are you after surgery?' Instead, she said, 'Do you remember when Abe ended up in hospital after that motorbike accident near Oxford?'

Zach's head still hurt from Ester's visit, and the triazolam he was on had wiped him out. He couldn't talk much, being half asleep, but it was better than climbing the walls.

All he said was, "Course I remember.' How could he forget? The first time Abe got on a bike, he nearly died.

'He was lucky.'

'Yes, he was.'

Hepzibah dried her eyes. 'Solly Benayoun rang last night. Remember him? President of the Association of British Zionists. He gave me the phone number of a guy called Jacob Vidal who's a regional manager at Maccabi Facilities Services, the housing repairs company owned by the Maccabi family. He has evidence of corruption.'

Zach knew he seemed uninterested, but he wasn't. He forced words out. They didn't sound like they were coming from him.

'That's great.'

'The company has contracts with more than a dozen councils, including six in London, and four of the biggest housing associations in the country. This guy Vidal says he has evidence the company regularly makes claims for work that's either not completed or not done at all.

The over-claiming covers *at least* 150,000 local authority and housing association properties. Can you believe it? The Maccabis have creamed off two million in the past twelve months alone. Of course, it only works if they've got corrupt officials working for their clients.'

He was drawn to Hepzibah's news, but he couldn't engage. He was interested, but too tired. He just wanted to be told the story. Hepzibah seemed to understand. She continued.

'It was two years ago that Vidal discovered they'd been over-claiming and overcharging on a contract with an inner London Borough. He hasn't looked at any earlier contracts, but he's been keeping tabs on the current ones. The practice is still taking place.'

Zach lay back and smiled. The Maccabis were cooked. He closed his eyes.

'I can see you're pleased. I'd have preferred to have got some evidence of his terrorist activities, something that linked him to the JLA in Israel.'

He opened them again. That was the easy bit. Thinking, talking, they were hard work. He had to push words out.

'Come.'

She put her ear close to his mouth.

'Fraud? That's jail.'

'Perhaps,' she replied with a smile.

~~~

At dusk when the nurse came to put the lights out and close the ward doors, she went to see Zach.

'Last night, I said yes to your sister, because she was leaving, but that's the last time.'

'Don't worry, she won't do it again.'

'You're a close family. I like that.' The nurse picked up his notes and read them. After some moments she nodded. 'Good. All normal. You're eating, drinking, managing the toilet.' She returned his notes to a peg at the end of the bed and came close.

'You're very tired. Shall I lower the dose of your triazolam?'

'No, no, don't do that.'

35

The doors to the ward were open, and Zach heard Neil arrive at the nursing station and engage in flirtatious banter with the all-female staff. Neil wasn't classically good-looking, but he had a chiselled face many women found attractive. He was young, fit, and strong, and walked with an endearing limp that drew people into his story. Was he a sportsman with a career-ending injury, or a soldier injured in battle?

When he walked into the ward, Neil didn't make eye contact. Something was up.

'Didn't you get it?'

'Don't worry. I got it.'

Zach sat up and put out the hand that wasn't in a sling. He was beginning to salivate.

'It's back at the pub.'

Now he was waking up. '*What the fuck?*'

His four elderly companions turned and stared.

'If you have a line you'll undo yer stitches, mate. You'll forget they're there.'

'*Bollocks!* Don't be fucking stupid. Nothing'll happen to my stitches.'

His fellow dwellers stared and stared.

'OK, nothing'll happen to yer stitches. Wait a few days. It'll be good for you.'

Now Zach was fully awake and completely pissed off. 'I don't *want* to wait a few days. For *fuck's* sake Neil, bring it in.'

'Listen, Zach mate, I'm starting to turn my life around. Maybe you should too. You can't stay on cocaine for the rest of your life. If you do, it'll be short.'

'I *know* that, but I'm supposed to be coming off the stuff *gradually*.'

'I should never have got it you. You're in hospital mate. It's the ideal opportunity. What are you on?'

'Fentanyl.'

'Jesus.'

'And triazolam.'

'*And* triazolam? You're joking?'

'Do I look as though I'm fucking joking? For *fuck's* sake, Neil. *Bring it in.*'

'No.'

'I'll *never* forgive you.'

'I can live with that.'

36

Zach opened his eyes. Once again, Hepzibah was sitting by his bed, gazing at him. Her elbow rested on the chair arm, and her hand cupped her chin. It must have been torment for her to see so much of Zach. Yet she put herself through the ordeal at least twice a day.

'How long have you been here?' he asked, feeling suddenly self-conscious.

'About a quarter of an hour.'

'Surprised you don't get bored as well as upset.'

'It's double-edged, you know. Sometimes it's unbearable. Sometimes I hate you for it, but sometimes, like this morning, it's lovely. I used to love bringing Abe a cup of tea and watching him wake up.'

For a moment Zach wanted to close his eyes and wish Hepzibah away.

She continued. 'You know, I told him, when he came back, I mean, I know he didn't come back to the house, but he came back to me. We didn't sleep together, but we became close again. I told him I'd never loved anyone as much. He was the only one. He'll always be the only one.'

Zach was tiring of this nonsense. For Abe, Hepzibah's help had been a means to an end. For Hepzibah, it had been encouragement to think they were rekindling their relationship. But now Abe was dead Hepzibah had no choice but to move on, surely? Unless she wanted to spend the next forty years on her own.

Zach sat up. He could do that now.

Hepzibah eyed him suspiciously. 'What are you smiling at?' she asked.

'They're letting me out tomorrow.'

'I know, I'm picking you up. I've left a bag of clothes by the bed.'

'What did you bring?'

'Boxers, flip flops, shorts, and a short-sleeved shirt. Oh, and a walking stick. You won't need anything else. And tomorrow night you can celebrate and crack open that Portuguese red you nicked. Miraculously, it was in one piece.'

Zach was to stay at her friend Paul's place. Actually, Paul had been Abe's friend, but he was happy to help a 'comrade'. Three in the house, Zach could see how that could work, even if two of them were trots. Having a third person around could make living with Hepzibah a lot easier.

'Zach, I've something to tell you, and I don't know whether it's good or bad.'

'Go on,' he said, warily.

'The JVF, they know I'm staying at Paul's. My new laptop was stolen last night, just hours after Jacob Vidal sent me incriminating documents. Vidal gave them my address, he must have been leant on, but that was my stupid fault for giving it him in the first place. So, Maccabi sent someone. In and out, while we were sleeping. Quiet as you like. The whole windowpane in the study taken out. Nothing else stolen. Déjà vu. They even left a note. It said, *Last Chance*.'

'Bet that went down well with Paul.'

'He was delirious. The point is, I wasn't killed. I wasn't attacked. I wasn't even threatened.'

'That's the good bit, presumably.'

'Maccabi was behind both break-ins. He could have had me killed.'

'Drop your investigation into Maccabi. Give him one less reason for being annoyed with us. We need to focus on finding Abe's killer, who is probably this Tamir guy, and prove he was working for Maccabi.'

37

The following morning, his last in hospital, Zach was showered and dressed for the first time in six days. He was sitting on the side of the bed, reading a text message from Neil whilst he waited for Hepzibah to pick him up. Goodbye stale air! Au revoir disinfectant! Fresh air was close. And sunshine. And cocaine! He'd gone six days without a line, managing because he'd been tranquilised for most of the time. Being pumped full of fentanyl helped as well. It didn't just relieve pain; it also took the edge off his anxiety. But now he needed to cut back on the triazolam and wake up. A line would help. Make no mistake, he fully intended to keep his promise to Rachel. He would wean himself off cocaine using the legal drugs he'd been given. Fentanyl, triazolam, and benzos.

Things were starting to look up, but there were still two blots on his horizon. His father's mental state worried him, as did his relationship with his sister. Ester was keeping to her word and not taking his calls.

Soon, Zach heard Hepzibah at the nursing station, bantering with staff. 'I've come to take him off your hands,' she said to much amusement.

'Finally!' they chorused.

'*I'll* have to listen to his moaning now.'

'Good luck with that,' they chimed. One of the nurses gave Hepzibah a piece of advice. 'Just give him a triazolam. That'll shut him up.' They laughed and laughed and laughed.

Hepzibah breezed into the ward and clapped her hands, waking Zach's elderly companions.

'Time to go, Zach. Chop chop.'

She was wearing a summer dress and had her hair up, baring bronzed shoulders – a reminder that Zach had missed a week of sun. He was raring to go, although he wouldn't be doing anything quickly.

'I'll be moving more like a tortoise than a hare,' he said, leaning on a walking stick to get up off the bed.

'I'll cope. Come on. I'll help you up.'

'No, this I can do.'

He hauled himself up. At the doors, he turned to the guys in the ward.

'Bye then,' he said.

'Do you know,' one of them said, 'those are the first words you've said to us.'

'Yeah, sorry. I wasn't really with it.'

'We saw.'

'Bye then,' Zach repeated.

None of them replied.

Zach walked out with Hepzibah. She suggested she put her arm round his waist and he his arm over her shoulder. But Zach had his stick, and he knew it was better to get used to it. They walked slowly, Hepzibah keeping to Zach's pace. They left the ward, said goodbye to the staff at the station, and took the lift down to the ground floor. In the lobby, Hepzibah paused at the news stand and flicked through the broadsheets until she found the paper she wrote for. Before she went in, Zach gave her a tenner for tobacco and cigarette papers.

'I shouldn't be getting you that stuff.'

'OK. I'll go in.'

Hepzibah sighed deeply and said, 'I'll get it.'

Zach leant on his walking stick and waited. When she came out Hepzibah gave him the baccy, skins, and his change.

'You're not smoking one before you get in the car. You'll have to wait.'

'Jeez,' he said, looking at the price of her paper.

'It's even more expensive weekends.'

'Do you get one every day?' he asked as he hobbled towards the hospital exit.

'Just Saturday and Sunday. Gotta get Sunday's,' she added with a self-satisfied smile.

'So ...?'

'I'm treating myself today. It's a bore reading online. We can sit in the sun with the paper.'

'Ah, domestic bliss.'

She held the exit door open, and he shuffled through. Outside, he screwed his eyes against the bright sunlight. Hepzibah put on dark glasses.

'Don't suppose you brought a pair of those for me, did you?'

'You suppose right. Funnily enough, I didn't think of that this morning.'

Zach stepped to one side and leant back against a wall to bathe in the sun's warm glow. He closed his eyes and breathed deeply. He could have stayed there forever listening to the hum of traffic on Homerton High Street, the buzz of an energised city. It felt great to be out of hospital and, best of all, the heatwave hadn't ended.

A flock of starlings swung through the sky. They circled half a dozen times before swooping down to land on an aerial where they lined up in rows. With sunglasses Zach could have watched them all day. He made a move towards Hepzibah, shielding his eyes with his free hand. He'd remembered something.

'This guy, Paul, I've met him. I think we got on.'

'I thought we could stay at my place, it's as safe as anywhere. We can pick up your stuff on the way.'

'Woah, slow down, the JVF are after us.' Zach pulled up sharply along with Hepzibah to allow a car to reverse out of a parking space. The movement had been quick and unexpected. Pain shot up his leg to the base of his spine.

'Yes, but are they after us?' Hepzibah asked once they were on their slow way again. 'If I publish and be damned, they'll be after me. But if I don't, they won't. As for you,' Hepzibah looked him up and down, 'I doubt they'll be after you, not for a while at least. Anyway, we're no safer at Paul's than we are at mine. They found me there, n'est-ce pas?'

They arrived at her car. Hepzibah brought her shoulder bag round and rummaged for her keys. 'Let's keep a low profile,' she said, 'I quite like being alive, and you've got to recuperate.'

'OK, I get that, but why are you so keen for me to stay with you?'

She opened the car door and helped him in. She even brought his seat belt round, knowing it was an awkward movement for him. 'You can look after yourself if you want.'

'What's the catch, Heps?'

'There isn't one. I don't want to be alone.'

'And you want my company? We'll drive each other mad.'

'You can help me find Abe's killer,' she said and turned on the engine.

'I thought we weren't working on that for the moment.'

She checked her mirrors. 'We need to keep our heads down, for sure, but I bet there's stuff we can do without putting our lives at risk. How long before you're properly better?'

'Two months, but I should be able to do most things in a couple of weeks.'

Ultra-carefully, Hepzibah backed out of the space. She checked her mirrors more than twice and inched out.

'Let's go pick up your stuff, get back and sit in the garden.'

'Mind if we take a slight detour first, to Kentish Town?'

Half stuck out, Hepzibah stepped hard on the brakes, pushed the lever out of gear, and swung round to face him.

'I've been waiting for this. It's about drugs, isn't it? This is how it's going to be, isn't it?'

'This isn't going to work, Heps. Just take me to Kentish Town and leave me there, or take me back to my flat.'

'Oh, it's *your* flat now, is it?'

'Oh for fuck's sake Heps, I'll get the bus.' As he undid his seat belt, he remembered he didn't have much more than three quid. He continued, through pride, and opened the door.

'I guess I'll just have to get used to it, won't I?' she said, resigned. 'Come on, let's go to Kentish Town.'

38

Zach sat under the rose arch in the middle of the garden, buzzing. He'd had his first line for a week and was puffing hungrily on a fag. He was out of hospital, he was high, the sun was shining, and he was rocking to *One Heart*, up there with the best psytrance hits of the year. What more could he want?

He could see Hepzibah. She was looking out onto the garden while she washed up. The windows were open. He thought he saw her lips moving, so he pulled his earphones out, but she was just singing along to Demi Lovato, trying to sound deep and soulful. Zach turned his iPod off and heaved himself up on his stick, figuring he should move a little. He headed slowly towards the house where *Heart Attack* was playing, a song about a woman who didn't dare show her feelings. It was four o'clock. Was Hepzibah already drinking?

Yes. Hepzibah drank to forget her life. Fair enough; Zach used cocaine similarly. But alcohol was a depressant to those prone to depression, and most evenings Hepzibah ended up dwelling on her life gone wrong, her promising career as a ballet dancer cut short by injury, her infertility, Abe's death, and the death of her father when she was still a teenager.

A month after her father watched her perform at the Royal Opera House, she left for school in the morning without saying goodbye to him. He hadn't spoken to her for four days. It wasn't personal – he wasn't talking to anyone, he was depressed, but Hepzibah wanted to demonstrate her unhappiness at his behaviour. Little did she know, she would never see him again. That morning her father didn't go to work.

Once he was alone, he went into the garage, sealed the doors shut, top, bottom, and around, attached a length of hose to the exhaust pipe and took it into the car with him.

Hepzibah was seventeen and needed help to come to terms with what had happened. When Abe met her twelve years later, he realised she'd received none. She had barely talked about what her father had done and how she felt about it. Her mother was useless, her sisters younger than her, her friends her age. She never thought to visit the doctor, and no one suggested it. Abe was no psychologist, but he could see a link. She hadn't processed her feelings about her father's depression and suicide, and now she bottled things up, until she exploded. Her behaviour sabotaged her relationship with Abe. The drinking, the bouts of depression, her refusal to seek help. She was consumed by bitter memories of her torn ligament, how she got it, and why. Whilst Hepzibah found her niche in journalism, she still dwelt on broken dreams. How many times had she told Zach she performed Myrtha in Giselle before her injury?

'Want some?' she asked, offering him some wine. 'Or are you high enough already?'

'I'm fine, thanks.'

Zach used his stick to get up from the kitchen chair. Amy Winehouse was now playing, and Hepzibah sang along as she checked the cooking.

For you I was the flame,

Love is a losing game.

Zach approached the open oven, his stick hitting the kitchen floor with a dull thud. Then, closing his eyes, he sniffed deeply. 'Mmmmm! Smells delicious.'

'It's been in the oven since nine this morning, slow cooking. Lamb marinated in pomegranate molasses, honey, yoghurt, lemon, herbs and spices.'

'Sounds great. Can't wait for some lovely grub. Heps, I've been meaning to ask, did you get in touch with Murrell?'

'I've left two messages this week and he hasn't got back to me.'

'Maybe he doesn't fancy you anymore. Shall I try?'

Hepzibah shrugged. 'You won't get through. You'll just be leaving a message like me.'

'Might as well give it a try. Shall I tell him about Tamir's nickname on the streets being 'the Israeli' because nobody knows his name?'

'If you get through, yes, but you won't.'

Zach sat in the late afternoon sun and phoned Detective Inspector Murrell. Hepzibah's cottage garden was filled with poppies, foxgloves, delphiniums, and rose campion. It looked an idyllic picture.

The DI soon picked up his call, the speed taking Zach by surprise. He hadn't thought about what he was going to say and started off on completely the wrong foot.

'Abe's killer is called Tamir and he works for Maccabi,' Zach told Murrell.

'I've told you before, no one killed your brother.'

Zach felt like strangling the phone. Through the window, Hepzibah saw Zach was wound up by something Murrell had said, and grinned.

'OK,' Zach said, 'the guy who was chasing Abe that night works for Maccabi.'

'How do you know?'

Once again, Zach wanted to strangle the phone, and Hepzibah tried not to laugh. Why was she finding this so funny? Had she been at his dope?

'All you know, Mr Peretz, is that someone called Tamir is using a phone paid for by Maccabi. All the rest is conjecture. You're giving me a headache. Zionism, JVF. Give me a break.'

They had no evidence. Murrell was right there, but nowhere else. Zach moved on. 'Maccabi and his family are using their company to cream millions off the top.'

'Have you any evidence of this?'

'We did have. They stole it last night.' He didn't tell Murrell they had copies stored in Hepzibah's cloud account. The inspector would be told when the time was right.

'They stole it. Who's they?'

'The JVF. Maccabi.'

'You're giving me a headache again. Anyway, I haven't got time to go on any wild goose chases.'

~~~

Later, in the dark, slowly, Zach went down to the bottom of the garden and made a call. He spoke quietly into the phone.

'Were we followed when we left the hospital?'

'Yes mate, you were, all the way. The good news is the tailer didn't realise he was being tailed as well. Connor does a good job.'

PART THREE

Under Surveillance

39

Zach could hear Janice Joplin's delightfully guttural rendition of *A Piece of My Heart* playing in the house. The song was a hit when originally recorded by Erma Franklin, Aretha's older sister, but nobody remembered the originals after Janis Joplin covered them.

Leaning on his stick, Zach let himself in. Hepzibah's MP3 player was in the kitchen by the bi-folding doors, which were fully open. She was lying on the lounger catching the last of the day's sun, a glass of wine by her side. Zach had been thinking about a drink for the last hour, along with a benzo and some dope. A tiring trio, but that was the point, to dull the craving for cocaine. In a perverse way Hepzibah helped as well. She didn't like Zach when he was stoned and on benzos, but she liked him even less when he was high. It meant he wasn't tempted by an evening toot. There were other benefits. She bought lots of wine. He went to the fridge and sampled the cool dry white she was drinking. Yummy, quite a tang. He could see how easy it would be to drink a bottle of the stuff. The problem was, for Hepzibah, that was too much.

Now that he had a filled glass in his hand, Zach realised how difficult it was to use a walking stick and keep the wine steady. But he made it.

'Nice,' he said, lifting his glass to Hepzibah.

'It's a Marlborough. Clapton mini market has it on offer at the moment. Moreish, isn't it? So, how did you get on with your stick today?'

'Yeah, you know, couldn't walk fast enough for Rachel, but it was great to see her.' He sipped at his wine. 'And you? How's your day been?'

She sat up and adjusted her bikini top. 'I've finished the article. Expect another invasion of Gaza soon, is my drift. Tensions on the border are electric, and Israel is itching for a fight.'

~~~

After three hours' drinking, Hepzibah was on the slide. She was looking at the TV, but not watching it. She barely moved. Her back and neck were straight as a die. A background in ballet helped, and Hepzibah was also an experienced practitioner of yoga. Even now, when she was drunk, the only movement was an occasional sway. From afar she looked serene, but up close you could see she wore the expression of a smouldering volcano.

Zach skinned up, fanning her ire. He went outside to smoke his joint and watched her through the windows. She kept perfectly still. Under different circumstances he'd be impressed, but he knew this could be the prelude to an explosion. He finished his joint and decided to nip her wrath in the bud. He steadied himself at the door as he went in. A spliff on top of wine and benzos made that necessary. When he walked into the living room he said,

'Hey Heps, you OK about, you know, the whole drugs thing, cos if you're not, well, you know, we need to be cool with each other, you know, chilled.'

She turned her head slowly and sneered. 'You're stoned out of your head. Do you know what you sound like?'

He said nothing.

Newsnight, by unhappy coincidence, carried an item on cannabis-induced psychosis. The subject was enough to tip Hepzibah over the edge. Out of the corner of his eye Zach could see her hitting rock bottom. The programme ended and she turned to face him with a scowl.

'I know you think cannabis is harmless.' Her tone was low and hard, and her words were slurred. 'But it's not. It's very dangerous.'

'What about alcohol? OK, cannabis is dangerous to a minority who are prone to psychosis, but it doesn't kill you or make you aggressive. Anyway, the tobacco I smoke with it is far more dangerous.'

'I *know* tobacco is dangerous.'

'But you don't think it should be made illegal, do you?'

She turned her face sharply away and sat in a huff. In the silence that descended, Zach wondered – exactly *what* was Hepzibah so angry about? Being alone? Why? She was attractive when she wasn't angry, and intelligent when she wasn't in denial. She was only forty and she was hot. A change of attitude and she'd have men falling at her feet. All the same, Zach couldn't help feeling she'd never be in a place to move on and be happy. And why was that? Zach could only guess, but he'd put his mortgage (if he had one) on it having something to do with her feelings about her father's suicide.

Hepzibah's slender neck remained motionless, and quite beautiful, yet it was twisted at an awkward angle, away from Zach. When she spoke again, she didn't turn to face him. Her eyes were fixed on a spot on the window blinds.

'You didn't see what cannabis did to Abe's best friend.'

Zach was getting weary now. 'No, I didn't.'

'His life's in ruins. Of course alcohol is harmful, but it doesn't induce psychosis. It doesn't render you useless.'

Zach raised an eyebrow at the sheer lunacy of what Hepzibah was saying. Somewhat like Tony Blair, she could convince herself that black was really white, or that alcohol didn't render you useless, or – even more ludicrous – that it wasn't dangerous.

'Anyway, you can't criminalise alcohol now,' she said. 'The mafia would come back if we had prohibition.'

'What, you mean a bit like drug dealers?'

That shut her up, until he rolled a joint. She heard the rustle of cigarette papers as he stuck three together, and whipped round.

'And what you're doing there is *illegal*.'

'Abe used to dabble now and again, you know.'

'I found a lump once, in his bedside drawer, wrapped up in a pair of socks so I wouldn't notice.'

'What did you do?'

'I threw it away, of course.'

Zach went outside to smoke his joint, taking his glass with him. Through the window, he watched Hepzibah sitting in the dimly lit room. She remained motionless, cross-legged on the sofa, arms folded, her face twisted away staring at that spot on the blinds. Zach inhaled deeply on his spliff and tried not to go over her stupid, angry comments. The dope couldn't block them out, but it did help soften the irritation he felt. He smoked quickly and drank. Soon, he was swaying. Before he stepped back inside, Zach steadied himself.

'Night then,' he said at the living room door.

'Night,' she replied eventually, barely audible, her face still turned away.

He took a triazolam and went to bed.

~~~

Zach was woken by a telephone. Hepzibah's landline. It was still dark outside. He checked the time. Almost four in the morning. The phone rang and rang. Bad temperedly, painfully, he got up, put a dressing gown on and made his way slowly down to the living room.

His mood worsened when he saw Hepzibah asleep on the sofa, snoring softly. He'd taken a heavy-duty sleeping pill. He'd taken benzos. He'd smoked dope. He'd drunk wine. He'd used a fucking walking stick to get down the stairs. How come he'd heard the phone and she hadn't? It was less than three feet from her ear.

The TV was on low. Some black and white film noir. The phone kept ringing. He answered.

'What?'

'Junkie? You listening?'

A Maccabi acolyte. 'I'm all ears.'

'You'll need more than a stick to get about if you fuck with us. You'll need a wheelchair. Understand?'

Zach knew a response was required. He gave the only one he could. 'Yes.'

'Same goes for sleeping beauty there.'

What? Zach stared at the blinds. They were down but not shut. Only up close could you see in. At least one of Maccabi's men was outside right now.

'You're wearing a blue dressing gown. Your dick's hanging out. You look like a wanker.'

Right enough, Zach hadn't tied the gown and his thingy was hanging out.

'Are you a wanker, junkie?'

Zach wanted to give this guy a piece of his mind, but he knew better.

'We're watching you.'

Click. The phone went dead.

40

The weather broke not long after the JVF's early morning call, coming with cracks of thunder and flashes of lightning. The rain beat down and the temperature plummeted ten degrees. For almost a month, everyone had lounged about in shorts and a T-shirt, or a top and a skirt. Today everybody would be in rainwear, murmuring darkly that summer was over.

A text arrived from Beth at a quarter to seven, waking him. 'Dreadful weather, but I have to go to London today. Taking Rachel. Brunch, 1pm, Carluccio's? My treat, obviously.' He'd had little sleep, but he texted back straightaway because Beth would be impressed he was compos mentis at such an early hour, and the name of the game at the moment was to impress Beth so he could see Rachel without a chaperone.

'Great. See you there,' he replied. Leaving his phone by the bed, he turned over and went back to sleep for over two hours. When he woke again, he showered, had toast, cheese, and olives, chatted with Hepzibah when she took a break from work, and checked the train times to Liverpool Street on her laptop. There was one at 12.27. Perfect. It was a ten-minute journey, then an eight-minute walk to Carluccio's. It would take him double that today. The longest element of the journey was the twelve-minute walk to Clapton station, which would take Zach half an hour in his current state. Fortunately, Hepzibah offered to drive him (very slowly) to the station.

~~~

He arrived in good time. The café was busy, but it buzzed with staff. He walked past the deli bar to the tables and soon spotted Rachel, easy to do with her thick black curly hair. She wore a dress, again, not pink this time, but white with a blueish blush. Why couldn't she wear jeans occasionally?

He waved as he approached.

'Daddy!' she shouted.

'Hi, darling,' he said when he reached her. He gave her a hug and a kiss. 'I missed you,' he whispered in her ear as he sat down beside her. He heard Beth call a waiter over. Typical. Always in a rush.

'I'll be with you in a minute,' he said to Rachel, 'I just need to look at the menu.'

The breakfast menu was still being served, so Zach went with a classic. A Royale. Smoked salmon with poached eggs and hollandaise on toasted ciabatta.

'And to drink, Sir?'

'I'll have a bottle of sparkling water with a slice of lemon.'

He turned back to Rachel and kissed her on the cheek. 'And what are you having?'

Rachel reached for a menu with a small hand and pulled one towards her.

'That one! Pa-ne-ttone,' she said, without emphasis on that final e.

Zach looked over at Beth. 'Really?' he asked.

Beth shrugged. 'She won't have anything from the kids' menu.'

Zach grinned at Rachel. 'Maybe you could start taking a stand against the clothes she makes you wear.'

They both said 'what?', only Rachel added 'Daddy' and didn't sound defensive.

'Only joking,' he told Rachel. 'Would you like to see some secret gardens that are very close by?'

'Why secret, Daddy?'

'Because you can't see them. Look,' he pointed through the window, 'there they are, on the other side of the square. Can you see a big green space?'

'No,' she said, her voice forlorn.

'Don't worry, darling, you're not supposed to. They're secret.'

She looked puzzled. 'But you can see them.'

'I can see them because I've been there. Once you've been there, you'll be able to see them too.'

'Can I go? Can I go?'

'Where are you going with this, Zach?' Beth asked. 'She thinks you're being serious.'

'I am. I'll show you when we leave. It's a lovely place.'

'We haven't got time. Our train's in an hour and a half.'

It was a surprise to hear they were leaving so soon. All the same, Zach wasn't convinced they didn't have enough time to visit the gardens.

'They're literally on the other side of the square.'

'Look Zach, you know I don't like rushing. It takes us more than twenty minutes to get to the station. Little madam here is easily distracted. We'll have to leave in less than an hour, because I'm not leaving it till the last minute. Even if our food arrived now…'

'Which it has.'

The young woman stopped at their table and unloaded her tray.

'Even so,' Beth said, making space for her smashed avocado dish, 'we'll leave it till the next time we're here. I've got to come to London in a few days. I'm not sure when yet. I'll text you. You better not be joking about these "secret gardens."'

'There's a small park on the other side of the square, called Elder Gardens, known locally as the Secret Gardens of Spitalfields.' He changed the subject entirely. 'You haven't asked how I'm doing.'

'How are you doing?'

'Pretty well.'

'You look well considering you're not long out of hospital, but I guess you're still taking that stuff.'

'What stuff, Daddy?'

'Sugar, darling, and you know how bad that is for you. I'm weaning myself off it and I'm on track to stop. Not long now and I won't be taking any at all.' He didn't tell Rachel he'd made a promise to her.

~~~

By the time Zach arrived back from Spitalfields, the temperature was higher than earlier in the day and Hepzibah was sitting under the rose arch, flicking through the monthly food magazine that came with the Saturday paper. He waved and went up to the bathroom for his first hit of the day. Leaning on his stick, he prepared a small line, smaller than the day before, and snorted it up. Wham! The rush came instantly and left Zach grinning from ear to ear. It was the best feeling ever. Would he miss it? Probably, but he was too high to worry, though not too stupid to know he needed to keep out of Hepzibah's way for a couple of hours. He slipped quietly out. As he shut the front door behind him his phone began to vibrate, then ring with a number he didn't recognise.

'Hello?'

'This is Seth Laskowitz.'

'Laskowitz my arse.' Zach leant heavily on his stick to negotiate the doorstep and keep the phone at his ear. He had intended to go over the road and get stoned, but now he turned left and headed for the park. 'Your name's Silberman. You're a fucking spy.'

Zach heard an announcement over a public address system in the background, a flight to Madrid. Seth was in an airport departure lounge.

'What are you doing? Escaping? And how the fuck did you get my number?'

'I don't need to *escape*. No one's after me.'

'My number, how the fuck did you get it?'

'Ralph gave it to me.'

'I never gave it to Maccabi.'

'You rang his house.'

'Well, why have you rung?'

'I wanted to talk and I could hardly ring Hepzibah or Fawz now, could I? But you're on my side.'

'I'm not on your fucking side,' Zach hissed.

'Well, you're not on their side, are you?'

'What the fuck do you want?' Zach snapped. A passing grandmother pushing a buggy looked over in disgust.

'To say I'm sorry about Abe.'

'Really? Well, if you're that sorry you can tell me why Tamir-whatever-his-name-is chased Abe into the road.'

Silence.

'If you were really sorry, you'd turn him in.'

'I'm not turning him in. Anyway, he's left.'

'Where's he gone? Back to Israel?'

'Look, we both feel bad about your brother. Tamir wasn't going to kill him.'

'Abe obviously thought he was.'

'Tamir has a bit of a reputation, but not for killing people.'

'Abe was scared out of his wits. Otherwise he wouldn't have run into the road. How well do you know this Tamir guy?'

'Very well,' Seth replied, in the manner of a best friend or partner.

'What's your relationship with him?'

It was a while before Seth replied. 'Friends. We met through work, I guess you could say.'

'What sort of work?'

'I was using the word euphemistically. Let's say he was my handler.'

'You mean when he got to spy on the Palestine Solidarity Movement?'

'He suggested it, yeah.'

'Who does he work for?'

Seth said nothing.

'Who were you giving your information to?'

Silence.

'You both work for Maccabi. Who does Maccabi send his information to?'

Still, Seth stayed silent. An announcement came over the tannoy, the last call for a flight to Lisbon.

'Where are you going?' Zach asked.

'Tel Aviv. I'm exercising my right under the law of return.'

'You want to leave home, everything you know, just because you did a bit of spying on the PSM?'

'You think I'm in trouble? You wish. Anyway, England's not my home. Do *you* feel at home here?'

'Yes and no.'

'*Yes and no,*' Seth mimicked. 'You sound pathetic. All Jews in the diaspora feel rootless. That's why we want to go home.'

'But where's that?'

'*But where's that?*' He mimicked Zach once more, but the jocular tone had gone. It was now between a sneer and a snarl. '*Israel,* you moron.'

Zach let the point go, but it was Seth who was being simplistic, wedded to the idea that Israel was home to the Jewish diaspora. Zach did indeed feel rootless, yet paradoxically had put down roots. England was his home, despite the xenophobic nationalism that bubbled under the surface.

The call to board the flight to Tel Aviv came through.

'Was Maccabi behind the attack on Abe?'

Click. The phone went dead.

41

The following day, after his interview for the postgrad course, Zach walked out of the Bartlett School of Architecture and stuck his earphones in. He chose a natty number, a fusion of house, dub and reggae, with a vocalist called Cheshire Cat. Zach needed to wind down, having just spent an intense thirty minutes in a small, airless room with two blokes and a woman firing questions at him from every angle. The half hour couldn't be called gruelling, but it had been full on. Zach was about to consider how he'd done when a man caught his eye. He was on the other side of the street, outside the UCL students' union. He clocked Zach and pushed himself away from the wall. The guy was built like a brick shithouse. He wore a crewcut, jeans, a white T-shirt tucked in, and a black bomber jacket. No self-respecting student would tuck in a T-shirt. He stood out like a sore thumb.

Zach pulled his collar up against the late afternoon drizzle and pretended not to have noticed the beefcake. He steadied himself on his stick as he negotiated the steps and switched his iPod off before Cheshire Cat could get going. Zach needed his wits about him.

The guy followed Zach all the way to Euston from the other side of the road. However, at the bus stop he stood close to Zach. And when the 253 came he breathed down Zach's neck and sat behind him. The man in a bomber jacket wasn't trying to be discreet. He was making a point.

We're watching you.

At Hackney Baths bomber jacket got off the bus with Zach and followed him across Murder Mile. They walked past the chemist, its doorway empty of rough sleepers for the moment. Zach couldn't walk fast, and bomber jacket was on his heels. It looked weird. People stared. The odd couple turned into Hepzibah's road and sidestepped a large puddle on the bend in unison.

When he reached Hepzibah's, Zach opened the spring-loaded gate and walked through. But it didn't shut behind him. Bomber jacket held it open, came in, and leant back against the gate post. He folded his arms.

Zach left him there. When he opened Hepzibah's front door he could hear Patti Smith, the punk poet laureate, singing *Because the Night*, a song she co-wrote with Bruce Springsteen.

Hepzibah was at the kitchen sink, swinging her hips and bringing in the next verse with a shake of her arms. Zach could smell cheese in the oven and looked around for evidence a cauliflower had been used. He found none.

'Macaroni cheese?'

Hepzibah swung round. 'Hey! Look at you,' she said, checking out the suit. 'You had your interview today. I guess you got the sympathy vote, being Abe's brother. So, how'd it go?'

'Good, I think. Hang on a sec.' He went up the stairs to the front bedroom. From there you could look down onto the gate.

'You up there for a line?' Hepzibah asked, getting the lingo right now it was about to become redundant.

'No, just need to check something.' He kept the light off, not wanting to alert the tough guy at the gate. He crept to the window, drawing back when a car pulled up. The driver leant over and opened the door for the guy in the bomber jacket. They shared a joke in the car before driving off.

'What's the matter?' Hepzibah asked.

'Nothing.' Why worry her?

'So tell me, how did it go?'

'Yeah, good. Fortunately, no one asked me why I'd needed an urgent appointment with a surgeon. What would I have said? After all, I jumped out of a first-floor window to escape two men with baseball bats. They'd have thought I was an addict who owed money to drug dealers.'

'Perish the thought.'

'Anyway, they seemed confident I could get funding from somewhere or other. Hopefully this will be the beginning of me getting my life back on track.'

Hepzibah drained her glass and went to the fridge for a refill.

'As in …?' she asked, pressing for some detail.

'Get back to doing what I used to do. I was good at it.'

She rolled her forefinger in the air, telling him she wanted more meat on the bone.

'Squeezing concessions out of developers, measly in the scheme of things I know, but you can't imagine how resistant they are, so it feels like little victories all the time. You know the sort of thing; x number of social housing units, a community hall, green space, safe play areas, larger gardens, fewer houses, I could go on, but I think you get the picture.'

'I do,' she nodded.

'So, are we having macaroni cheese?'

Hepzibah ignored his question. 'Is that all you're going to do?' she demanded to know, folding her arms and pushing out her chest.

Zach knew exactly what she meant, but he didn't like her tone. 'Is that all what?' he asked.

'You're going to do to get your life back on track. What about the cocaine?'

She had some chutzpah, Hepzibah. But then Abe always said she lived in a parallel universe.

'I'm down to one small line a day.' *Usually*, he should have added. If he went out in the evening, or more to the point, if he wasn't in Hepzibah's company, he'd more than likely have another toot.

'You only manage that because you take those infernal benzodiazepines. They pretty much knock you out.'

Zach was looking forward to the day he didn't take a benzo, but they only knocked him out because he combined them with alcohol and dope. He didn't point that out.

'I thought you preferred me to be on benzos.'

'I do,' she conceded, taking a sip of her wine. She had not yet offered Zach any. Was she making a point? When was the last time he bought a bottle of wine? Come to think of it, when was the first?

He popped a benzo. 'So, what's for dinner? Macaroni cheese?'

'I'm worried about Fawz. I messaged her a few hours ago, and I haven't heard back.'

'A few hours? I'm sure there's nothing to worry about. Anything could have happened. She could have left her phone at a friend's this morning and now she's out for the evening.'

'You know Fawz. She has her phone with her all the time. Her Facebook page hasn't been opened since yesterday evening.'

That did not sound good. Fawz had Facebook open all day every day.

'I've been in touch with ... someone in Tel Aviv. She used to work for B'Tselem and has useful human rights contacts.'

'I know Lila,' Zach said.

'How do you know Lila?'

'Well, I don't *know* her, but Abe used to talk about her.'

'I bet he did,' she said, the bitterness in her voice clear.

Abe was close to Lila and stayed with her whenever he was in the region. Hepzibah had met her a few times in London and Tel Aviv, but it was safe to say they weren't bosom buddies.

'Yeah, well let's hope she can help, but I'm sure Fawz will be fine,' he said optimistically.

'You haven't heard, have you? Three Israeli teenagers were abducted yesterday. Israel has launched a military operation to find them. The IDF has arrested hundreds of Hamas members. Hamas, of course, has responded with rockets.'

'What's that got to do with Fawz? She doesn't support Hamas.'

Hepzibah gave him a scornful look. 'It doesn't matter if you support Hamas or not. There are demonstrations every day now. The military is on high alert, anything can happen. If you get caught up in a protest the IDF doesn't ask if you support Hamas before they arrest you.'

'OK Heps, I get it.'

'Do you, Zach? Do you? Over the past twenty-four hours ten Palestinians have been killed in retaliation.'

Zach saw tears forming. Who she was crying for wasn't clear. Everybody, probably. Fawz, the ten Palestinians, and the three Israeli teenagers.

Hepzibah opened the oven to check on the macaroni cheese.

42

The following evening, Hepzibah was watching a recorded episode of her favourite, a police series fronted by a female duo. She looked relaxed. Zach wasn't. He was looking at the TV, but he wasn't absorbing its content. Appropriately, because he couldn't keep still, he was in the rocking chair where he could sit and move. It helped a little.

By now Zach would have taken a benzo and had a glass of wine, but he needed his wits about him that evening. He stared at the TV. The two detectives did their best to hold his attention. They shouted at each other in the police station toilets before bursting into tears and hugging each other. But what the cops were up to, or up against, wasn't clear to him, and he realised why. He couldn't care less. All he wanted was for Neil and this guy Connor to hurry the fuck up.

He looked at his phone again. Two minutes. Was that all? Time passed slowly whilst your life passed you by. The irony didn't impress him. He rocked harder. Surprise, surprise, he was irritating Hepzibah.

He paced the back garden, his walking stick doing the damp grass no favours. The heatwave was now a distant memory. It was July and the temperature was rarely higher than twenty. Tonight, the sky was heavy, a sign of more rain to come. Zach pulled his phone out again. Still another five minutes to go.

He heard a Beep! Beep! They were early. As quickly as he could, he went back into the house and opened the front door. Neil waved from the passenger seat of a macho red convertible truck. The driver looked tough enough. Zach put his thumb up and went back in. He popped his head round the living room door. Hepzibah was watching both detectives intently. They were in a parked car talking earnestly to each other in very low voices.

'See you later, Heps.'

Hepzibah pressed the pause button. 'You're going out?'

'Yeah.'

'You haven't taken any benzos today, have you?'

'No.'

'I knew you hadn't, you've been hyper since you got in. You're planning something. Where are you going?'

He couldn't tell her, she'd either freak or take control, or both. 'Out for a drink,' he said.

'Who's paying? You haven't got any money.'

'See you later, Heps,' Zach said and closed the door behind him. Now he had a forty-minute journey, thirty-five if he was lucky. Would he cope? He'd have to. He climbed into the back of the car and joined Nellie.

'*Drive*. Just fucking drive, as fast as you can.'

~~~

Connor, who was driving, pulled over. Zach already had his seat belt undone. 'Thank *fuck* for that,' he said and prepared a line.

Every speck of cocaine was hoovered up, despite Nellie's constant nudges. Now his scowl disappeared, and he grinned at Neil. His friend did not grin back. A minute ago, Zach wouldn't have noticed, but now he was as alert as an eager young trot learning the forty different ideological positions on the Korean Workers Party.

'So, were we followed?'

'I told you we were being followed earlier on. Don't you remember?'

'I don't remember much from the journey here.'

'Want me to enlighten you? You swore a lot. You upset Nellie and you need to apologise to Connor. Go on, apologise.'

'Sorry Connor for whatever I did or said. And, also, thank you for helping me out this evening, and the other day.'

The driver turned round. He had a scar down his right cheek and his black hair was slicked back cowboy style. Zach was tempted to ask where his hat was, but he was an ex-soldier and he'd fixed Zach with an inscrutable look. He could have been thinking anything. Zach told himself not to say anything if Connor called him a junkie.

'No problem, mate,' Connor said instead.

'Connor's too forgivin'. Mate, you just wouldn't keep still. You were pissing everybody off, including the dog. Conversation was out of the question. You only had one thing to say – "when the fuck are we going to get there?" You need to sort yourself out, mate.'

Zach ignored the comment. 'Where are they?' he asked.

Neil sighed in resignation and said, 'They're parked up about twenty yards behind us, outside the house. Remember, no awkward questions. You're here for one reason only. Forget about Abe for the moment.'

Zach tracked back to the black four-wheel drive and waited for the window to lower. He raised his hands, one with a walking stick, and said to the two heavies inside, 'I'm not looking for trouble, I just want to deliver a message, in person.'

'Who's in the truck up ahead?' the guy in the window asked as he sized Zach up. At the wheel, his partner looked both bored and tough. If everyone was sensible tonight there'd be no problems, and Zach was hoping that was just how it was going to be.

'Two ex-army guys and a staffie with a grip like a vice. They're my protection. I want them parked up here just in case anything happens to me.'

They conferred until the bored one at the wheel made a call. Zach waited for what seemed an eternity but was in reality little more than a few minutes.

The one with his arm on the open window stepped out of the car. 'Hands up,' he said, and patted Zach down thoroughly. He turned to his partner and nodded. The information that Zach was clean was relayed to Maccabi on the other end of the line. His agreement came through and Zach waved the truck over. Once Connor was in place by the entrance to the house, Zach made his way down the drive accompanied by the heavy who had searched him.

Maccabi's dog came out first and was immediately attracted to the smell of Nellie around Zach's ankles. Maccabi shooed it inside with a foot. He wore slippers, a tad incongruous as he was still wearing his waistcoat and tie. Zach wasn't invited in. Instead, Maccabi smirked at Zach and his walking stick.

'You're like the cat with nine lives,' he said, 'or maybe you've just got two.'

'That's why I'm here. I don't want to have to jump out of any more first-floor windows. Can we just call it quits? You sent two guys round to hospitalise me. I got hospitalised. I've learnt my lesson, and I'm re-habilitated. As for Hepzibah, she likes staying alive too. She's dropping all her investigations into you.'

'You're both on trial,' Maccabi said, and closed the door.

43

Abe used to say, 'You can gauge Hepsie's mood by the music she plays. If she puts *Heroin* or *Candy Says* on you should be concerned. When she doesn't play it again you should be worried.'

It was a comical allegory. Hepzibah loathed drug-induced music or music about drugs and wouldn't listen to The Velvet Underground in a month of Sundays. But if the lyrics were heavy and the tone downbeat, she was on her way down. When there was no music on at all, she'd hit rock bottom.

Billie Holiday was playing. Zach could take or leave her. Easy listening, the sort you have on in the background. But the song was one of Hepzibah's favourites and she wasn't singing along. A bad sign. Zach had toyed with the idea of telling Hepzibah about his doorstep conversation with Maccabi last night. No longer. She was on the slide, and Zach needed to tread carefully.

He finished his meal. 'I enjoyed that, thanks.'

'Obviously, you wiped the plate clean with a piece of bread. And now you're licking your fingers.'

'You sound like you disapprove.'

'Abe used to do that.'

'You still sound like you disapprove.'

'It wasn't one of the things I liked about Abe. It's a bit pig-like.'

'Yeah, well, you're an Ashkenazi. You don't know how to enjoy your food.'

'Abe used to say that too.' Hepzibah's eyes welled up. Zach smiled sympathetically, even though she was drunk, sullen, and feeling sorry for herself.

'I miss him so much.' She dried her eyes and went to the fridge for more wine.

'That won't bring him back.' As soon as the words left his mouth Zach regretted them.

Hepzibah slammed her glass down. 'You can talk. What did you do when Beth and Rachel left? You took to drugs and now look at you, you're a cocaine addict. Don't you dare lecture me on how to deal with loss. At least I've managed to stay in employment, good employment I might add, employment that keeps you in food and wine, and train fares to Wivenhoe. And *you're* lecturing *me?*'

'You're a pain, Heps. I'll go back to the flat tomorrow. I can look after myself.' He stuck three cigarette papers together to roll a joint, metaphorically sticking two fingers up at her.

'Yeah, and you're a pain too, you noisy junkie.'

She played another recorded episode of her favourite TV programme, thinking it would annoy Zach, but he'd grown to like the implausible police series. It lived in a parallel universe (a little like Hepzibah), where the station was run by women. The two central characters were good enough to allow you to suspend belief, sit back and enjoy.

But Hepzibah wasn't in the mood. She was too angry. She stared at the TV screen and seethed. She pressed the pause button. Was she about to give him grief? No, she needed a refill and a pee. He went outside with his joint and had a couple of tokes before going back in. When Hepzibah came back down he waited for her to press the play button on the remote control. She didn't. Instead, she folded her arms and stared at the frozen image on the TV screen.

Zach left Hepzibah to her bad mood, went back outside and relit his joint. There were no stars that night, but it was warm. He sat under the rose arch to smell the myrrh and think about what he would do without any money. Not much, was the brutal answer. Beth asked him that very same question when they met yesterday. He'd had no idea then, though he'd smiled at Rachel as he said so, and he had no idea now.

Zach popped his head round the living room door.

'Night then,' he said quietly, hating scenes.

'Don't you 'night then' me. I want you out of here *tomorrow.*'

'Don't worry, Heps. I'm going.'

44

The clouds rolled by and the sun came out. Zach took his coffee outside, sat under the rose arch, and lit a rollie. He pondered his situation. Hepzibah's moods were stressful, but he had no money. All he had was thirty quid, most of which he was about to spend on Rachel, and he had to keep a fiver back to snort cocaine up his nose.

He finished his fag, went round to the front of the house, and looked up and down the road. No black four-wheel drive, no heavies. Maccabi had kept his word.

Back in the kitchen he made two decent-sized sandwiches. One thick with a strong cheddar, slices of cucumber and tomato, a little salt, and loads of pepper. The other filled with a tasty French blue cheese and Parma ham. He heard the toilet flush. Hepzibah was up. Quickly, he wrapped the sandwiches and popped them into his small rucksack. That way, no arguments about it being her food.

Hepzibah was wearing a short silk Japanese kimono, tied at the waist. Her legs were a picture, the ballet dancer in her still there. She stood at the door, yawned, and made eye contact. She was feeling bashful.

'Morning, Zach.'

'Morning.'

'We argued last night. What about?'

'Your drinking. Apparently, I don't have the right to say anything because I'm a drug addict.'

'I'm never going to touch another drop again.'

'Yeah, right.'

'No really. I asked you to go, I remember that much. I didn't mean it.'

'What, you want me to stay?'

'Yes.'

'Why?'

'I feel safer with you around. I promise I won't behave like that again.'

'Yeah, right.'

'I'll make something nice tonight.'

How would he buy food? Or wine? 'I'll be back around seven.'

~~~

Zach and Rachel found a free table outside Stella Coffee on Old Brompton Road. They were on the rich side of town. The area heaved with tourists and people with money. It had been cloudy earlier, when they'd been inside, but now the sky was blue and Zach was bathed in a warm glow. He sipped at his flat white and watched his daughter from across the table. Rachel only had eyes for the is Hwaiter who she could see coming towards her. She bounced up and down and clapped her hands.

'Yummy, yummy, yummy!'

Rachel hadn't done anything to earn the treat other than ask nicely, but there it was in her hand. She drooled. Her little legs dangled a foot off the ground. She swung them backwards and forwards and stuffed the prize into her mouth. Zach grinned at her, and she broke into an ice cream-covered smile. She licked around her lips but hardly made a dent in the white mass around her mouth.

'Enjoy yourself today, darling?' He already knew the answer but asking her was fun. After a film, The Wizard of Oz, they went to see the dinosaurs again.

'Yes!' she replied in between licks.

'Would you like to go and see granddad Dov?' he asked. On reflection, he had no idea why. Dov was still depressed, not talking, not eating, and he hadn't expressed a desire to see anyone, let alone a granddaughter who wasn't Jewish. And would Ester want to see him?

Rachel looked up. 'Now?' she asked.

'No, not now, darling, but soon maybe, I'll check with Ester.' But when would he check with Ester? Ester wasn't talking to him and hadn't since he went into hospital.

'Who's Ester?'

'Your aunt, my sister.'

Out of the blue a stern voice called out.

'Zach!'

From the crowds Beth appeared at the table, hands on hips. She stamped her feet, and her dress flew into an angry swirl.

'She's not going to eat her tea now! Look at the time. It's almost six o'clock.'

Beth wrapped a reassuring arm around Rachel and kissed her messy face, then she glared at Zach once more.

'You're early,' he said, 'fifteen minutes early.' Zach had intended to tap Beth for money. Had the chance gone?

'Yes, and I suppose you thought you'd have the deed done by then. You've been with her all day. Why didn't you give her one earlier?'

He did, but he made no mention of it, and nor did Rachel who was too busy finishing the rest of her second ice-cream of the day.

Zach shrugged and said, 'She's had a lovely day, haven't you, darling?'

'Yes!' she replied in between licks.

Beth stuck her nose up in the air. 'Right, well, we have to go. Come on, darling,' she said, chivvying Rachel along. 'Kiss your father goodbye.'

Rachel planted a sticky ice-creamy kiss on his cheek.

'Love you,' he told her.

'Love you,' she replied.

'Beth, I've spent a lot of money on Rachel today ...' He broke off, having made his point.

'I'm sure you have. Maybe next time you won't buy her an ice cream.'

She took a firm grip of Rachel's hand and pulled her away. Rachel waved on the turn.

'Bye!' she said.

~~~

The benzo Zach popped half an hour earlier when he got on the bus had kicked in. He'd slowed down, both physically and mentally. It was either that or let paranoia set in. He pulled himself up from his seat whilst leaning on his stick and walked slowly down the bus with all the energy of an overweight elderly person.

At Hackney Baths, his stop, Zach was helped off with a hard shove. He fell into the arms of three toughs. They pulled him to one side. The street was busy, but everybody pretended nothing untoward was happening. The thug on the bus joined his mates and the four of them pushed Zach around quickly, laughing at his inability to react. One of them caught and pulled him till their faces were barely an inch apart and held him there. The man moved into position to head-butt Zach. In his hazy state, Zach considered his options and plucked for heading him right back.

He didn't expect the knee in his groin.

Ooooof! Zach yelled in pain, doubled over, and grabbed his testicles. The man yanked him up. Zach let out an agonised groan.

'Message from Ralph Maccabi. Don't *ever* think of breaking your word, or we'll do more than tap your balls. Same goes for the commie journalist.'

45

There's been another attack on the brother. It was restrained, I guess. The JVF had wanted revenge for their beaten comrade, but were restricted to a knee where it hurts. Believe me, they wanted to go a lot further.

Correct me if I'm wrong, but the brother had been attacked from behind and kicked in the head. Well, the biter got bit. That's how it goes sometimes. But then twenty-four hours later he jumps out of a first-floor window to escape a beating for having flattened his attacker. When he leaves hospital, he promises both he and the journalist are dropping all their investigations. And I believe him.

I bumped into Ralph earlier today. I put my dog on a short lead. He did the same. Our dogs don't get on.

'Leave the guy alone now.'

'I should listen to you?' A rhetorical question because Ralph never does. 'Zach Peretz has got my goat.'

'He's suffered enough.'

Ralph shrugged. 'Shit happens. Hopefully he'll be sensible now, and more importantly so will she, and we'll all be OK, won't we?'

I guess so. My conscience isn't great, I'm too much of a coward, but Ralph doesn't have one. We've known each other since I moved to Finchley twelve years ago. We're both members of the tennis and golf clubs. We're not pals, we mix in different circles. Some of my friends would walk out if he walked in.

It's not just his politics, it's his business ethics. He doesn't have any. Just like his father, they say.

We used to do no more than say hello, but then the professor died and we were thrown together, because we both fear Hepzibah and Zach Peretz.

46

'You're still walking funny,' Neil observed twenty-four hours later.

'At least I'm not still talking funny.'

Zach was looking on the bright side. Those JVF thugs could have done him a lot more damage. He lit a joint and inhaled deeply. To add to the effect, he kept the smoke down for a good few seconds before exhaling ever so slowly. *Boing!* Stoned again. He toked once more, a long one, swayed under the effect, and handed the joint to Neil. His friend was sitting under the rose arch, pushing a branch back into the trellis so it didn't bother him anymore. Once he'd succeeded, he took a drag on the spliff.

'Nice!' he said with a grin.

Hepzibah called them over for coffee at the patio table. They both had another toke before leaving the joint in the ashtray for later.

Neil puffed his words out. 'Don't think she likes me. Or Nellie.'

'She's got a lot on her mind at the moment. She hasn't heard from Fawz for three days. Of course she likes you,' Zach glanced down at the staffie strutting alongside them. 'I'm just not sure about the dog.'

Zach was also worried about Fawz, and beginning to think something must have happened to her. He'd seen the email Hepzibah sent to Lila in Tel Aviv, as well as her correspondence with her editor and other contacts in the media. Hepzibah was looking for commissions. She was going to Israel.

Zach sipped at his coffee and wondered if he'd manage to drink it. It was too milky, but now was not the right time to criticise Hepzibah's rubbish attempts at a flat white. She'd probably burst into tears.

'Zach,' Hepzibah began in her nicest voice. 'If I can wangle you a ticket, will you come with me?'

'We'll argue. You'll piss me off. I'll piss you off.'

'I know, but I don't want to go on my own. I'd feel safer going with you. I'm feeling pathetic at the moment. That knee in your testicles was aimed at me as well.'

'Are you still in pain?'

'What?'

'Never mind. But I'm not fully recuperated. I won't be much use for another couple of weeks.'

'That's OK. I'd still feel better if you came with me.'

'If I went to Tel Aviv, I'd want to track down Seth Silberman and hopefully find this Tamir guy.'

'I want to track him down as well, but how? You can't tackle Seth on your own at the moment, never mind the Israeli.'

'One step at a time. Let's track them down first.'

'So, you'll come?'

'Yep.'

'Good. I just hope we find out what's happened to Fawz before we leave. Everywhere's under military lock down, so I just don't know.'

The operation to find the missing teens had shut down the West Bank. In response, protests sprang up everywhere. In the Wadi al-Joz neighbourhood, close to Fawz's home in the old walled city, rocks, petrol bombs and flares were thrown at passing cars. Riot police responded with rubber bullets, fatally shooting a sixteen-year-old youth between the eyes from ten yards. The video went viral, sparking more violent protests across the West Bank. Had Fawz been hurt in the ensuing chaos? Had she been arrested?

~~~

It was nine o'clock in the evening when Lila's email arrived, eleven in Tel Aviv.

'Shall I read it out?' Hepzibah suggested.

'That's good by me.'

Lila Dohan July 07 2014 9:02 PM (1 min ago)

To me

Dear Hepzibah

I have to confess I have known about Abe's death for some time. I thought about contacting you, but I did not think you would appreciate a message from me. Please accept my apologies, and my deepest sympathy. Abe was a wonderful man.'

Hepzibah broke off. 'Have you noticed she doesn't contract words. Did not rather than didn't.'

'I'm surprised you're surprised. Nor does Fawz. And have you noticed that both Lila and Fawz used the same adjective to describe Abe? One we'd never dream of using.'

'Go on.'

'Wonderful. Interesting, eh?

'I guess so. It's not a word I'd use. Shall I carry on?'

'Sure.'

To answer your questions. First, why did I leave B'Tselem? I was scared for my children, not so much for myself. I could put up with the harassment from the IDF, and the trolling from the ultras, but not my children's fear of school. Remember, this was Jerusalem, not Tel Aviv. They were targeted by their peers because I was a human rights worker. Now they are known as the children of the receptionist at the vets, and they are left alone.

We live in Hatikva. Literally translated this means Hope. The irony has not escaped people. There is little hope here. It is the poorest part of Tel Aviv and has the highest unemployment. There was an anti-immigrant protest earlier this evening and now men with clubs roam the streets vandalising African-owned businesses and beating any unfortunate African out on the streets.

It has its pockets, like Hatikva, but Tel Aviv is called The Bubble for good reason. In general, it is tolerant, secular, creative and liberal. It is a city separate from the rest of Israel. Jerusalem, dominated by the ultra-orthodox haredis, is another country, Tel Avivians joke, requiring a passport. But it is Tel Aviv which is out of step with the rest of Israel, not Jerusalem.

I will write again tomorrow after work. First thing I will contact B'Tselem to find out what has happened to your friend Fawz.

Lila x

~~~

That night when Hepzibah's landline rang at three thirty in the morning, she got up and answered. Zach had an idea what might have been said by the JVF creep. Afterwards, Hepzibah came to his room. She was white as a sheet. He lifted the duvet and she climbed into bed. His body fitted snugly around hers and he had to stop himself getting aroused. After a while he fell asleep.

47

It was late the following evening when Zach peered out of the bus window and saw they were passing Pentonville prison, where conditions were somewhat harsher than those he experienced at Feltham, and those were pretty shit. People who pontificated that prison was soft had never been incarcerated. At the same time, prison didn't work. During his time there, Zach learnt the only thing he needed to. How to survive. What about those who couldn't look after themselves? Was prison too soft for them?

Zach was on the number 56 from Angel station on his way back to Hepzibah's, feeling troubled. The day had started well. Zach got a text from Beth suggesting he met her at Sinead's in Islington for dinner, but early enough to see Rachel. Sinead was a friend of Beth's, and someone Zach had known for years, along with her partner, Bill. They didn't keep in touch after the split out of solidarity with Beth, but Zach had always got on well with both of them.

The trouble began over dinner when Bill asked Zach who he'd been running away from when he jumped out of the first-floor window. Sinead remained silent, giving Zach the impression she already knew the answer, from Beth.

Once he'd been told, Bill said, 'Don't know what to say, mate,' and reached for the wine bottle. 'It all sounds a bit heavy.'

The trouble deepened when Bill asked Zach what he was going to do next. He did not expect to hear Zach say he would carry on investigating.

'Jesus, Zach. These guys are dangerous.'

Beth, along with Sinead, had remained quiet throughout the exchange. The episode unsettled Zach, but when he pondered his situation, he found there was only one conclusion. Yes, the guys were dangerous, but if he didn't carry on, he'd never forgive himself. He had to do it, for Abe.

What did he know so far? Seth Silberman and a man called Tamir worked for Ralph Maccabi. Maccabi had links to a Jewish terrorist group that wanted to blow up the Al-Aqsa mosque and funded Tahor Yisra'el in the UK, a party dedicated to an Arab-free Greater Israel. The JVF, controlled by Maccabi, had attacked Zach three times already. First, down by the river in the park when Zach fought back. The second time, twenty-four hours later, when Zach escaped attack but sustained serious injury bolting from two men armed with batons, and third, the recent knee to his testicles, which was a warning. If there had to be a next time, he'd be permanently damaged.

What did he believe, without knowing for sure? That Tamir was the man who chased Abe to his death, whilst working for Maccabi.

Zach got off the bus at Hackney Baths and turned into Lower Clapton Road. Coming towards him were four testosterone-filled skinheads. They talked loudly and all at the same time, demonstrating their presence to everybody on the street. Zach checked Murder Mile both ways. He no longer used his stick, and could run across, but he wasn't sure how fast. The white guys were still shouting over each other, aiming to intimidate people on the street rather than communicate. As they passed, the nearest one turned and scowled at Zach. Zach didn't imagine it, because he wasn't coming down from a hit. Nor was he high.

He crossed Murder Mile at a trot and turned into Hepzibah's road. There, he ran, for the first time in weeks.

He could run.

He could also go a whole day without a line. He'd just done it. OK, he wouldn't have been able to without a fentanyl, mid-afternoon, but he did it without benzos. He felt a swell of pride in himself. And he was no longer taking triazolam. Now, all he needed was fentanyl in the afternoon and dope and alcohol in the evening. A sad state of affairs for most people, but not half bad for someone coming off cocaine.

He was relieved to open Hepzibah's wrought iron gate and step onto the black and white Victorian tiled path, gasping, as he was, for a glass of wine and a big fat spliff.

48

It's been nine weeks since the professor died, and I haven't heard a thing from the police. I'm getting more and more confident I never will. And I'm sure his brother and his ex have been scared off. That doesn't mean I won't pay for my role in the professor's death. I pay each day, every time a car crunches unexpectedly up the drive. And my first thought when the phone rings? Is that the police?

As she passes, Ella touches my hand. It's not a caress, it's cursory, fleeting, almost meaningless but not quite, because she's making a point. At the moment, I don't deserve her love because I'm drinking too much. That's why she hasn't kissed me today. In all the time Ella and I have been together, I have never known her not to give me a peck on the cheek at least once in a day. Of course, if I were to kiss her, she'd kiss me. The problem is, I don't feel much like kissing right now. It shouldn't be terminal to our relationship, my current behaviour, but it's certainly not helping.

She turns. 'Why won't you talk to me?'

Do I tell her I'm responsible for a man's death? I look away. I didn't want the conversation earlier, and I don't want it now. I want a drink.

'If you won't talk to me, at least talk to someone else, maybe the doctor. We can't go on like this. We barely have a relationship.'

I shift about and avoid Ella's gaze.

'I'm off to bed,' she says. 'Please don't drink too much more.' The dog joined Ella and left the room without giving him as much as a glance.

'Promise I won't. Night, darling.'

'And try not to make too much noise when you come up.'

'OK, darling. Night.'

No reply. Even Ella has her limits.

49

Zach heard the toilet flush. Hepzibah was up. She'd missed yoga. What sort of mood would she be in? Full of self-loathing because she'd given in to alcohol-induced fatigue when the alarm went off at eight thirty? Irritable, because she would have felt better had she gone to yoga? She was already grouchy because she had a deadline to meet for an article on the thawing of Iranian/US relations under Obama.

'Morning,' she said at the doorway, covering a yawn with a hand. Zach took his earphones out, pulling the plug on Groove Armada.

'Morning,' he replied.

Still yawning, and moving slowly, Hepzibah went to the cupboard for cereal, mixed seeds, and dried fruit. She piled the ingredients into a bowl and added strawberries and raspberries. She was about to mix yoghurt in when she reconsidered the prospect of nuts, fruit, and toasted buckwheat, and popped the yoghurt back in the fridge.

'Cup of tea first. Want one?'

'Yeah, I'll take a cup of tea.'

'Did we argue last night?' she asked popping tea bags into the mugs.

'No, but we could have done. Do you want me to stay?'

'Yes of course, till things settle down with Maccabi.'

'Yeah, well, if you want me to stay it's got to stop. You get cross every evening when you hear me rolling a joint. I haven't had a hit for over twenty-four hours. More like thirty-six. And I'm no longer taking benzos or triazolam. You should be pleased, for fuck's sake.'

'OK Zach, OK. Keep your hair on. I'll try not to get annoyed.'

'You mean you'll try to *remember* not to get annoyed.'

'Whatever.'

'I'll remind you later, when you forget.'

Hepzibah fired up her laptop, saying nothing. She opened her inbox. 'There's a reply from Lila here.'

Lila Dohan July 08 2014 7:04 AM (2 hours ago)

To me

Dear Hepzibah

It is six thirty in the morning …

Hepzibah broke off to repeat a bitchy point she'd made before. 'Her first words and she's at it again. It is, not it's.'

Zach was about to say, 'And what's your Hebrew like?' when he remembered it was very good. Better anyway if he said nothing that could be construed as defending Lila.

'Get back to the email, Heps.'

It is six thirty in the morning and the air raid sirens have been wailing for half an hour now. I am looking out of my window at the traffic down on the street. It remains as busy as ever. The cars have not sped up, slowed, or stopped. No one has abandoned their vehicle and run to the nearest air-raid shelter. Life goes on. It helps that most of the rockets are taken out in mid-air by our missile defence system. Also, it is too hot in the shelters. There is no air conditioning. Maybe in the rich areas, but here in Hatikva?

Search teams have found the bodies of the three missing teenagers in a field north-west of Hebron. They were killed shortly after their abduction. I am worried for the future. Hamas has denied responsibility for the kidnapping. I do not know what this means. Perhaps the kidnapping was not sanctioned.

And now we are attacking Gaza from the air and sea. In just a few days we have killed two hundred people, mostly civilians, many of them children. Their deaths are presented as entirely the fault of Hamas. Children die in airstrikes because Hamas is a terrorist organisation. This is now an acceptable argument. The deaths are put out of mind with a collective shrug. Jews are a superior people to Arabs, more entitled to life.

Have you heard of 'Sderot cinematheque'? Israelis go to a hill in the western city of Sderot to watch missiles rain down on Gaza. They sit in lawn chairs, eat popcorn and drink beer, and watch people, barely bigger than ants, run for their lives amid deadly explosions. I have never heard of this Tamir, but I imagine he has been there. I will give his name to B'Tselem, with the name he is known by in England, and let us hope they can help without a last name.

It is good that you are coming. Dori, my eldest, remembers you. Lev you have never met. Yes, I can recommend a decent hotel that is not expensive, I am just sorry I have no room for the two of you. It is interesting what you say about Zach. For many people an affecting personal event can lead them to question beliefs they have held all their lives. Your job is threatened, your relative is killed and it is covered up, your brother, a Jew, is a target for Jewish extremists for standing up to Israel.

Be prepared. There is a lot of tension here, and it is always worse in poor places like Hatikva. There was another race riot here last night. Now, in the morning, I can see Eritreans down on the street. Men, no women. They are sitting in circles drinking coffee. Israelis pass them, some smile, most don't. The Africans will not be out on the streets after dark, for sure.

I am certain B'Tselem will have news of Fawz by the end of today.

Lila x

As Zach prepared lunch for the two of them, he began to wonder why he, alone amongst everyone around him, didn't have a belief. The God thing passed Zach by, despite Him saying Israel belonged to the Jews. Religion, spirituality, they were ideas from another planet, not one he inhabited. Socialism, the little he knew about it, he found attractive, but he wasn't a socialist or any other -ist, he thought. Until Abe called him a Zionist for supporting the Jewish state, and he realised he was an -ist after all. If Abe were to talk to Zach now, would he still think him one? Yes: a not-so-sure Zionist.

It was the *idea* of Israel that had always been important to Zach. Jews needed somewhere safe, right? But was Israel safe? Zach's conclusion was now 'no', despite its overwhelming might. The country was on a permanent on/off war setting. How could that be considered safe? To keep the country 'safe', Israeli aggression continuously increased, and so did Palestinian hatred. How could that keep Israelis safe? Fawz was right. Safety could only be achieved through peace and equality.

Over lunch, a second email arrived from Lila. Hepzibah read it as she finished her cheese and spinach omelette with the last of the salad and some bread.

Lila Dohan July 08 2014 1:58 PM (5 mins ago)

To me

Dear Hepzibah

A terrible thing has happened. Early this morning a sixteen-year-old Palestinian was kidnapped, it is thought by settlers. His charred body has just been found. The news outlets are saying he was set on fire.

The boy was from the Shu'fat neighbourhood, the same as your friend Fawz. He left the mosque at three forty-five this morning for a pre-dawn meal. It is Ramadan. His friends and family saw two men bundle him into a vehicle. His father heard him scream.

You are coming in bad times. The three boys kidnapped and killed by Hamas were buried yesterday. After the funeral, settlers assaulted Palestinians across the Occupied Territories, often in the company of soldiers. They went on the rampage in East Jerusalem alongside violent football fans. In Bethlehem they chased and ran over a nine-year-old child. In Jenin a teenager was shot dead. The response on social media has been disgusting, a revenge Facebook page, that sort of thing. At times like this, liberals and the left are at most risk. I am not a brave person. In this climate the bad feel able to be very bad, and the good just keep their heads down.

I have a headache. The sirens have not stopped since early this morning. Nobody bothers going to the shelters as most of the rockets do not get through. But every day we kill hundreds from the air and sea.

Gaza is being softened up for a ground invasion, for sure. Who knows when it will start? A week? Two weeks? Maybe when you are here. Reservists are being called up. We all get called up. For some of us it is too much. It was too much for my cousin Gev. He killed himself two years ago, the night after his patrol went into the Al-Arroub camp near Hebron. I do not know the circumstances, the IDF would not say, but a five-year-old Palestinian boy was killed. Gev was not responsible, thank God. That is the only comfort we have.

I look into it. Israeli soldiers are fifteen times more likely to kill themselves than die in battle. Whether we are at war or simply imposing Israeli authority on the Occupied Territories does not seem to matter. They feel obliged to carry out actions that go against their moral principles and beliefs. For many it is too much.

Are these suicides a reflection of Israeli society? I do not know, but many of us are appalled at the way we impose our authority on the Palestinians. We can see we are creating the terrorists of tomorrow.

A friend in B'Tselem knows of a Tamir Bachar, who is often in London. He is a member of Tahor Y'Israel, an extreme right-wing party with a couple of members in the Knesset. Be careful with him, he is known to be violent.

I have kept till last news about your friend Fawz. She was arrested with her younger brother four days ago at a disturbance in Ras al-Amud, near the Church of All Nations. It is a spot where youths congregate to throw stones after morning prayers at the Al-Aqsa mosque. There are often clashes there. But they are being held in a detention centre here in Israel, not the Occupied Territories. It is wrong, but the authorities do it, particularly to those they suspect of being a security risk. Tell me, is she close to Hamas or Palestinian Islamic Jihad? You are unlikely to befriend an Islamic ideologue, so why take her to Israel to be interrogated? Is she left-wing, a member of the PFLP perhaps? If I learn anything more before you arrive, I will tell you.

Lila x

'Shit, she's in trouble,' Hepzibah said. 'She's been taken to Israel. Why? She's definitely not an Islamic ideologue. Fawz wouldn't be

PFLP, would she?' Hepzibah didn't expect an answer. 'I don't know why I'm asking you, you're hardly likely to know. You probably don't even know who the PFLP are.'

'The Popular Front for the Liberation of Palestine, not to be confused with Popular Front for the Liberation of Palestine – General Command, which is based in Damascus.' Zach said, showing off his newly acquired knowledge gained, in this instance, from Wikipedia. 'Secular, Marxist-Leninist, revolutionary socialist. She could be.'

'*Marxist-Leninist? Revolutionary socialist?* My arse. Where does the PFLP get all its money and weapons from? Tehran and Damascus. Fawz support them? No way.'

'So why did you ask?'

'I just wasn't sure for a moment. They favour a one-state solution. So does Fawz. So do I. But she wouldn't touch the PFLP with a ten-foot bargepole.'

'A one-state solution? What's that?'

'The two-state solution was born out of the idea that the "two sides" can't live with each other. But why not?'

Whilst Zach grappled with the idea of Jews and Arabs living peacefully together in a future Israel/Palestine, Hepzibah continued. 'Israel, in its current state, will never allow an independent Palestine. We can see now with Gaza; it doesn't allow an independent Gaza. The two-state solution is a dead duck in the water. A one-state solution is the only solution. Jews and Arabs have to learn to live together, equally, in peace.'

'Sounds completely utopian.'

'People said that about the dismantling of apartheid in South Africa.'

'That was a walk in the park compared to this.'

Hepzibah didn't disagree, but she repeated her point. 'Jews and Arabs still have to learn to live together. They did so for thousands of years. The relationship broke down less than seventy years ago. It's time to rebuild it.'

PART FOUR

A Trip to Israel

50

The landing at Ben Gurion was smooth, prompting applause from an infantile section of passengers.

'Welcome to Tel Aviv,' the Easyjet announcer said over the tannoy system. 'The time is one twenty and the temperature outside is thirty-nine degrees centigrade. Once again, we apologise for this plane's late departure from Stansted, which has led to our late arrival here in Tel Aviv.'

Zach stretched. It had been a long day already, and he'd lost two hours somewhere in the stratosphere. He got his bag – Hepzibah had hers – and they headed slowly for the door along with everybody else.

Once she was at the top of the stairs, Hepzibah turned and said, HH'I'll go through security first.'

'OK, but why?' Zach asked. He stepped off the plane and hit a wall of heat. He donned his Wayfarers and grinned at the sun. Tel Aviv, early July, and the weather was sizzling. Just as he liked it.

Hepzibah waited till they were down the steps and walking side by side to reply. 'It's much better we don't ... Hey!' A bag knocked her, or rather brushed her. '*Excuse* me!' she said. The guy apologised. He had a connecting flight and was in a hurry due to their late arrival. Zach put his hand up in acknowledgement for Hepzibah and waved him on. She was fussing about a barely visible scratch on her leg. That guy could miss his plane.

Inside the airport they joined a queue. It moved slowly. Soon they were level with three soldiers leaning against a wall keeping an eye. They cradled their guns and assessed the passengers.

'You were going to say, it's better if we don't what?'

'It's better if we don't tell them we're here to visit Fawz. Tell them you're staying with my sister. I'll have already told them.'

The queue kept moving. Up ahead Zach could see two border policemen in booths for the queue. 'You know we'll end up seeing different guys?'

'Yes, but if there's a problem, they'll talk to each other.'

'You anticipating a problem?'

'No.'

Now they were approaching passport control there were more soldiers. Soon Hepzibah was at the head of the queue. A moment after she was called, it was Zach's turn. He handed his passport to a portly guy with a beard who stared at the photograph, then at Zach.

'What is the purpose of your visit, Mr Peretz?'

Zach faltered. 'Er, I'm staying with her sister [he pointed to Hepzibah] here in Tel Aviv.' Hepzibah was let through, and the two policemen did indeed confer.

'And the purpose of your visit, Mr Peretz?' he repeated.

'The purpose? Um, I got the opportunity to come, and I love Tel Aviv. You've got the beach day and night.'

'Day and night? Do you like to rave?'

Zach had made a mistake. He wasn't going to make another. 'No, I like peace and quiet, and the moonlight.'

'Do you take drugs, Mr Peretz?'

'Not anymore.'

The border policeman pulled at his beard. Was he about to ask Zach to step into the arms of an inquisitive soldier or two who would do more than ask questions? No, thank God. He handed Zach his passport.

'Enjoy your time in Tel Aviv, Mr Peretz.'

'Thank you.'

Hepzibah had a quizzical look on her face. 'What was all that about?'

'He asked if I took drugs. I told him not anymore. After a couple more questions he gave me my passport, and here I am.'

'I might have known it would be about drugs.' She didn't know the half of it.

'Shall we go?' Zach swung a bag onto his shoulder. He was keen to meet Lila. Over the years, Abe always talked fondly of her. They met through her work at B'Tselem, but Abe had been relieved when she put that life behind her and moved to Tel Aviv. He stayed with her whenever he was in Israel or the Occupied Territories doing research at one of the universities. Once he'd separated from Hepzibah his visits became more frequent, and Zach had assumed they were having a relationship, until Abe told him different. They'd been good friends, nothing more.

The airport terminal thronged with travellers, but Zach managed to walk alongside Hepzibah as they passed into greeters' hall.

'We're looking for a younger version of me,' she said with a pinch of bitch, 'but without the hair and with two kids in tow. They'll be near gate three. There they are, can you see?'

They were about ten metres away, a small woman in her late twenties with two young children. The boys wore shorts, as did Lila, but hers were more in the style of culottes. Her hair was short and swept across like a boy's, showing off an open, happy face.

Lila went to Hepzibah first, as she knew her, but she'd already given Zach a big smile. Zach said shalom to the boys and shook their hands, but he couldn't help noticing Hepzibah embrace Lila stiffly and not engage afterward. He stepped in quickly and left the boys to deal with Hepzibah.

'Hi,' he said to Lila.

'I recognised you straight away,' Lila said, and her smile widened. She opened her arms in a welcome and Zach found himself hugging her as if she'd been Abe.

'Thank you,' he said, 'for finding out what happened to Fawz.'

'In the end I made little difference. She was released less than twenty-four hours later.'

'All the same, thank you.' Hepzibah threw him a glance, which he ignored. 'Knowing where she was twenty-four hours before her release was important to us. At least we knew she was alive.'

'Let us go home and eat,' Lila said.

'Yes, let's,' Hepzibah said, without making clear she was correcting Lila. She sounded like she was hissing. What Lila and the boys thought was anyone's guess.

~~~

Dori, the youngest, took his guests on a tour of the apartment conducted in superfast non-stop Hebrew. Even Hepzibah had difficulty keeping up. At odd moments he would stop and look quizzically at them, before carrying on talking ten to the dozen. Meanwhile, Lev called out to his younger brother. It sounded like: 'Shut up stupid, they can't understand a word you're saying.' Zach couldn't have been far off, because whatever Lev had had said prompted Lila to tell him off. Dori smirked at his mother's rebuke of his elder brother and ushered them into the living room, which was large and light. He talked and pointed. Upwards, to the ceiling fan that hummed, across to the sewing area, over to the wide-screen TV, round the corner of the L-shaped room to the dining area where Lila was setting the table.

Lev brought out ice-cold beers for their guests and opened the doors to the balcony. Zach left Hepzibah with Dori and took his drink outside, where there was a small table with two chairs and a couple of recliners further along. Zach looked out at Tel Aviv and the Mediterranean sea, pulled his shades down and smoked a fag.

He had just stubbed his cigarette out in a small saucer-like ashtray when he was called in. On the table were three bowls of garlic soup, a traditional Czech dish apparently, and two cheese and egg-filled bread boats for the kids, with cherry tomatoes on the side. 'Khachapuri,' she said, a 'Georgian dish. The boys love it.'

'And they're not so keen on garlic soup,' Zach quipped.

Lila nodded her head and laughed. 'And they are not keen on garlic soup.'

Zach tried it, not knowing what to expect. At the first sip his taste buds came alive. If it had been in a mug, he would have drunk it in mouthfuls. It was delicious.

Goulash was brought out. 'Don't tell me,' Zach said, 'Hungarian.'

'This one is Czech. It has been cooking slowly since this morning.'

Zach took a mouthful. 'Wow! Best goulash I've ever had. This is scrumptious.'

'Scrumptious. What is this?'

'It means delicious.'

The boys certainly thought so. They were wolfing theirs down. As for Hepzibah, she wanted a drink, so perhaps felt obliged to approve the food.

'Is there any chance of a glass of white to accompany this lovely meal?'

'Of course,' Lila replied and went to the kitchen. She returned with a bottle, a wine glass, and two more cold beers. Once Hepzibah's glass was full, Lila put the bottle back in the fridge.

'So, where's your family from?' Zach asked when she got back. 'You've mentioned Czech food twice.'

'Prague,' she replied, looked down at her plate, patted her mouth with a napkin and said nothing more. Her tone and manner suggested she didn't want to. The boys asked to leave the table and ran to their bedroom when told they could. Silence descended. Lila was curiously silent, Hepzibah belligerently so.

Zach filled the void with small talk. 'You're an excellent cook. You missed your vocation. You should have been a chef.'

Zach's behaviour was irritating Hepzibah. She demonstrated this by snorting derisively at him. Then she finished what was left in her glass and said to Lila, 'It's not at all bad, this Israeli stuff. Can I have another?'

Whilst Lila was in the kitchen getting Hepzibah's drink Zach said, 'Careful how much you drink Heps. It's the middle of the afternoon.'

'Don't worry, Zach. I just need enough wine to fall asleep, so I don't have to listen to you behaving like some obsequious Lothario.'

Obsequious? Perhaps. But Lothario? The last time Zach looked, he and Hepzibah were not in a relationship. Why should she care who he liked? He was about to ask when Lila came back with drinks. Hepzibah took hers to a recliner outside. Lila and Zach sat at the small patio table and talked about how much happier her boys were in Tel Aviv.

Hepzibah soon finished that second glass. She leant round from her chair and asked, 'The stuff I'm drinking now, is it local or from a supermarket?'

'Both. I bought it from the supermarket, but you can find it in the shop on the corner.'

'Great, I'll buy some later, but in the meantime can I have a little more of the delicious stuff?'

'Of course,' her host replied, taking the glass for a refill.

Zach waited till Lila was in the kitchen. 'What was all that obsequious Lothario stuff about?'

'Have you listened to yourself?'

Was Hepzibah jealous? He was just about to ask when Lila returned. Hepzibah took her drink with a smile. She finished her third glass without engaging in their conversation about the boys. Her eyelids soon fluttered shut and she began snoring lightly. The empty wine glass rested on her chest, held there by a fingertip. Deftly, Zach took it away. Her hands twitched and her lids quivered, but her eyes stayed closed.

'She will burn,' Lila said and moved the umbrella. She stationed it fully over Hepzibah and said quietly, 'We could go inside.'

'Good idea.' Out of the sun but away from prying ears.

'Coffee?'

'Another good idea.'

'I have a machine.'

'Now it's a great idea.'

'How do you like your coffee? Espresso? Cappuccino?'

'A flat white?' Zach said both tentatively and hopefully.

Lila smiled. 'Less milk, stronger. Sure.'

Zach sat back on the sofa and waited, looking forward to his coffee. When it came, he wasn't disappointed. 'Nice,' he said, lifting his cup up to Lila in appreciation. It wasn't up to barista levels, but neither were his. She sat the other end of the sofa, flicked her sandals off, brought her feet up and faced Zach. He did likewise.

'I'm sorry you won't see Abe again.' Zach had no idea what prompted him to say that, but as soon as he'd said it a tear formed in the corner of his eye.

'I loved your brother.'

Zach was shocked.

'Not in that way. Abe was a *good* person. There are not many. He was special. You see this apartment? It is mine. But really it belongs to Abe. Without him I would not have a home.'

This story, so typical of Abe, brought another tear to Zach's eyes. 'I miss him so much. I'd love to be able to tell him I'm cocaine-free.'

'You are no longer taking cocaine?'

'Haven't had any for more than a week.'

'That is fantastic! Abe would be so pleased. He was worried about you.'

'I know. I guess his death woke me up. I'd lost Abe, and I was going to lose Rachel as well. She's nearly four now. I started a bit later than you. Anyway, enough of that. Tell me about you. Single, two kids. Why don't you come and live somewhere sane, like England?'

'I would have to come back and do my national service, unless you married me.' She grinned. So did Zach. 'But yes, Israel is a mad country, perhaps the most mad in the world. The only country where black is white.' She emphasised her Israeli accent: 'Can you not see how much Israel wants peace?'

That made Zach laugh.

'You are not the Zionist Abe said you are.'

'That's because I am not the Zionist I used to be.'

'What are you now? A different Zionist?'

'Yes, perhaps.'

'What, a nicer one?'

'Probably, and you?'

'I am not a Zionist. I *accept* Israel, I do not *believe* in it. Do you?'

'I don't know anymore.'

Lila smiled. 'I have to check on the boys for a minute. Would you like anything? More coffee? More beer? Wine?'

'I'm fine, thanks. You go ahead.' He sat in the sun and rolled a fag. Hepzibah was still asleep. Before Zach lit his rollie, he walked down to the end of the balcony, as far from Hepzibah as possible. He wouldn't put it past her to wake up and give him grief.

Lila joined him, and Zach offered his cigarette. 'You smoke, right? It's just that you've got an ashtray, which is in regular use by the looks of it.'

She nodded. 'But not too much these days.' She took the fag and looked at it. 'What is this strange thing?' she asked, knowing full well what it was. She dragged on it a couple of times and handed it back.

'So, you haven't told me. A good-looking woman like you, on your own for years. What's the story?'

She took another couple of drags and passed the cigarette back. 'I will tell you inside.'

The good thing about roll ups was that they were easy to put out, and Zach made sure it had finished burning before dropping the cigarette into the ashtray on the table.

He settled on the sofa once more, facing Lila, their feet almost touching.

'It took me a long time to get over Lev's father leaving. I was six weeks pregnant with Dori.'

'Wow. Did you get any support at all during your pregnancy?'

'He has always helped. He still does.'

'Dori's what, five years old? You been on your own all that time?'

She nodded.

Hepzibah woke. 'Fucking umbrella,' she said, prompting both Lila and Zach to laugh. After she'd moved the offending item, Hepzibah stuck her tongue out and said something about interfering busy bodies, before settling back into the recliner.

'Let's let her sleep in the sun for a while. Then maybe give her a coffee. We'll get going to the hotel after that and get out of your hair.'

'Get out of my hair?'

'Leave you alone.'

'Of course not. You must stay to eat. Do you mind more soup and goulash?'

'On the contrary.'

'There will be salad as well, and cheese and fruit.'

'Great.'

'Would you like to go out? The boys will go for a walk if they are bribed with a small ice cream. We can leave a note for Hepzibah.'

'Now that sounds like another great idea. Let's go.' He had his Wayfarers. He didn't need anything, as long as Lila didn't mind buying all four ice creams.

~~~

Lila's balcony faced south-west and Hepzibah was still bathed in sun on their return. Zach joined her whilst Lila went to the kitchen, and the kids their bedroom. He found Hepzibah in good spirits. All the same, he told himself not to mention Lila. This was more difficult than he anticipated and only avoided through small talk, which began to irritate Hepzibah. Zach moved over to the end of the balcony and smoked a fag.

She shouted over. 'So, enjoying yourself here?'

Zach wasn't sure how to take the question. Was it genuine or was it provocative? Indeed, was it small talk? He played it straight, with a sting.

'If you're asking whether I like Lila, the answer's yes.'

'And you want to let her know by shouting it out?'

'Yes.'

'Subtle.'

He finished his fag, grabbed a chair, and joined Hepzibah. 'You don't seem to be OK about it.'

Hepzibah straightened up and adjusted the straps on her top. 'About what?'

'Me liking Lila.'

With perfect timing, Lila came out. She acknowledged their conversation with a smile. 'Would you like something to drink? We will eat soon.'

They both nodded.

'That white was very nice. But I don't think there was very much left.'

'There is another bottle in the fridge. And you, Zach?'

'I'll have a beer.'

Once Lila had left, Hepzibah said, 'You're trying to impress her.'

'Yes, is that a problem?'

Hepzibah was about to enlighten him when Lila came out with their drinks and now all she was interested in was her wine. She sipped. 'This really is very nice. I promise I'll buy half a dozen bottles tomorrow.'

She was on her second. At that rate she'd need to buy a few more than six. During the meal, Hepzibah restricted herself to one glass, but once the boys had left the table, she pushed her empty glass out and said,

'Do you have any more of that delicious wine? I really will replace it all.'

'Of course.'

Zach waited till Lila left. He leant towards Hepzibah and whispered. 'Do you know how expensive wine is here? I know you'll replace every bottle, that's not my point.'

'Of course I do. I've come here often enough.'

Another glass arrived, and she tucked in. It wasn't long before Zach and Lila were more than innocent bystanders. They shared a bottle of red.

Hepzibah watched Zach sip his wine at the same pace as Lila. 'My my, we are being moderate. Normally he'd quite happily keep up with me. Has he told you about all the drugs he takes?'

Zach couldn't be bothered retaliating or defending himself. Hepzibah was making a spectacle of herself. 'I'm going for a smoke, one of the many drugs I take.' He picked up his tobacco and an already rolled fag and left. Lila joined him on the balcony, and they smoked his very thin cigarette together. She lifted an eyebrow at Hepzibah's behaviour and talked about the stars and the lights of the city.

'I love sitting here in the evening when it is cooler.'

'Yeah, it's great.' Zach rolled a fatter cigarette, which they shared, and they drank their wine.

'You know, sometimes I sit here, and I think how lucky I am to have this, the balcony, the apartment, and then I always think of Abe.' She kept her voice low.

So did Zach. 'So, when was it he helped you?'

'Three years ago.'

Zach lowered his voice even more. 'So just before his separation. Did he want to be more than friends?'

'Yes.'

'And you?'

She shook her head. 'Abe knew. He helped me because he wanted to.'

'That's Abe.'

They went in for refreshments. Hepzibah was leaning back against the sofa, her eyes closed. She snored lightly. Lila opened another bottle of red, which they took back out. They drank, loosened, and got closer.

Two hours later, they'd polished off that second bottle and were shaking Hepzibah awake.

On the walk back to the hotel, Zach realised he was falling for a woman he'd probably never see again once he left in a few days' time.

51

There was a time when Tel Aviv liked to think it could vie with Ibiza as the party capital of the Med. At sunset, ravers took over the beach and DJs whacked the volume up. Fourteen years earlier, seventeen and freshly out of prison, Zach had partied all night. It was the tail end of the first summer of the new millennium and the Occupied Territories were in rebellion. A couple of days before Zach arrived, Ariel Sharon stood outside the Al-Aqsa mosque and repeated a declaration made at the end of the Six-Day War: 'The Temple Mount is in our hands!' Palestinians were enraged by the threat to the mosque, the third holiest site in Islam, and the Second Intifada was born.

Back then, Zach could taste belligerence in the air. Israel, having lit the spark, poured petrol onto the conflict by provoking widespread violence, giving the army a pretext to hit back hard. The Palestinians were bullied into unconditional surrender.

He could taste that same belligerence now.

This morning, their first, they were on a crowded bus heading for Central Station. The windows were open wide, but there was no breeze as the number 204 from Hatikva barely moved in the heavy traffic. The sun beat down on the tin roof. Zach sizzled. He guessed Hepzibah, who was hungover, did too.

And it was noisy. The passengers fought for supremacy with the wail of the air raid sirens outside. Israeli voices were loud and aggressive. The harshness of the language didn't help. Requests sounded like commands. Strangers, asking the time of day, would bark the question out like a head teacher who knew full well the answer and was only testing. Even when quiet, or speaking English, or both, there was a hard edge to the Israeli voice. Like the bored hotel receptionist who couldn't be bothered to accompany a question with inflection when he said, 'You will stay another night.'

Zach stuffed his earphones in, switched his iPod on and played an old favourite, the Chemical Brothers' *Come with Us*. The phenomenally high beat per minute matched the madness of the city.

It wasn't long before Hepzibah tapped him on the arm with the map of central Tel Aviv Lila gave them last night. He pulled his earphones out and heard a voice louder than all others, filled with anger. Towards the front of the bus a beefy guy with a thick beard was shouting at an old Palestinian man.

'I didn't take much notice in the beginning, you know how noisy Israelis are, but this is horrible.'

'What's he saying?'

'He's calling him a dirty Arab.'

The old man pretended nothing was happening and looked away. He was joined by the busload of passengers. The poor guy found it more difficult to ignore the situation when the Israeli moved forward. Now the big guy was in the Arab's face. Insults were accompanied by a jabbing finger. He spat out verbal abuse, spraying the old man's face with spittle. His finger drew back, then suddenly his hand opened out and he smacked the old guy round the head. The crowd gasped and looked away. Another smack came. More verbal abuse. Zach didn't have to understand Hebrew to get the gist.

'You're a dirty Arab. What are you? A dirty Arab.'

Zach packed his sunglasses away. 'How do you say "stop" in Hebrew? I've had enough of this.'

'Atsor.'

'Atsor? Fuck that.' He stood up and shouted, 'Stop!'

The bearded man stopped and so did time. The look of surprise within the bus froze, from the passengers to the bearded man and the Palestinian. The beefy Israeli turned slowly round to face Zach, as did everyone on the bus. He was in his thirties, big and intimidating, but overweight. How would the busload of Israelis react? That was the bigger worry. The big man with the beard looked Zach in the eye and moved for him. Would the crowd join in? Zach pushed past Hepzibah and scanned the faces around him. He saw confusion, surprise, but he didn't see anger.

'*Englishman,*' the bearded man hissed and quickened his pace. He pulled people aside to get to Zach. One too many. A middle-aged man with a pot belly took umbrage. He said something. An argument ensued. Others joined in, then more, till everyone on the bus was having their say at the top of their voices. Zach had become irrelevant, and so had the old man.

The driver stopped the bus, pulled up the handbrake and swung away from his seat. He waved his arms about and shouted over the rumpus. Then he leant into the driver's cab and pressed a button. The doors opened. Seizing the opportunity, the old man ran out. The driver brought his arm up high and swung it back. He showed them all the bus keys and yelled,

'Shut the fuck up, or I'll throw the keys away!'

Or something along those lines. The crowd quietened, and the driver took to his seat. He started up. The argument resumed, with the volume turned down.

Zach squeezed past Hepzibah and sat down. 'They're mental, this lot. One minute they're doing nothing, looking away, the next they can't stop arguing.' He popped a fentanyl. Immediately, Hepzibah threw him a look. 'It's prescribed,' he told her.

The cocaine he'd brought over wasn't. Zach had that packed away in his nether regions. Safe as houses until his stupid mistake at airport security. Would they have strip-searched him? They should be looking for bombs, and it wasn't often you had those hidden up your bum.

Now he had the option of a line, which he probably wouldn't exercise. He'd left it alone for a week already and was doing great. The hitch? Zach had managed to convince himself the best way to give up was to have a gram of coke available.

The addict in him was hanging on.

'What's it for?'

'What?' he asked, concerned he had a cocaine conversation coming.

'The fentanyl.'

'Takes the edge off,' he replied, breathing a sigh of relief.

'Takes the edge off what?'

'You know, life.'

'No, I don't know,' she replied testily and peered out of the window. After a while, she nudged him, harder than was necessary. 'Come on, we're there.'

Passengers were using the middle doors to get off. The argument was still going on at the front of the bus, held together by a rump of three. The guy who attacked the old Palestinian and the pot-bellied man, who were clearly never going to agree, and a younger man who somehow managed a say occasionally.

The bus was almost empty now and the big man with a beard and a violent temper clocked Zach. He moved quickly. Too quickly for the guys he was arguing with. He let Hepzibah progress to the doors after scaring her, but he barred Zach's way.

'*Englishman*,' he snarled and swung a fist, but Zach stepped back, and he hit air. Zach was ready to smack the guy in the head, but curbed his instinct and the big Israeli was pulled away.

'I can see what you need the fentanyl for,' Hepzbah said from the pavement.

'Blimey, Heps, you don't often crack jokes.'

'Come on, we don't have long.'

The moment Zach stepped off the bus into the fierce mid-morning heat, his ears were assaulted by a cacophony of claxons from the taxi area outside the Central Bus Station, where the car horn was used to express every emotion under the sun. He followed Hepzibah to the ticket office.

52

A little over an hour later they were in East Jerusalem, occupied territory. Soldiers and police patrolled the streets, rubbish-strewn due to a strike over lack of funds. The temperature gauge had smashed forty degrees, yet these guys were wearing battle fatigues, helmets, visors, and vests thick enough to withstand all but a bomb. They must have boiled.

The city heaved with tourists, somewhat incongruous, given the security situation. The majority, no surprise, were Christian, there for Bethlehem and the churches, and what the heck, the synagogues and mosques as well. They walked slower than a family of snails meandering home after a night out on Special Brew, making it hot work to weave around them. Beads of sweat gathered on Zach's forehead.

He was told they'd just crossed from the Jewish to the Muslim quarter. You wouldn't have known. Nothing changed. Traders continued to call out, 'Hey! Come! Look!' The narrow, crowded cobblestone alleyways remained the same, and Zach was still forced to walk behind Hepzibah, and she behind their guide, a fourteen-year-old Palestinian boy who kept to the shade when he could.

The air was filled with more than the smell of perfumes and street food. Zach could feel tension above the hustle and bustle of the souks. Their guide explained, in broken English, that yesterday armed police had raided the Al-Aqsa mosque and clashed with Palestinian worshippers. There was trouble after evening prayers at sunset, and more was expected today.

They left the old city through the Damascus Gate, where their papers were scrutinised by soldiers. Hepzibah and Zach were allowed through. Their guide, carrying his ID card in a bright green folder, went to a separate security check and had to walk into a steel cage. Zach looked away from the boy's nervous face, up to the ramparts of the old city. He wasn't surprised to see soldiers patrolling at that vantage point, their automatic rifles trained on all entering and leaving. Nevertheless, he was shocked to find himself in the sights of more than one gunman.

Their guide came through the checkpoint and hurried them. They crossed Sultan Suleiman Street, passed a tomb cut out of rock, the bus terminal, the US consulate, another tomb cut out of rock, and turned right. Now they were off the tourists' beaten path. Three corners in quick succession, left, right, left, and the boy pointed to a house on the other side of the street. Hepzibah gave him a twenty-shekel note and folded his hand over it. He'd only asked for two, worth less than fifty pence to Hepzibah.

'Too much,' the boy said.

'Take it, go home, and give it to your mother,' Hepzibah told him.

The boy smiled, bowed his head, and ran off.

Zach's eyes were shielded from the sun by his Wayfarers. Still, he squinted. The house the boy had pointed to came in and out of focus. White walls against a deep blue sky, classic Mediterranean. But he wasn't on holiday. The roof appeared to have a hole in it, he couldn't quite tell. Tiles were missing and the windows were mere rectangular holes in the wall. They had no glass, or shutters.

Next door the Israeli flag flew. There, the roof was intact, and the windows set with glass. Soldiers stood guard outside. A group of male settlers came out wearing shawls and kippahs. They carried assault rifles and greeted the soldiers, 'Shalom! Shalom!' slapped shoulders and joked with them.

Their humour deserted them when Zach and Hepzibah approached. A soldier stepped forward. He pointed a gun and said, in English, 'What do you want?'

'We're visiting a friend.'

'There?' He looked at the house next door with barely disguised disgust.

'Yes, she studies in London.'

'Papers,' the soldier demanded. He looked at their passports and radioed through to central command. Then he used the end of his rifle to push Hepzibah and Zach into the group of soldiers.

'Wait,' he said.

They were surrounded by unfriendly armed men. One of them was American, whose English was now heavily tinged with an Israeli accent.

'Do you sympathise with *them?*' he asked, looking over at the house.

Hepzibah pulled herself up to her full five foot something and a bit. She stuck her chest out and raised her chin.

'Yes, I do, and so should you. It's dreadful that you have no sympathy for them.'

'They are extremists, *Islamists*. You know nothing'.

The soldier who stopped them came back with their passports. 'Go, go and see your terrorist friends. But how do you say? Your cards are marked. Expect delays wherever you go.'

Hepzibah's bravery surprised Zach. These guys were armed to the teeth. He looked at her as they approached Fawz's house, but she was turned away and he couldn't see her face.

The front door was covered in woodworm. Hepzibah stayed her hand and knocked gently with her knuckles.

Fawz was dressed traditionally, in a matching dark grey hijab and long-sleeved dress. She looked frail and thin, and her eyes were sunken and lined with dark circles. Hepzibah hugged her. In the embrace Zach could see only sadness in Fawz. When it was his turn to hug, he felt her hipbones dig into him. She led them through to a small, stoned courtyard where two men sat on wooden chairs. One was in his forties, the other in his seventies. Both wore keffiyahs wrapped around their heads. The older man rested his hands on a stick, the younger one smoked. They both got up and shook hands with Hepzibah and Zach. The younger man's smoke distressed Hepzibah, but she said nothing.

'As-salamu alaikum,' they said.

'Alaikum as-salam,' Hepzibah replied.

A woman in her seventies came out with Turkish coffee. Fawz's grandmother. She was joined by Fawz's mother, dressed conventionally but with more colour than the family matriarch, and her two youngest daughters. The girls wore jeans and T-shirts.

'As-salamu alaikum.' They bowed their heads.

'Alaikum as-salam.'

More wooden chairs were brought out. They drank and sat in polite silence for longer than Zach was comfortable with. He put his cup down and leant forward so Fawz could see him. He didn't want to say, how are you? It was obvious how she was. Not good. With his options limited, he found himself saying, 'Are you managing to eat?'

The question surprised Fawz but she quickly regained her composure. 'A little,' she said.

'You need to eat more.'

'It is difficult. My brother is being tortured.'

'You know for sure?'

'For sure, believe me. I am too tired to explain how it works, the system, just believe me, I can assure you my brother is being tortured.'

'Did they torture you?'

Fawz shook her head. 'Torture, no. They punched me, on my arms.' She pulled up her sleeves. The skin around her upper muscles was a yellowish brown.

'What happened? Why did you get arrested?'

'I went to the Damascus Gate to get my brother. He was there, throwing stones after prayers.'

'Your brother's a *jihadi?*'

Everybody glared at Zach.

'You are quick to judge when you know nothing,' Fawz snapped. 'Our homes are being stolen from us day by day. Come. Let me show you.'

They climbed the stoned spiralled staircase. Hepzibah joined them.

'Look,' said Fawz, pointing to a hole in the roof the size of a sink. 'We have the tiles, we have the money, thanks to your brother, but we need a permit to renovate. They will not give my father one, nor for anything else, not even the front door. He will soon be forced to sell our home. They know this, of course. It is their plan.'

She walked over to the window hole. Glass and shutters leant against the wall, waiting to be hung. Fawz pointed to the house next door, where the Israeli flag flew. 'Our neighbour was denied a permit. He was forced to sell. When a settler family bought the house, the permissions were granted immediately. The city is being stolen from us, house by house.'

The evidence for that was right before Zach's eyes.

'Are there always soldiers outside the house next door?' he asked, looking out of a different window hole.

'Of course, they are settlers.'

'Is it normal for there to be so many? There's maybe a dozen down there, just hanging around, double the number earlier.'

Fawz and Hepzibah came over to look. Things Zach had seen before, but never registered, were now hitting him square in the face. Settlers and the army working hand in glove. The local authority dishing out assents to settlers like confetti, after having previously denied them to Palestinians who owned the houses and whose families had lived there for centuries.

'I count *thirteen* soldiers,' Hepzibah said, disbelieving.

'Something is happening,' said Fawz.

Five male settlers came out and greeted the soldiers. Many shaloms and much back slapping ensued, then they left, accompanied by ten of the soldiers. Three remained outside the house.

Fawz rushed down the stone stairs. Zach was right behind her, though he had no idea what was going on. Hepzibah was on his tail, as much in the dark as he. They followed Fawz into the courtyard where she retrieved her phone from a small wooden table. She yelled for her sisters. They ran out to the courtyard. She said something in Arabic, and they rushed back into the house. It had been said too quickly for

Zach to understand. But he got one word. Father. The girls came out with a phone and began reading a message. Fawz joined them and put a hand to her mouth as she read whatever was there.

'The phone belongs to my father,' Fawz explained. 'He received a text urging him to defend the mosque. He knew there would be trouble and he has gone, without his phone.'

Fawz had messages. She read them. She also had a video, which she played. A rowdy group of settlers in prayer shawls were encircled by a phalanx of soldiers.

'What are they doing?' Zach asked. 'They're at the Western Wall. Why aren't they praying?'

'They want to pray outside the Al-Aqsa mosque. That is why they have so many soldiers with them.'

The mosque was on a site called Temple Mount, which had been holy to Jews for three thousand years.

'Despite the history, it's a bit provocative.'

'Exactly, when tension was already very high.'

Another message arrived for Fawz along with one more video. She read with a look of resignation, steadied her trembling hand and played the short film. Teargas and stun grenades rained down on Palestinians throwing stones, disorientating them. A teenager, no more than fifteen, fell to his knees. It was unclear why. If he'd been hit by a rubber bullet he would have yelled in agony. He was still there when the police charged. He put his arm up in defence, but the baton came down anyway, hitting him on the shoulder. Then he was dragged away, along with others. The rest ran. The gates to the Al-Aqsa compound were clear and could now be opened.

~~~

An hour later Fawz's father, Mahmoud, had not returned. Everybody tried to help find him. Everybody apart from Zach and Hepzibah. They sat watching a family in panic. Zach felt distinctly uncomfortable, and he imagined Hepzibah did as well. There was nothing either of them could do. Soon, there was nothing anybody could do, except wait. Fawz had contacted the East Jerusalem Hospitals Network. If he was anywhere receiving treatment, they'd locate him quickly. She'd heard nothing and was coming to the conclusion he'd been arrested.

Food was prepared. It was, after all, eight o'clock in the evening. Zach was careful not to eat too zealously while everyone around him had lost their appetite. It was difficult. The *musakhan* was delicious. It was a first for Zach, but Hepzibah said it was the best she'd ever had. Palestinians called it a quiet meal. Chicken legs cooked in layers of onions with the softest of spices. It didn't sound much, but boy was it tasty, and with yoghurt and salad the meal was a treat. Zach ate as slowly as he could, but what he really wanted to do was wolf his food down and ask for more. The serving dish was, however, empty, so he might as well eat at a snail's pace. Also, there was something missing. Alcohol. He was sure Hepzibah felt the same. Of course, neither of them asked for any.

After the meal, coffee was made, and the grandfather smoked more cigarettes. Hepzibah had to make sure she was always as far away as possible from him, something she did for another two and a half hours. This was no easy task. He was sprightly for an eighty-year-old smoker, and anxious for his son, so he paced the courtyard as much, if not more than the rest of his family.

It was dark when they heard the door open. The family stopped and stared. No one said a word or moved a muscle until a second later Mahmoud appeared and they went mad with joy, kissing and hugging him.

'I'm so pleased for you,' Zach said when Fawz came over. They embraced and Hepzibah joined in for a group hug. 'What happened to him?' Zach asked.

'He was detained at the Damascus Gate checkpoint, with many others. It happens.'

Food was brought out for Mahmoud, along with beer for the men and Hepzibah. But now, when they finally got a drink, it was time for them to leave. Zach downed his in two goes, as did Hepzibah. They said their goodbyes to the family. When Zach hugged Fawz, he told her again how happy he was Mahmoud was safe, and wanted to say something hopeful about their lives in East Jerusalem, but couldn't.

'See you soon,' he said, and she smiled, probably at the thought of London.

Once they were outside Hepzibah checked her watch. 'We need to get a move on.' They walked quickly. At the house next door one of the soldiers, a young woman, stepped out and barred their way. Her two colleagues moved to back her up in case Zach and Hepzibah were thinking of ignoring the one gun. There were three now.

'Passports,' she said.

As they handed them over Hepzibah said, 'We have a bus to catch. It's the last one.'

'And what time is your bus?'

'Midnight.'

She looked at her watch and raised an eyebrow.

'So you can see we need to leave now,' Hepzibah pointed out.

The soldier slapped her hand with their passports and said, 'Checks.'

'We'll be too late.'

'There is another bus from Arlozorov. You can get that.'

'But that's at ten past twelve and it's a twenty-minute walk, it's eleven-forty-five already. And we haven't got any tickets.'

'You can buy tickets on the bus,' she said, and walked away. She appeared to talk into her lapel and kept her back to them.

Hepzibah turned to Zach. 'If she brings them straight back, we can make it. But she's not going to. Remember what that other soldier said? Expect delays wherever you go.'

'So, what are our options? If we go back to Fawz's we'll only have to pass the soldiers again. A hotel near the station?'

'A taxi. It normally costs about fifty quid. This time of night might be more like seventy. But it's worth it. I can't wait to get back to Tel Aviv. I need a proper drink.'

'Amen to that.'

53

The next day, Zach and Hepzibah left for a late afternoon coffee at a place Lila recommended. They kept to the shady side of Arlozorov, heading west towards the sea, before turning into Dizengoff, Tel Aviv's most famous boulevard. It was a ritual for the city's residents 'to Dizengoff', to stroll down the city's north-south street from the port to the Mann Auditorium, the country's most prestigious concert hall and home to the Israeli Philharmonic Orchestra. Tourists took all day, distracted by designer shops, natural food stores, a mammoth shopping centre, avant-garde museums, and galleries galore. Lunch was expensive, but hey, this was Dizengoff. And if the tourists were spiritually inclined as well as loaded, they could visit Madonna's Kabbala Centre after dessert.

There was also great coffee to be had, according to Lila. 'Café Castel, trendy, young, and the coffee is good.' Word must have got around. There were no free tables.

Hepzibah pointed to the gallery over the road. 'We can keep an eye from there.'

'I think we should stay here, that way we'll definitely get the next table.'

Hepzibah shrugged. 'Suit yourself, but I've heard about this place. It's an Israel nostalgia gallery. There are photographs and posters from the early days and before.'

Zach joined her, of course. They found they could stand in the window opposite the café and browse. Hepzibah looked through posters from the early socialist and workers movements. Zach flicked through the photographs. One in particular took his eye. A mixed group, Arabs and Jews, taking a break for lunch. They were building a kibbutz together. The photograph was dated 1910.

'*Bastard,*' Hepzibah hissed, loud enough for people to turn and stare.

'What?' Zach asked.

'Look. On the café terrace.'

It was Seth Silberman. Zach's adrenalin rocketed. Why was Hepzibah angry? Seth was their link to Tamir. He was carrying a tray loaded with drinks through the crowded terrace, negotiating the tables with the panache of a seasoned waiter. Indeed, he was a waiter, judging by the natty black waistcoat he wore over his white shirt. Matters were sealed when he left a bill under the sugar bowl and walked away to take another order.

'That rules out coffee at Café Castel,' Zach said.

'Why? I'd like to have a few words with him.'

'*What?*' Zach was taken aback by her stupidity. 'What's the point in that? He can lead us to the Israeli.' Zach needed answers. Why was Tamir chasing Abe that night?

'We're going to follow him? I don't really think that's my forté.'

'It's not mine either, but I'll give it a go. My guess is Seth's staying with the Israeli.'

They sat at a terrace on the other side of the street. Café Castel was twenty yards away but in their sight. Zach ordered a flat white, Hepzibah a glass of white wine. It was six in the evening.

~~~

Four hours later, Seth left Café Castel in the opposite direction from Zach and Hepzibah, towards Dizengoff Square. He was wearing black padded earphones, which contrasted neatly with his blond locks. Zach mopped up the remaining salad dressing with bread, something he knew annoyed Hepzibah.

'See you later,' he said.

'The money I've given you, I want it back if you don't spend it.' Hepzibah's tongue was thick with alcohol.

Zach had managed to lay off the booze and was compos mentis, if still not fully fit. He followed, at a discreet distance. In the underpass beneath Dizengoff Square, Seth took the Pinsker Street exit and stopped at a bus stop a short way down. He hung his earphones round his neck and made a call. Zach stopped on the corner, about ten metres away, outside a gaudy 1940s theatre. He contemplated his situation. It was quite simple. If he followed Seth onto a bus he'd be seen. Nevertheless, when the number 29 came and Seth got on, Zach joined him, staying behind a small group. Seth paid and sat two rows back, looking out of the window, his head moving almost imperceptibly to the music he was listening to. Could Zach have struck lucky? He gave what the guy in front of him had given the driver, three shekels, and moved smartly to a seat near the middle doors. In the meantime, Seth listened to his music and stared out of the window.

They left the city centre and crossed a river. The surroundings became residential as well as commercial. Soon, Seth made his way to the doors near the driver. Zach got up as the bus stopped and followed Seth along a wide road lined with smart apartment blocks above expensive clothes stores, cool coffee places, Italian shoe shops, and high-class jewellers.

Seth pulled down his earphones and began chatting to someone on the phone again. He quickened his pace and ended the call. The headphones stayed where they were around his neck, and he turned through a gap in a low hedge towards a block of flats. Zach stopped and took in his surroundings so he'd remember where he was.

He walked through towards the flats. In the dark, sitting on steps leading up to an entrance hall, was Seth.

'You've been following me.'

'I want to ask Tamir some questions.'

'Maybe he doesn't want to answer any.'

Out of nowhere a fist smashed into the side of Zach's head. He lost consciousness before he hit the ground.

54

The number 29 negotiated the heavy evening traffic around Dizengoff Square as best it could. The renovations were still going on and so were the jams. Zach stared out of the window and listened to *Firestarter*, a great advert for combining electronic music with punk rock, which was helping him ignore Hepzibah's bad mood. Sure, she was sorry Zach got knocked out, but she'd worried all night and got no work done. After some hours, Lila located him. She'd phoned police stations and rung hospitals, eventually tracking Zach down at Ichilov Hospital at 4am. She put her sleeping kids in the car and they drove to Weizman Street to see Zach. Meanwhile, looming, was Hepzibah's five pm deadline for the article on Fawz's father being refused permits to repair his house (she was writing a separate piece on Fawz and her brother). She made it, just, but late enough to condemn them to travelling during the rush hour. And now they were stuck inside a sweltering, stationary vehicle stuffed with hot sweaty bodies.

Hepzibah attracted Zach's attention with a hand on his knee. He pulled an earplug out.

'What are we going to do when they open the door? Ask them nicely to tell us why they killed Abe?'

'I don't know, but for the second time in a little over two months I've been found lying face down in my own vomit and I don't want ...'

'I know, you don't want to make a habit of it. You said earlier. But what are we going to do? We can't fight them, even if you have been given a clean bill of health.'

'We need to know why he was chasing Abe that night. At some point he'll tell us.'

The bus sped up and Zach yanked up the volume. Hepzibah gave him a nudge. He pulled an earplug out.

'Turn it down, Zach.'

'Why? It's an iPod.' His backside lifted off the seat as the bus went over a bump in the road.

'Because I can hear it. Are we nearly there?'

He looked out. They'd crossed the river and were in the right neighbourhood.

'It's not far.'

Soon they passed an office tower, tall but not elegant, with little glass, which Zach remembered because he was looking at it when Seth got up from his seat.

'It's the next stop.'

They left the bus and walked along the wide street lined with smart high-rise residential blocks. Zach soon saw the one he was after and, just as he had remembered, a café on the corner before.

'Let's have a drink,' he said on arrival and headed for the toilets inside. 'I'll have a Goldstar, if I'm not back.'

He brought out a wrap from his back pocket and the tip of his tongue tingled. Saliva built up. How long had it been? Nine days. He felt good he'd been able to last that long. He felt even better as he prepared a small line to get onto his toes. The addict in him was alive and snorting.

The rush hit him in less than a second. Energy surged through him. Parts of his body he'd forgotten he had came alive. Zach flexed muscles and stretched joints from his fingers to his toes. When he walked out of the toilet cubicle, he was reborn. Now he could face Tamir-whatever-his-name-was with equanimity.

Hepzibah had folded their table's umbrella and sat facing the evening sun. She looked dead sexy leaning back, her elbows resting on the table. Her top had risen revealing a flat, hard tummy. Zach was staring at her belly button, but she was staring at his eyes. He quickly brought down his sunglasses. Too late.

'Is that it? Is that the plan? You get high and talk him to death with endless inanities?'

'You cracked a joke there, Heps. What's that, second this year?'

'Where did you get it from? You didn't bring it over, did you?'

He nodded.

'My god, Zach. Is there no end to your stupidity?' She shook her head in disbelief. 'Anyway, I thought you'd given up.'

'I have.'

'Doesn't look like it.'

'It's only for special occasions. This is one. I can't afford to be scared of the Israeli.'

His cold beer arrived, along with a large glass of house white for Hepzibah. She took a drink.

'God, I needed that!'

'What's it like?'

'It's OK. Takes the edge off,' she said, mimicking Zach.

'Heps! That's two jokes in a minute!'

'Maybe I get funny when I'm nervous.'

'Maybe you should be nervous more often.'

'I keep thinking about Abe and how scared he must have been to have run into Euston Road. What I'm nervous about is not remaining cool.'

'Alcohol's not going to help there. You can't provoke this guy, Heps. He'll knock you flat.'

Hepzibah drank quickly, easily. So did Zach. 'I know,' she replied and left fifteen shekels on the table. They crossed the road and turned through the gate to the flats. Hepzibah examined the names by the doorbells. Most were in Hebrew, a language she could read. In the meantime, Zach rolled a fag and stood well away from Hepzibah to smoke.

'His name's not here,' she said after some time. 'I'm certain.'

'How come your Hebrew's so good?'

'I went to Jewish school till I was thirteen where we spoke only Hebrew. Then there were all the trips to Israel to see family, none of whom spoke English, only Hebrew and the old language.'

A woman leant out of a first-floor window. 'Erev tov,' she called. In her seventies, she had a shock of white hair and a friendly face lined with years. She said something to which Hepzibah replied, 'Ken, beseder,' and the woman disappeared from the window.

'She's coming down. She says she has something to tell us.' They waited, some minutes.

'Shalom! Shalom!' cried the old woman when she saw Zach. She took his hands, brought them together, and asked, in Hebrew, 'How are you?' Hepzibah told her he was fine. 'Good,' the woman said, 'because he hits very hard.'

'You know Tamir?'

'Yes,' she replied, clearly unhappy that she did. 'My son Levi, God knows how, is a football hooligan. They drink and fight together.'

Hepzibah was translating everything. 'And you saw him hit Zach?'

'Yes, and I saw him earlier. Levi had just come home, smelling of beer. They'd been at the club together. I don't know why I looked out, but I saw Tamir receive a call when he was at the gate. Instead of walking on, he stayed right there and had a conversation. I didn't linger, but a few minutes later I looked and he was still there, talking. Then suddenly he put his phone away and crouched down out of sight, this side of the hedge. A blond man walked past him after a couple of minutes and sat at the steps. Then, moments later another man arrived, you,' she said, pointing at Zach. 'Some words were spoken between Zach and the man on the steps before Tamir sprang up and hit Zach.'

'Do you have an address for Tamir?'

'No, but he's at the supporters' club on Hatikva Street every day, it's up near the market.'

'Which club?'

'Bnei Yehuda, of course.'

55

The reputation of the Bnei Yehuda fans went before them. Like Beitar Jerusalem, the club was a hotbed of violent Israeli nationalism. Of course, Tamir supported Bnei Yehuda. He had every reason to, not least because he was from Hatikva, the working-class neighbourhood in Southern Tel Aviv that was the beating heart of the Bnei Yehuda fan base.

Lila spluttered into her cappuccino. 'Walk into the supporters' club? You will be trapped in a room full of right-wing thugs, *drunk* right-wing thugs. I pass it every day. This evening I will pass it. But never on that side of the street. Never. The thump you got the other night will be nothing compared to what will happen to you in there.'

Zach squinted in the sun and watched her. She licked the end of her thumb to rub at a spot on her cotton skirt. Zach took in an eyeful of her legs. After a while she sat back from the café table, tipped her head to one side, and gave Zach a questioning look from behind her sunglasses. He soon realised he was staring at her and blushed into his flat white.

'Do you have to make it so obvious, Zach?' Hepzibah said. 'Since we got here you've been fawning over Lila. It's a bit, you know, yuck.'

Lila stood to leave. Her lunch break was over, and no doubt she was beginning to feel embarrassed. She looked at Zach, but sunglasses to sunglasses he couldn't see what was in her eyes.

'So, what will you do?' she asked.

'I think Heps and I should go and see if Seth's at work. It's not far to Dizengoff. Heps could use her feminine charm and persuade him to ring Tamir and get his friend to agree to see us peacefully.'

'I thought I didn't have much female charm,' Hepzibah chipped in.

'You don't, but I'm sure you can pretend.'

'I'm going to have to be nice to him.'

'Yep.'

'Even though I don't like him.'

'Yep.'

'I used to like him. I'll try and remember why.'

~~~

They struck lucky, three times. First, Seth was working. Second, they saw him, but he didn't see them. And third, there was a free table outside, with the umbrella already down. They waited till Seth went back to the bar, then sat down.

'Make me cry,' she said.

'What?'

'Make me cry, hurry up.'

'Shall I hit you?' he joked.

'I said make me cry, not hurt me. Say something emotional.'

'Heps, I didn't know you had a sensitive side.'

'I'm working on it. Say something emotional. *Quick.*'

Zach had been using Hepzibah's phone earlier to look up stuff on the internet while he waited for her to get ready. She'd given it him, temporarily, as his was cheap and nasty and barely worked in Israel. He came across a picture. A pygmy elephant riddled with bullets by a watering hole in Borneo. Shot seventy times, it had been shorn of its tusks and left upright, legs splayed out like a puppy. The image brought tears to Zach's eyes, but he didn't think it would do the trick for Hepzibah. Then it came to him.

What Zach said next was almost true. He added two words at the end, and they changed everything.

'Abe said one of his biggest regrets was not having children with you.'

On cue, she burst into tears, got up and walked into the café. With Hepzibah gone, Zach grabbed the opportunity to roll a fag and light up. As the other waiter passed, he ordered a flat white and a cappuccino, pulled on his fag and looked about. The place was stuffed full of middle-class Israelis, dressed casual to smart, eating shakshuka.

The arrival of their drinks coincided with Hepzibah's return. Zach stubbed his fag out.

'He's agreed to do it. We're more than halfway there.' She dragged her cappuccino over. 'He could see I was really upset. I think he took pity on me. Said he'd do what he could. I'm still upset. Is it true? Did Abe really regret not being able to have children with me?'

'Yes.'

'Why didn't he tell me?'

'He knew it would upset you. You know, because ...'

'Because it was my fault, you mean.'

'It's not a question of fault, Heps. But it wouldn't have helped if he'd told you. You'd have just felt bad.'

The answer seemed to satisfy Hepzibah. 'Oh well. No point dwelling on what could never have happened.' She looked at her watch. 'Now we just have to wait.'

'How long?'

'Don't know. Half an hour? An hour? I suggest we eat while we're waiting. But we have to be careful how we behave. No jokes, Zach. You mustn't make me laugh.'

'How often do I do that?' he asked, sipping at his coffee.

'I don't know. Just no jokes.'

'Lila was right,' he said, thinking he'd keep the conversation light. 'This is an excellent flat white.'

Hepzibah pulled a face. 'Does *everything* have to be brought back to Lila?'

She was jealous. But why? Did she want a relationship with Zach? The question couldn't be taken seriously, surely.

'You're overreacting, Heps. Lila was talking to both of us when she said this place does good coffee, don't you remember?' He had been about to ask what her cappuccino was like. Now he couldn't care less.

Hepzibah turned away and said nothing, her nose pointed up in the air. Zach saw the waiter nearby and called him over.

'Heps,' he said, bringing her round, 'do you know what you want? I'm having shakshuka. Everyone's eating it, so it must be good, unless the café's run out of everything else.'

After a quick look at the menu Hepzibah ordered in Hebrew. To his surprise, a few minutes later a large glass of white arrived.

'I have to steel myself for this meeting,' Hepzibah said. 'This man killed Abe.'

'Yeah, well don't get so drunk you get an attitude and get *me* hit, because the next time I see you, I'll hit you, and that's a promise.'

Hepzibah leant forward. 'And I'd slap you right back. You take cocaine when you need to. I drink when I need to.'

Their food arrived. The smell of herbs and spices wafting from his plate calmed Zach. He moved closer to the table and leant into his lunch.

'This shakshuka looks great and smells great. Truce while we see if it tastes great as well?'

'Agreed,' she replied, and they both tucked in to their identical meals.

'It's fantastic,' Zach enthused, his mouth full. 'Truce till we finish?'

'Agreed,' Hepzibah replied and dived into an egg yolk with a chunky piece of bread. When she ate the gooey end, Zach saw the hint of a smile. Over her shoulder he saw Seth leave the bar and head in their direction.

'He's coming over,' Zach told her. He'd never liked Seth's type, the ones who were handsome as well as good at stuff. Seth didn't quite fit into the category, because there was nothing he was particularly good at, but he was tough as well as Hollywood handsome. Today, he'd dispensed with the waistcoat and wore a short-sleeved white shirt.

'He says he'll do it,' Seth told Hepzibah.

'Safe passage into and out of the club for both of us and no violence while we're in there?'

'Yes, on one condition.' He looked at Zach. 'No drugs, junkie, otherwise the agreement is dead.'

Hepzibah put her glass down. It was empty. 'Is alcohol acceptable to him?'

'Only if you can take it,' Seth said. Did he know about Hepzibah's drunken moods? From Fawz perhaps?

'A glass of the house white for my junkie brother-in-law, and I'll join him, to keep him company.'

'A small one for you,' he said and left.

If Zach said the wrong thing now, or rather the right thing, an argument would ensue. He finished his shakshuka and pushed his chair out a little. He said nothing of substance, because he needed to tread carefully, yet he still managed to wind her up.

'Let's talk about our approach to the Israeli,' Zach suggested.

'What do you mean by our approach? This isn't a business meeting. He was chasing Abe and we want to know why.'

'I mean the way we approach him.'

Their wine arrived and Hepzibah immediately pulled at hers and said, 'What do you mean the way we approach him?'

'Well,' he said, watching her drink her second glass, 'we mustn't provoke him in any way.' He drank some wine. In truth he didn't want to, but rather that than leave it for Hepzibah.

'You say 'we' but you're referring to me.'

'What?'

'You say we mustn't provoke him, but you really mean me. I mean, why tell me when you know you don't have to tell yourself. So, the only point in you telling me is you're worried I'll provoke him.' She drank more wine. So did Zach, reluctantly.

'I've met him,' he said, 'and you haven't. Believe me, it's not difficult to provoke him.'

Even Hepzibah didn't argue with that. Instead, she caught the waiter's eye. When he came over, she asked for a macchiato, to 'sober up a bit.' Zach joined her.

~~~

Half an hour later they were on a bus heading for Hatikva market, travelling at the hottest time of the day. The air stank of sweaty armpits. Zach tried to take his mind off the uncomfortable odour with chit chat.

'Lila says the market here is not only cheaper but better than the famous Shuk HaCarmel across town.'

Hepzibah swung round. 'Will you stop with the Lila says this, Lila says that crap?'

'Are you jealous?' he asked with just the right amount of incredulity to sound surprised but not offensive.

She looked confused, then the penny dropped. 'Of *course* not.'

'Then what's this behaviour about?'

'It's like watching history repeat itself. Abe was exactly the same. *Lila says this, Lila says that.* It got on my nerves then, and it's getting on my nerves now.'

Zach said nothing. He wasn't surprised at how Hepzibah felt. Abe travelled to Israel and the Occupied Territories a number of times without Hepzibah. It was easy for her to draw conclusions.

'You ready for this?' he asked. 'We're nearly there.'

She nodded, but Zach wasn't convinced. They got off at the market and walked up Hatikva Street. The club stood out. Flags fluttered from the rooftop, orange and black, the club colours, alongside the blue and white flag of Israel. Drinkers milled around outside in groups, many of them smoking. The pavement was wide enough to accommodate them alongside passers-by, but they were still an intimidating sight. Most crossed the road.

Hepzibah held Zach's hand tightly as they walked past the guys out on the street. One blew smoke at them. It hit Zach first. He gave Hepzibah's hand a squeeze in case she was thinking of saying something. Another muttered misogynistic insults, which Hepzibah understood. She let go of Zach's hand and was just about to say something when Zach pulled her into the club.

Pictures of the football team through the decades adorned the walls. Scarves and flags hung everywhere. The all-male clientele ended conversations and put games of pool on hold. They manoeuvred themselves into position and stared at the newcomers. A TV, suspended from the ceiling and out of harm's way, played a goal the home team scored over and over with the sound turned down low. No one said a word. All eyes were on Hepzibah and Zach.

A big man with a thick beard came in. He had the club's logo tattooed on his arm, a black lion on an orange background, and he reeked of both alcohol and tobacco. He stood by Hepzibah, closer than he should. For her this was too much. She spoke to him in Hebrew, which surprised him, in a tone Zach recognised only too well. She was telling him off and putting him down. He blushed, prompting sniggering in the crowd. This turned to laughter when Hepzibah came in with her crescendo. The guy looked over to Tamir, who had joined in the laughter. He turned and left.

Once the man had gone, the smile disappeared from Tamir's face. Now it was deadpan. He leant back, his elbows on the bar behind. As Zach walked towards him he stared at his huge biceps, on which the colours of the national flag were tattooed.

The Israeli ignored Zach. He was looking squarely at Hepzibah. 'You have been drinking,' he observed, in English.

'And what have you been doing? Playing tiddlywinks?'

Her retort prompted tittering from those who understood, and was translated through the crowd. Soon, everyone in the bar was in on the joke. Even the Israeli saw the funny side. But then his smile disappeared once again. 'Yes, I have been drinking, but less than you, clearly.'

'Listen to you, the voice of moderation. You're the man responsible for the death of my husband. You chased him to his death.'

The bar went deadly quiet, except for the whispered explanations into Hebrew. The Israeli clenched his fists. The muscles and veins in his arms bulged, along with those in his neck. His eyes fixed on Hepzibah. He was about to move.

'*Hepzibah,*' Zach hissed. 'Shut the fuck up. *You're* going to get hit, not me. Stay back there, out of harm's way.' Surprisingly, she did as she was told. Zach turned to the Israeli. 'Will you talk to me?'

'Ask your questions and leave.'

'Why were you chasing my brother?'

Tamir looked Zach in the eye and his face softened. Zach saw anguish at the turn of events that night. Tamir sighed and said quietly, 'I was brought in to slap him around a little, but it did not go to plan.'

'You can say that again. You were working for Maccabi, right?'

'No, not that night.'

That took Zach by surprise, and no doubt Hepzibah too.

Zach cleared his head and asked, 'So, who wanted my brother slapped around?'

The Israeli shrugged. 'I do not know.'

The reply was a blow to Zach. He took a moment and tried a different approach. 'You said you were brought in. Who by?'

'Yes, and at the last minute. I have been trying to remember his name. Ralph knows him. He recommended me. Latvian, small guy.'

Zach turned to Hepzibah and said, '*Juris fucking Neilands.*'

She stepped forward and joined him. 'Juris Neilands,' she echoed, without the expletive.

'Juris Neilands, yes. He is the reason things went wrong that night.'

'Juris Neilands was there?'

'Of course. It was his plan. But he is sloppy and a coward. He was following your brother when your brother saw him and became angry. Neilands was scared and told him I was coming. Your brother had heard of me and ran. Straight into my arms, almost.'

'So, it was Neilands' plan to attack Abe that night. Who was he working for?'

'He never told me.'

'You said you felt bad about Abe. How bad? Does it stretch to giving me Neilands' address?'

'I will have to speak to Seth for his approval and the address.'

The pool players went back to their games whilst Tamir made the call. Conversations broke out with nods in the direction of Hepzibah and Zach.

Hepzibah received a call. To Zach's surprise, she stepped to one side and took it. Zach was left waiting for Tamir. The Israeli soon came off the phone. 'We have to wait a few minutes.'

'There's a few things I need to ask,' Zach said. He paused, seeking approval, which he got through the Israeli's silence.

'Was it you who nicked Hepzibah's laptop, twice?'

'If by nicked you mean stole, yes.'

'You stole them both times?'

Tamir nodded.

'For who?'

'Ralph Maccabi.'

'So you were working for Maccabi then, but not when you chased Abe.' Once again, Zach tried and failed to get his head around this.

Tamir nodded once more.

'And the stolen chapter? What was that all about?' Zach asked.

'I hoped to put you off the scent. It did not work, clearly.'

'Clearly,' Zach acknowledged, and pressed on. 'Seth said you were his handler. Are you a spy?'

At that the room burst into laughter. 'Spy' was a universal word.

'I'll take that as a no,' Zach said. 'So, what are you? Hired muscle?' The room went quiet after those two words, barring the whispered translations into Hebrew. 'I'll take that as a yes, which is how you come to work for Maccabi. Seth, presumably, was already a member of the JVF, but I'm guessing it was your idea he join Jews Against the Occupation.'

'Yes, which is why we joked about me being his handler. He was perfect. Good-looking, clever, and he can look after himself.'

Hepzibah returned, having finished her call. She was grinning from ear to ear. Zach stared, unsure whether this was Hepzibah. She was still beaming when Tamir's mobile pinged with a text, then rang. He answered in English and handed the phone to Zach.

'It's your lucky day,' Seth told him.

'Yeah?'

'Yeah. I've texted the address. He lives in Arnos Grove. A word of advice. We don't like him, but Ralph does.'

'Aah, it's lovely to know you're thinking of me.'

'You're growing on us.'

'The feeling isn't mutual.'

'Fair enough. Your brother's dead. We understand, but Ralph, see, he can't be bothered understanding. You see what I'm getting at?'

56

Zach was close to Hepzibah as they passed the smokers on the pavement. He couldn't help noticing she was still smiling. Indeed, she appeared to bubble with joy. He never thought that possible for Hepzibah. For his part, Zach was feeling smug. He'd been right about Neilands all along. Next stop Arnos Grove.

'I always said the Latvian was involved.'

'I was wondering how long it would be before you mentioned that. I might have known it would be less than a minute.'

'I'll gloat no more, just look forward to the moment I knock on his door. Anyway, what's with you? You've gone all weird. You seem *happy*. By the way, taking that call was pretty rude.' He said nothing about her stupid drunken behaviour when she provoked the Israeli.

'I had to take the call. It was Solly Benayoun. Was I really rude?'

'Yes.'

'Good!'

Zach groaned in despair at her foolishness. If she hadn't worked out by now how stupid it was to annoy the Israeli, he wasn't going to tell her again.

'So, what was so important about the call?' he asked.

At that Hepzibah stepped in front of him and danced a jig. She also sang. 'Maccabi is fucked! Tra lala lali! Macccabi is fucked! Tra lala lali!'

Zach had never seen Hepzibah like this in the thirteen years he'd known her. 'Tell me.'

'Israeli security services have traced a donation of half a million dollars to the JLA back to Maccabi. Tra lala lali! They've been in touch

272

with the British police. He doesn't know it, but he's going to be arrested tomorrow morning. Tra lala lali! And then the Israeli government will ask for his extradition. Tra lala lali!'

They turned right off Hatikva Street at a bicycle shop and passed a synagogue, not much bigger than a house.

'I don't have much time to get the article written, but I'm going to make sure it's done. Tra lala lali!' She got her phone out. 'I need to phone my editor.'

As she dialled, Zach said, 'I know someone else who's fucked. The Latvian. He's lost his protector, and he doesn't know I've got his address.'

Once she'd stopped laughing alongside Zach, Hepzibah stepped to one side to talk with her editor. Under the Tel Aviv sun, it was fun watching Hepzibah. She was a picture of happiness. Her dress was light and swirled when she turned. The dancer in her wanted to get out. When she came off the phone, she did another little jig.

'I'll be on the front page! Tra lala lali! They're putting it in the daily sister paper. And I can do an in-depth on Maccabi for Sunday, after I've given the evidence of corruption to the police. It means the company is fucked, as well. Tra lala lali!' She did another jig.

'You're a journalist in demand, Heps!'

'I am. And what with the papers here thinking the ground invasion of Gaza is imminent, I'm going to be a busy bee.'

Another synagogue loomed, but not before Lila's apartment block. Zach rang the bell, and they were buzzed in. When the lift arrived, they took it to the ninth floor. Dori was waiting at the door and invited them in.

'Bevakasha,' he said and stepped aside as they entered.

He gave them another guided tour, again conducted in superfast Hebrew, only this time, quite bizarrely, he took them to the bedroom he shared with Lev. It turned out they were massive supporters of Hapoel Tel Aviv, the Red Demons, the antithesis of Bnei Yehuda. The club's paraphernalia was everywhere. The red and white hammer and sickle badge, pictures of Bloomfield stadium lit up with red and white flares before a Tel Aviv derby, and the dozens of championships and cups they'd won. But what Dori really wanted to show them were photographs of their best European moments. The wins against Chelsea, AC Milan and Paris Saint-Germain. Then he listed other notable victories, using the club's names. Both his pronunciation and the speed at which he spoke made it difficult, but Zach could make out three. Benfica, Rangers, and Celtic.

Soon Dori took them to the balcony where he pointed twice to a lit barbeque. Each time he said the same word.

Zach turned to Hepzibah. 'What's he saying?'

'No idea.' Hepzibah wasn't listening. From her expression she was dreaming of the expression on Maccabi's face when the police knocked on his door in the morning. And who could blame her? She plonked herself on the sofa in the living room, got her laptop out and began writing an article depicting the fall of Ralph Maccabi, now that Solly Benayoun had sent the information she needed.

Lev, Dori's older brother, came out. 'It is a fish,' he said. 'We will eat fish tonight.'

Lila was right behind him. She kissed them both on the cheek and dashed back into the kitchen. Her baggy cotton trousers ballooned as she rushed, a sexy contrast to her skimpy white top. She checked something and came back with three bottles of cold beer.

Zach took his onto the balcony and rolled a fag. He lit up and leant against the railings. Ignoring the hum and clatter of the street below, he looked out at Tel Aviv, densely packed, busy, some old, most new, and beyond, to the vast expanse of the deep blue Mediterranean sea.

Lila joined him. 'Can I help you smoke that very thin cigarette?'

'Of course,' he said and handed it over. 'Where are the boys? They're very quiet.'

She took a drag on the roll up and exhaled the words: 'Game time on the computer.'

Then, she smiled, perhaps at the freedom that gave her, or maybe just because she liked to smile. She poked at the fire, levelling it off.

The coals looked ready. She placed the grill on the pit to warm up. 'I hope you like marinated catfish.'

Zach blew smoke out slowly and handed the cigarette back to Lila. 'Sounds lovely.'

'It is,' she said, and her smile broadened. She picked up her bottle and clinked his. 'L'chaim. It was good to meet you, Zach.'

'Likewise.'

'If you come back, you are most welcome.'

Their eyes met. He edged imperceptibly closer and so did she. Their lips were inches away. They could so easily have kissed, but acknowledgement and a lingering look were enough. Also, Hepzibah was watching. Lila stepped back and took a cheeky drag on his cigarette before handing it back.

'What will you do now?' she asked.

'Go and see Neilands.'

'Is that not for the police?'

'I want a word with him first. Just a word, then I'll go to the police. He's going to tell me who he's been working for.'

~~~

Later, Zach saw he had a missed call and a voicemail message from Ester, the first contact from her in six weeks. Something had happened to his father, surely. Why else would she call? He played her message back immediately.

"Your father's asking to see you, Zach. No one else will do, apparently. I have no idea why, given how much worse you made him. He won't speak to anyone, even me, but he's going to talk to you. Imagine how that feels. But it's done now, and we will talk of it no more. When can you come? The day after tomorrow? If you need money to get here, ring me.'

Ester left the message at eleven thirty his time, nine thirty hers. What had he been doing when she rang? Having a last drink with Lila before he and Hepzibah left for the hotel. Zach would have walked straight back, had he not got a 5.30am taxi for an eight o'clock flight. He knew he'd think about Lila and wonder when he'd next have enough money to fly back.

Once he was back at the hotel and getting ready for bed, he considered that missed call from Ester. What would have happened if he'd taken it? Immediately, she'd have realised it was long-distance.

Where are you?

Israel.

What are you doing there?

Talking to the man who chased Abe into the road. He's a militant Zionist.

That would end the conversation. Abe's death ignored, the conversation sent elsewhere.

Ester worked by evasion. She confined herself to the superficial, her exhaustion from running the house and looking after Dov, and gossiping with the best of them in the tightly-knit community of South Manchester Sephardis, even though tradition frowned upon the scandal-monger. But all talk of how she felt about Abe's death, or her unfulfilled life, was avoided. Ditto Nissim. They had been conditioned to shut down thought, to not think about uncomfortable matters. It didn't suit that Abe's killer was a Zionist and not an anti-Semite, and so they didn't reflect on it. And what had they said to Dov? Nothing, in all probability.

And Zach? He'd say nothing as well. What would be the point? Not even Ester could hear the truth. It was inconvenient, as it often was for the narrow-minded.

PART FIVE

Back home

57

Ester was standing in the open doorway watching Zach walk up the drive. Her arms were folded, and she looked stern. Zach had seen this behaviour many times. Ester needed to show him she'd been very cross indeed. A few moments later, with Zach standing in front of her, grinning, Ester cocked her head and opened her arms. In that moment, Zach forgave Ester her stupidity, her bigotry, her narrow-minded life, and welcomed her embrace. She had always been more than a sister to him, having taken the place of his mother in childhood. Zach would always love her for that. And he couldn't fail to feel for her. He was the nearest thing she had to a child but had never been enough to fill the void in her empty life.

Not knowing he'd been under the Tel Aviv sun for a week, Ester said, 'You look *so* well.'

She held Zach's hands and beamed. Her hair was wrapped in a white woollen tichel that looked like an untrendy beanie, and she was dressed in a shapeless dark blue cardigan, a white neck ruff, a long grey skirt, and thick stockings. It was July, and Zach, in contrast, was about to unzip the bottoms on his lightweight convertibles. Ester had never done herself any favours, covering her body from head to toe in formless clothing, and shoving all her hair into a headscarf that hung down the back of her head like a sack. Her hair was long and black and curly, but when it was shunted into a bag at least her face shone through. Strong-boned, dark-skinned, large brown eyes, a big smile. Ester always had her admirers, and no doubt still did.

Not for the first time, Zach wondered why it was Ester had never married, given how much she'd wanted children. She'd had her pick of orthodox men from across the city and beyond. Dov and Malka arranged countless meetings for her. Yet she remained resolutely single and, as far as Zach knew, untouched. Why? Was it love she'd been looking for rather than an arranged marriage? Zach broached the subject with her on a couple of occasions but, just like his mother, she refused to talk about how she felt. And if he were to raise the issue again now, and tell her there was still time for happiness, would she listen? No, for it would mean breaking out of the insular life she had lived for fifty years.

Pastries were cooking in the non-meat oven. He could smell melting cheese. A Fattoush Salat lay in a bowl on the kitchen table. Zach picked at a piece of flatbread and dug it into the minty yoghurt. Before he had a chance to lift his hand, Ester dealt him a light smack on his wrist.

'Wait till we're at table,' she ordered, as she had so many times. But Ester wasn't cross. She was delighted Zach was there, picking at the salad. She squeezed his hand and kissed him on the cheek. 'It's lovely to see you, Zach.'

Instinct told him not to ask questions, such as 'Does that mean you missed me?' or 'Am I forgiven?' He guessed he was, so long as he didn't bring the subject up.

He popped the flatbread into his mouth. 'Mmmm, nice dressing, Es.'

Smiling at her, he went for a slice of radish whilst she pretended to be angry. After that, he left the food alone. Ester got plates and cutlery but kept an eye on Zach's straying fingers all the same.

'Nissim doesn't want to see you, Zach. Might as well get that out of the way. I'm sorry.'

'Don't worry Es, I'm much more bothered about you.'

'Yes, it's not as though you're especially close to him or his family.'

'Especially? I'm not close at all. How's Dad?' he asked, expecting the worst.

'Not good, getting worse. His bronchitis is bad, he's coughing a lot. He's barely eating, a bit of soup now and again. And it's difficult to get him to drink. He has his mouth round the straw, but I have to tell him to suck. And then he does it reluctantly, and I have to badger him to suck again. It's hard work.'

'He doesn't want to.'

She shrugged. 'He's lost interest in everything, eating, the garden, life.' She opened the oven and pulled out a tray.

'Shouldn't I go and see him first?'

Ester brought out cheese and spinach bourekas, the perfect accompaniment to the salad. 'No, let's eat.'

Zach bit off a piece. 'Es, you are the best. This is delicious, so light. I tell you Hepzibah is good, but you are even better.' He didn't tell her he knew someone who could rival her baklava. Ester had no idea that he sometimes lived with a Palestinian woman.

As they ate, Ester talked about the family, though Zach was only interested in the bit about Dov. Thankfully, she didn't give him the latest gossip in the community, but she did tell Zach about the missing cat from three doors down. The rumour was it had moved in with an elderly neighbour, but nobody was quite sure, because the neighbour kept to herself. One thing they didn't talk about was Abe's death, the elephant in the room. Zach wasn't surprised, not after Ester's performance at the hospital. Along with the attack on Zach, Abe's death would remain un-talked about. However, Zach found it interesting that Ester hadn't asked about his cocaine habit. Preoccupied with Dov probably.

'I haven't had any cocaine for over two weeks,' he said, embellishing the truth a little.

'Zach, that is fantastic! I am *so* pleased. Mazeltov, mazeltov,' she said, and went over to embrace Zach and kiss him on the cheek.

'Don't suppose it'll mean much to Dad, but I'll tell him anyway. How does he call you when he wants you?'

'He never wants me,' she replied tartly. 'He has a stick to bang on the floor, but he never uses it. It wouldn't bother him if I never went in at all.' The resentment in her voice was plain. 'I go in every couple of hours or so. If he's awake I try with soup and something to drink, get him to the bathroom if he needs to.' She turned her nose up and screwed her face. 'He won't shower, because he doesn't want me to see him. Sometimes Nissim manages to wash him, or one of the boys, but other than that I wash his face and hands, at least he lets me do that.'

'I might pop my head round the door in a minute, see if he's awake. Does he know ...?'

'About you coming? Oh yes. We even discussed it. He actually asked me questions. That was a surprise, I have to tell you, the first time in a while. He asked what time you were arriving and for you to wake him after lunch.' She narrowed her eyes and looked at Zach quizzically. 'He hasn't talked to anyone in weeks, he hasn't asked to see anyone, and then this. It's all a bit strange.'

Zach didn't know what to make of it either. His relationship with his father had always been volatile, but it had also been more demonstrative than with the others, except, perhaps, Abe. Odd though it may sound, Dov was closer to Zach and Abe, the two children who rejected the life he wanted them to have, in comparison to Nissim and Ester, who didn't.

Zach mounted the stairs two at a time and opened the bedroom door. Stale air hit him in the mouth. He gagged. The room was dark, the curtains drawn. He opened them all, as well as two windows, fully.

Dov was in bed, awake. His breathing was rapid and shallow. He lifted his head. 'Zachy ... come. I have been ... waiting.'

His father gave off an unpleasant odour, a sweaty, sick smell, and his breath hadn't been freshened in weeks. Zach bent down and kissed his father on the forehead. Dov looked ghastly pale. His face was emaciated, the skin around his jaw stretched tight, and his chin jutted up, out of all proportion. His mouth was open slightly, enough for Zach to have to move away from Dov's rasping sour breath. He brought a chair over and sat by the bed.

Dov began to cough. Zach sat him up and it eased.

'Come close,' Dov said, his voice faint.

Zach leant in. His father's acrid breath crept up his nose and into his mouth. Zach gagged a little, feeling guilty for not wanting to be close.

He also felt cheated. He'd been looking forward to this moment. He'd felt favoured, and had wanted to hug and kiss his father.

Dov put his hand on Zach's arm. It was hot and clammy. Unpleasant. Again, Zach reproached himself for being physically repulsed by his father.

'Zachy,' he squeezed Zach's arm, 'my Zachy.' Despite his weariness, there was real warmth in Dov's voice. He looked at Zach with watery eyes and a palpable tenderness. Guilt flooded through Zach at the distance he wanted to keep, for these were moments he craved. His father squeezed again. 'Always ... I've loved you.' Breathing was painful for Dov, talking even more so. A couple of words, then he had to get his strength back. 'Such a lovely boy ... despite everything,' by which he meant the drugs, the thieving, the family shame.

Dov began to cough. When he stopped, he said, 'This bronchitis ... will kill me. Maybe not now ... but soon.' He gripped Zach's arm. 'I want to tell you.' His father was almost whispering now. 'Abe and I,' he glanced upwards, 'God knows how much I love him ...we argued ... two weeks before ...' Dov closed his eyes. When he opened them they were moist. 'I never saw him again.' Tears formed in the corners of his eyes.

'What did you argue about, Dad?'

His breathing was ragged. 'We had *an agreement* ... after more than ten years ... he broke it.' His father looked away, pained by the memory, and began wheezing heavily.

'What agreement?'

Dov turned to face Zach, his lips peeled back ghoulishly, revealing more gum than teeth. As he spoke, Zach was hit by bursts of hot fetid breath. 'He promised ... to keep ...his views ... quiet.' Dov's face was etched in pain. He closed his eyes.

'What are you saying, Dad?'

His father's mouth twisted and bitterness crept in. He roused himself in anger. 'He broke his promise ... when he spoke ... at *that* meeting.' Dov had summoned up enough strength to spit the word out. Abe's lifestyle had never disgraced Dov. He hadn't been a drug addict, a criminal, or a low life. Abe's differences with his father were ideological. His views on Israel were anathema to Dov and dishonoured Dov in the community.

Zach started to feel uneasy. His heart began to pound. He turned to face his father. Dov's face had softened. He smiled and said: 'I was lucky … thank God,' he said, looking upwards in appreciation.

'How's that, Dad?'

'I did a bad thing … but I got a letter …. it wasn't me.' He looked skywards again. 'Thank God.'

Zach could feel his anger rising, as well as his worry. 'What are you talking about, Dad?'

'Abe needed … to be … taught a lesson … for bringing shame … upon the family.'

Zach grew cold and dizzy as the full horror of what Dov was saying dawned on him. He brushed his father's hand aside and got up. He felt faint, but fury kept him on his feet.

Zach looked at Dov in disgust, with contempt. Hatred even. '*You* were responsible. You were working with Juris Neilands.'

'Who is … Juris Neilands?'

'Tamir Bachar, then.'

'Who is … Tamir Bachar?'

'The man responsible for Abe's death. Apart from you, that is.' Zach wanted to shake his father, violently. He wanted to scream at him. He wanted to drag him by his white hair to Abe's grave and rub his face into Abe's battered skull.

Dov raised himself a little. 'No, no, you don't understand! I was assured … it was not us.' He looked up again. 'Thank God.' He fixed Zach with unfathomable watery eyes. His voice begged for empathy. 'After the warning … I said enough. It was stopped.' He motioned Zach to him, who didn't move. Zach was scared he would throttle his father if he went close.

Instead, he shook with rage. 'You *stupid* old man!' he screamed, alerting Ester. 'You *stupid* old man. Abe is dead because you were shamed by his views.'

Dov lifted himself higher, his breathing heavy. He looked frightened and his eyes beseeched Zach. 'No!' he cried. He had more to say, but was catching his breath. 'He told me ... it had nothing ... to do ... with us.'

Somehow, Zach managed a sarcastic tone. 'Who told you? *God?*'

The name crashed through Zach's ears as Ester burst in. 'What's going on?' she asked, looking from Zach to Dov and back again. Zach glared at her. What could he say? Abe was dead because their stupid father couldn't tolerate his views? She wouldn't listen. Zach rushed out of the room, brushing past her. Downstairs, he picked up his bag and fled the madhouse.

He ran to the park in a state of despair, as he had so many times as a teenager. It had been a favourite haunt for Zach and his mates to forget about home and get stoned under the trees near the café, so they didn't have to go far when they got the munchies. He headed in that direction as if on autopilot, or maybe because he knew there were toilets nearby. It was early afternoon. Mums chatted, rocked prams and watched toddlers in the play area. Adults walked dogs in the leafier parts, and seven young men played football on one half of a pitch. One goalkeeper and two teams of three playing defence and attack. Zach sat on a bench near the small café, caught his breath and phoned Neil. His call went through to answerphone.

'It's Zach. I need ... Can we talk?' He ended the call and sat with his head in his hands. His father killed his brother, good as. All for honour. Shame, to be more accurate. Could Zach ever forgive him? Probably, but Dov would be long gone by that time.

Zach fingered the wrap in his back pocket. Should he? He'd have some relief from the hopeless fury he felt. It would be temporary, but better than nothing. He marched over to the toilets. There were two cubicles. He chose the one he thought least dirty, placed the wrap on top of the cistern and got out a fiver. His phone rang. Zach looked at the five-pound note and the wrap of cocaine, and back again, then ignored them both and answered his phone. It was Neil.

'Hey mate, you sound like you wanna talk. Where are ya?'

'Rock bottom.'

'What's happened?'

'I'm in a public toilet about to have a line. Let me ...'

'Wait mate, yeah? Pack it away. Is there somewhere you can talk?'

'I'm in a park, there's a bench nearby. I'll ring you back in a minute.'

'You won't have that line?'

'I won't have that line.'

Zach put the wrap in his pocket, the fiver in his wallet, and left the toilets. The truth was, he knew Neil would intervene. Hepzibah would have done as well, and Beth, but crucially, Neil's tone didn't grate.

The bench near the café was free. It looked down on the pitch where the seven guys were having a fairly serious kick about. One end of the bench was shaded by a large oak tree. Zach sat in the sunny bit, rolled a fag and lit up. When that was going nicely, he rang Neil and told him his story. In the end Ralph Maccabi and his militant thugs had nothing to do with Abe's death. That night Tamir was working indirectly for his father. Why? Because his father had been shamed by Abe's views. Dov felt dishonoured. He hadn't meant to kill Abe of course, but he was responsible.

'Shit, that's heavy, mate. You OK?'

'No. Finding out my Dad killed my brother hasn't been great.'

'No, 'course not mate. An' I agree, there's no point the cops goin' round to talk to yer Dad.'

'I'm going to ask them not to. I'm sure they'll agree.'

'Where are ya?'

'Manchester, about to make my way to the station.'

'Come round fer a drink later. They're on me.'

'OK. I'm about to ring Heps and suggest she meets me at the police station. I need a chat with Inspector Murrell. I'll come over soon as I'm finished.'

'Great. So where is it?'

'Where's what?'

'That cocaine.'

'In my back pocket.'

'D'ya wanna another line?'

'I've got to stop.'

'Throw it away mate, otherwise you'll 'ave another one, an' another. It has to stop now.'

Zach knew Neil was right. He would have another one, and carry on. It had to stop now, otherwise it would never stop. 'You know what? I am going to throw it away.' Zach fished the wrap out of his pocket, opened it up and shook it. He watched the cocaine fly away. 'It's done.'

'Great! 'How d'you feel?'

'Relieved, believe it or not. That's it now.'

'Proud of you mate!'

'We'll have a drink later, and I'll forget about my stupid family.'

'Man, family's family, yeah?' Neil intoned, like it was a mantra. 'You can't give up on your sister, *right?*'

A young black lab burst into the game of football. There was a loose ball. The dog got to it first, but couldn't fully control it, so he sank his teeth into the expensive leather and ran off with it, shaking it from side to side. Soon, he was distracted by a bird and decided to give chase. He dropped the punctured ball and forgot about it altogether. The incident amused Zach, but it didn't please the young men who remonstrated with the owner when he finally arrived on the scene.

'What's 'er name, yer sister?'

'Ester.'

'You should tell 'er, mate.'

'I know. The problem is she'd only really understand if the police went round, and they're not going to.'

58

Car headlights sweep the living room. Tyres scrunch to a halt on the gravelled drive. Lights shut down, an engine dies. Two doors open and close. Voices, both male. The dog starts to bark and runs to the front door.

Panic propels me out of my chair. I scan the room. I'm looking for something, anything that can save me. But there is nothing, no one, no salvation. Newsnight is on, and Mark Regev, the Israeli spokesperson, is smoothly absolving Israel of any responsibility for the deaths in Gaza. But not even he could talk his way out of this one.

The dog is still barking at the door. There's a knock now, spelling my doom. Ella appears at the top of the stairs tying her dressing gown.

'Who can it be at this time of night?' she wonders.

Poor Ella. She will be devastated. I say nothing, but I'm sure she can see the miserable look on my face.

'Darling, what's the matter?'

She comes down the stairs. 'What's the matter, darling?' she asks again, but the other way around, demonstrating more urgency. I ignore her and open the door to two policemen out of uniform, one a young Chippendale look-alike with an eager face, the other a scrawny middle-aged bloke who'd seen it all before. They flashed badges and introduced themselves. DI Murrell and DC someone or other.

'Solly Benayoun?' the older one said.

Ella is pulling anxiously at my arm. 'Solly? What's going on?' The girls appear and start asking questions.

'Come in,' I say to the policemen and then I turn to Ella and the girls. There's no detail to their faces through my moist eyes, but I can see their anguish. I kiss each one of them on the cheek and whisper, 'I love you.'

I've gone cold. I have no strength, not an ounce. I am defeated. With permission, I get my fleece jacket from the cupboard under the stairs, and make a pot of tea. They sit at the kitchen table and wait. Ella, my poor love, wants to know why the police are here. So do the girls. I can't tell them bluntly, they're here to take me to the police station to make a statement that will be handed to the CPS for prosecution. Let it come out slowly.

I'll get some relief, at least. Finally, I can talk about what happened. That it span out of control and ended in disaster.

I sip at my tea, keeping the saucer close by. 'Over two months ago, it seems an age now, Juris told me about a professor he knew, an anti-Zionist Jew who was about to speak at a public meeting organised by the Palestinian Solidarity Movement. Juris was letting off steam. I'm fairly long in the tooth, you hear about that sort of thing far too often, I'm afraid, and I wasn't taking too much interest, until he mentioned the professor's name.'

I can feel Ella's anxiety mounting. The wait is killing her.

The older policeman leans forward. 'When you say Juris do you mean Juris Neilands?'

'Yes.'

'And your relationship with him is ...?'

'I first met him two years ago when he joined the Christian Zionist movement. I bump into him frequently in my capacity as President of the Association of British Zionists.'

'You were saying about the professor's name, go on.'

'Yes, Peretz. My father went to school with Dov Peretz in Damascus. They were friends. I've met Dov a number of times and knew how he would feel, so

I rang him. Obviously, now, I wish I hadn't, but at the time it seemed I was doing the right thing. Dov was furious. Apparently, they had an agreement and the professor had promised not to speak publicly about his views.' I can feel Ella begging me to go quickly. The girls too, but I can't.

'Dov asked me to stop his son. I'm not the type to threaten people, not even alongside others. I told Juris that. Juris said he'd do it on his own. But of course, the professor took no notice of him. Have you met Juris? He has a lot of anger in him, but he is not at all tough. He asked me did I know anyone, and of course I don't, so I stupidly suggested he contact the JVF, Maccabi's plaything.'

At this point I lose everybody in the room, and so I explain, briefly, who Ralph Maccabi is and what the JVF does, emphasising the defensive nature of the group.

'Which is how this Tamir character got involved. He works for Maccabi as a thug.' I sip at my tea, suppressing the urge to groan. How stupid was I? 'Then Dov said he wanted nothing more done, and I felt immense relief. I told Juris, and he said OK, but obviously he didn't mean it. It was on the eve of the public meeting that he told me they were going to follow the professor and slap him around a little. I protested, told him that Dov Peretz wanted no more done. But, he laughed at me and said the issue was beyond the father. Stop the professor and people like him will think twice, was what he said. Tamir was right behind him. So they followed the professor to the pub after the meeting and waited.' I shiver at the memory of what took place next and look up at the policemen. I didn't expect sympathy, but a little pity wouldn't have gone amiss. 'And what was I to say to Dov?'

It's the older one who speaks. 'And what did you say to him?'

'I lied. He'd wanted no more done after the warning. He deserved a white lie, so I wrote to him. He's an old man. I wanted him to live the rest of his life in peace. It might not be long. I told him the police didn't have enough evidence but were sure a neo-Nazi chased him into the road. He believed me, why shouldn't he?'

'Why a letter, why not call?'

'A letter can't be traced. I told him to get rid of it as soon as he'd read it.'

'I think we've heard enough,' the older one says. 'Niall, read him his rights.'

My account might have satisfied the policemen, but not Ella and the girls.

'What happened?' they ask.

To my relief, the older policeman takes up the story. 'The professor, Abe Peretz, ran into Euston Road to escape his assailant. He was fatally hit by a car.'

'Oh my god, that's terrible!' Ella exclaims. The girls gasp. 'But Solly's not responsible. He tried to stop it.'

'No, Mrs Benayoun, he didn't. Read him his rights.'

'But Solly doesn't like fighting.'

'No one is suggesting your husband should have physically confronted anyone. But he should have warned the target of the impending attack or, failing that, he could have contacted the police. Read him his rights.'

Epilogue

July 22nd, 2014

Beth opened the door and Bitz squeezed past, his tail wagging furiously. Zach paid him some attention before Rachel ran out. They hugged, exciting the dog, who jumped up and licked their faces.

Zach resurfaced from the melee and Beth handed him a Tigger rucksack. 'Everything's in there, animal torch, projector, the sparkling mosaics set, clothes, and some other stuff. She's just eaten, so she'll be fine till she gets to yours.'

Beth gave him a heartfelt hug. 'I'm proud of you Zach, cocaine-free, and dealing with that terrible stuff about your father. What a thing to find out. It's a lot to cope with, a lot to deal with. What are you going to do about your dad?'

'You mean will I see him? Not for the moment, I don't know when. The complication is Ester. I'm hoping she hears about Solly Benayoun. I might be able to talk to her then.'

'Beneath it all, she's no fool, but she won't want to talk about it.'

'No, I guess you're right.'

'Tell me, how's Heps?'

'Classic. I met her at the police station on my way back from Manchester and told her about my dad. She screamed at me about my mad bigoted family and beat me on the chest, in the middle of the reception area. Of course, it caused a commotion. A policeman came out, but by that time she was sobbing into my chest rather than hitting it. By the way, she didn't ask how I was, finding out that my father was responsible for my brother's death. Yeah, I know. Then she started crying again, saying it was all her fault, because she'd pushed him to speak, telling him he'd be great. Apparently he said, "You're right. Enough is enough, I'll speak." Heps didn't attach any meaning to that other than he'd speak at the meeting. She knew he'd be great, and apparently he was. She's got a recording.'

'Why do you think he did it?'

'What? Make a promise? Family. You know Abe. He was attached to Dad and Es, just like me.'

'Yes, I guess you're right. But poor Heps. She knew nothing about the promise Abe had made when she encouraged him to speak.'

'Even I feel sorry for her. Oh yeah, she texted me later. No apology for any bad behaviour, of course. By that time, she had her journalist head screwed on. After all, it is a big story. Solly Benayoun is a pillar of the Jewish community. Quite a coup, after her exclusive the day Maccabi got arrested.'

'I read her piece. That guy's in real trouble. But is Solly Benayoun?'

'The police think it very unlikely the CPS will press charges. Not so with Juris Neilands however. They think it highly likely in his case, particularly with Solly Benayoun willing to testify against him.'

~~~

On the bus, the last leg of the journey to his flat, they sat upstairs at the front. Rachel tried to copy Zach and reach the rail underneath the window with her feet. But she couldn't stretch all the way without slipping off the seat. She tried again. Each time she slipped, she laughed.

They got off near the park on Lea Bridge Road and walked home. The flat was spic and span. Every photograph had been reframed and hung in the right place, and the timber-framed bay window had been repaired and painted.

Zach put the shopping bags down and went through the post. Rachel helped. Actually, she delayed the process, constantly asking, 'What's this?' Most of it was junk, so they played a game where she got to throw the mail onto the floor if Zach gave it the thumbs down. The trick was to do it *really fast*, he said. Amongst the rubbish was crap he couldn't ignore. Bills and the like. To that stuff he gave a horizontal thumb. Carefully, almost reverentially, Rachel placed that mail in the darkest corner of the table. To one envelope he gave a thumbs up. It was white and stamped: University of Central London.

He took it from her and ripped it open.

'Dear Zach Peretz. We are pleased to offer you a place ...'

Zach threw the letter into the air, picked Rachel up, and danced around the room.

GLOSSARY

Ashkenazi - A Jew with a European heritage

Baba ganoush – A smoky aubergine dip

Biscochos – A traditional Sephardi ring-shaped cookie, also known as biscochos de heuva

Christian Zionism – The belief that the creation of the state of Israel is in accordance with biblical prophecy

Clause 4 – The original clause, adopted in 1918, called for the nationalisation of all industry

Fattoush Salat – A Middle Eastern salad

Goyim – Non-Jews

Heuvos haminadoes – Sephardi-style eggs, traditionally served at Passover

IDF – Israeli Defence Forces

JLA – Jewish Liberation Army (*fictitious*)

JVF – Jewish Volunteer Force (*fictitious*)

Kapo – The term used for Jews who worked as 'trustees' for the Nazis in the concentration camps

Keffiyeh – A black and white chequered headscarf which has been a symbol of Palestinian nationalism since the 1936-39 Arab revolt in Palestine

Kippah – A brimless cap, usually made of cloth, traditionally worn by Jewish males to fulfil the customary requirement that the head be covered

LSI - Labour Supporters of Israel (*fictitious*)

Labneh – A Middle Eastern soft cheese made from strained yoghurt

Mogen Dovid – The Star of David

PSM – Palestine Solidarity Movement (*fictitious*)

Sephardi – A Jew from the Middle East or North Africa, most probably of Spanish or Portuguese descent, their families having fled The Spanish Inquisition in the fifteenth century

Shemira – The Jewish ritual of watching over the body of a deceased person until burial

Shiva – A period of seven days mourning for the dead, beginning immediately after the funeral

Tichel – A headscarf worn by orthodox Jewish women

Torah – The first part of the Old Testament, the central and most important bit of Judaism

UCL – University College London

Zionism – The belief in a Jewish state for the Jewish people

Zionist – Someone who believes in a Jewish state for the Jewish people